end times

end
times

michelle
syba

Freehand Books acknowledges the financial support for its publishing program provided by the Canada Council for the Arts and the Alberta Media Fund, and by the Government of Canada through the Canada Book Fund.

 Canada Council for the Arts   Conseil des Arts du Canada   Alberta Government   Canada

Freehand Books
515 – 815 1st Street SW   Calgary, Alberta   T2P 1N3
www.freehand-books.com

Book orders: UTP Distribution
5201 Dufferin Street   Toronto, Ontario   M3H 5T8
Telephone: 1-800-565-9523   Fax: 1-800-221-9985
utpbooks@utpress.utoronto.ca   utpdistribution.com

Library and Archives Canada Cataloguing in Publication
Title: End times / Michelle Syba.
Names: Syba, Michelle, author.
Description: Short stories.
Identifiers: Canadiana (print) 20230152422 | Canadiana (ebook) 20230152465 | ISBN 9781990601286 (softcover) | ISBN 9781990601293 (EPUB) | ISBN 9781990601309 (PDF)
Classification: LCC PS8637.Y25 E53 2023 | DDC C813/.6—DC23

"End Times" was originally published in *The New Quarterly*, Summer 2017.

Edited by Naomi K. Lewis
Book design by Natalie Olsen
Cover artwork: Pieter Brueghel, the Younger. *The Peasants' Wedding* [detail], mid-16th to mid-17th century. Art Gallery of Ontario. Gift of Mr. and Mrs. Redelmeier, 1940. Photo © Art Gallery of Ontario.
Author photo by Alex Tran
Printed on FSC® recycled paper and bound in Canada by Imprimerie Gauvin

for my mother

contents

end times

If an earthquake struck now, she would grab Katy's arm and huddle with her under the doorway to the fitting rooms. When the walls and racks of cashmere tumbled down, Katy would have a few extra moments to repent, and surely the Lord would forgive a mother for trying to save her child from His judgment.

As it is, they are stuck in line behind two young men who cannot stop touching each other. Amid the rhinestone hairclips and socks festooned with martini glasses, she fingers a T-shirt. The fabric reveals the pink of her fingertip, that's how thin it is, so what is the point of wearing it? You might as well go topless.

In moments like this, she imagines Christ's return, how the world will be transformed from glittering chaos to radiant order, from empty pleasures to a deeper, stabler bliss. All in the twinkling of an eye.

But the laughter of the young men yanks her back to the present. One of them has placed a clip in the other's hair. It sticks out like a horn.

"I'll wait by the front door," she tells Katy. In the company of an umbrella stand, she watches damp snowflakes spatter the cars that crawl along Robson Street. Bewildering weather for Vancouver.

When she and Katy are back outside, she mentions the young men. Katy does not recall them at first, so she must describe their antics in detail.

"So what?" says Katy. "Maybe they were on MDMA, who knows."

"MD — what?"

"It's a drug that makes people very touchy. Touchy in a good way." Katy draws her to the side, and pedestrians stream past.

"How can you say that a drug does anything good when you know what they've done to Matthew?"

"Matthew was on something different."

It is appalling that Katy can speak of drugs so carelessly, when hundreds have died in the past few months from that toxic super-drug. It's on the news daily. Every time she hears a siren she thinks, Another overdose. She thinks of Matthew and wonders if he is working at the café or walking the dogs.

Even now, in the absence of any siren, she wonders if Matthew is on his way to the restaurant, or if he will be late and make up some excuse. If he is relapsing again or about to. If he is still trying to lead a normal life, or if his life is coming to an end.

At the restaurant they find Matthew on a circular velvet bench, surrounded by iron bars. Whenever Matthew is on time, she is relieved but apprehensive too, wondering how long such normalcy can last, not that anything feels very normal in a restaurant where bare, dim bulbs glow inside miniature birdcages.

Katy is paying for lunch. Because this is the life Katy leads. Most weeks she flies out to a distant city to give expensive advice to a company. Sometimes she flies to San Francisco, where the man she is dating lives. Katy calls him her boyfriend.

One day Katy will realize that flying around the world every week is not a real life, not at age forty-three.

Katy insists on an appetizer, even though nobody is hungry. But the appetizer is only a few sheer slices of fish that disappear on the tongue — almost nothing, which impresses Katy and even Matthew, this experience of eating something nearly imaginary for twenty dollars a plate.

Soon the subject of American politics comes up between her children. They bulge their eyes at each other and share an exhalation of despair.

They know that she admires the new American president. Yes, he is flawed and worldly, but also a man of action committed to his country's prosperity.

But today she wants no argument.

"Chaos," says Matthew, and this she can agree with. Yes, the world is chaos, she replies. Perhaps they are in the end times.

The moment she brings up anything related to Jesus, her children behave as if she has released a powerfully dismaying fart. They hope it will dissipate soon, though they are also a tiny bit amused that it has erupted, yet again.

"So does that make him the Antichrist?" her daughter asks, of the American president. Matthew laughs.

"He is not the Antichrist."

"Then it's not really the end times, if the Antichrist isn't here yet." Katy likes to insist on her superior logic, as if logic defines God's plan. "But it would be funny if he *were*, because then you'd have a bunch of evangelicals who voted for the Antichrist." Katy has swaddled herself so tightly in her logic, is so charmed by her own cleverness, that it is impossible to talk to her. Matthew is calmer.

"Isn't the Antichrist needed for Christ's return later on?" he asks. "Maybe the Antichrist doesn't just suck."

"He's like a really spectacular opening act," says Katy, "while Jesus keeps everyone waiting." Her children are laughing, it is unclear at what, exactly. Concerts, things sucking. Yes, things suck. She would not put it that way herself, but she agrees with the general idea.

She never imagined that a child of her own would become an addict. Matthew was a beautiful and open boy, an exuberant snuggler who delighted in helping her with ordinary tasks — watering the African violets without wetting the leaves, even sweeping the kitchen floor. When he turned to drugs, it was like watching a songbird get thrown into a blender.

That is what humans do when they lack God's guidance. They ruin things.

Katy cannot understand how painful it is to watch your own child become so lost. Katy acts like everything is normal again since rehab barely a year ago. Rehab is fine, but it is not somewhere you can spend your whole life. In life you need a deeper support system. That's what Jesus is for.

When Matthew asks how she has been, she talks about the preschoolers — their faces sweetly receptive when she reads to them — and the latest hiking club controversy, about whether a long uphill trek is safe for seniors. She does not understand what the fuss is about. She has always taken care of herself. How some people can let themselves go until they need a scooter, she does not know. The fat people spilling out of scooters, even in Vancouver.

She asks Matthew about the dogs. When he isn't working at a café, he is walking a big black mutt and a small silly dog, as if the point of life is to walk your dogs.

Matthew reveals that the little dog just had a tooth removed. Fortunately, the big dog, Crow, has never needed medical care. "Crow is an ox," he says.

When she brings up the pastor's sermon series on the book of Matthew, she pretends to address Katy to take the pressure off her son. "You would find it interesting, Katy. The pastor gives a lot of history. At the Christmas service he talked about the Roman Empire. How Herod built up Judea's infrastructure to improve his reputation."

"I could just read Wikipedia."

"But it's a whole way of understanding the world too."

"I fly to Jakarta on Sunday."

When she invites Matthew, he gives her a sad smile and tells her it's not for him. He always says that.

"But it *is* for you!" she replies, her voice filled with a great hopeful enthusiasm, like when he was small and she'd coax him to try a new food, and finally he'd take a bite and concede that it wasn't so bad, in fact it was rather tasty.

He was obviously lonely, otherwise he wouldn't need those dogs. He was no longer in touch with his drug friends, and his school friends were busy with their families. He'd had a very nice girlfriend, but once the drugs took over again, she left.

He could find a new girlfriend at the church. He was still handsome, and many of the younger people at church were kind, and good looking too.

When Matthew leaves for his shift at the café, Katy is also ready to say goodbye. Before hugging Katy, she asks, "How did Matthew seem to you?"

"You just saw him. Why are you asking me?"

"He must tell you things he doesn't tell me."

"He's fine."

"Katarina, your brother has a serious problem."

"Yes, and what do you want me to do? Ask him whether he's done drugs lately every time I see him? That won't make him not do them. It might have the opposite effect."

"I just want to know." Was it so wrong, a mother's desire to know that her child was safe?

The pastor is a fine man, knowledgeable and well spoken. The sermon series on the book of Matthew sharpens her own Matthew's absence. He should know what his namesake wrote. Not that she named him after the disciple. When Matthew was born she was not yet saved.

Today's topic is the blind men and the power of faith. How Jesus told them, According to your faith be it done to you. And their faith made them see.

If only America were governed by a man like the pastor. The pastor unites authority with compassion, and passion too. The way he strides along the stage in crisp jeans. A man devoted to practical ideals that change lives.

He is Anglo-Saxon like her first husband. When her first husband proposed, she was flattered that a native-born Canadian wanted her, an immigrant from a communist country. Her fondness for him grew after they married, though she was never in love with him, strictly speaking. A settled man, fifteen years older, well into his forties. Matthew was ten when his father died of a heart attack. Katy grew more stubbornly independent and Matthew began to skateboard obsessively, sliding along benches and railings, crouching behind cars. Ordinary movement was not enough for him. When she recalls how she worried about Matthew then, she pities herself. How little she knew.

She thought the second marriage would be good for Matthew. Her second husband was an energetic man, a Pole who oversaw a block of apartments. He was interested in everything—Mayan history, Arctic geology, the length of a day on Saturn. She thought his energy would break the pall in the household. He was also her only real love. When she recalls how much she loved him, something in her ribcage blooms, even now, so she asks God to turn that selfish love into a force less destructive and more universal—Jesus's love.

The pastor is telling congregants to stand on God's promises. By your faith be it done to you, he reminds them, inviting everyone with a need to walk to the altar for prayer. She places a hand on the pew in front of her and pushes herself up.

She calls Matthew every second day. If she called as often as she wanted, she would call him twice daily, but it's better not to overdo it. The fact is that if he overdosed on the super-drug, he'd be dead long before she could save him. Nonetheless, when they talk she listens for signs that he might have lapsed, or be about to.

Sometimes she takes the bus to his neighborhood and they walk the dogs together. The conversation comes more easily then, as the dogs sniff and piss tranquilly. The little one is called Tootsie, a rescue dog Matthew inherited from an old woman found paralyzed in her own filth after a two-day ordeal. Tootsie is nearly as old as her original owner, though very devoted to Matthew and to Crow, whom Matthew calls his guru. "Crow helps me stay in the present," he'll say, or "Crow keeps me sane," to which she replies, "You were never crazy." As for living in the present, there is nothing wrong with that, but one must think about the future too.

The only future that preoccupies Matthew is the environment's. If there is one thing Crow cannot soothe, it is what humans are doing to the earth. The strange weather has not helped, all the snow that makes Tootsie trot ever more daintily. Matthew gestures towards a terraced rock garden where a granite Buddha reclines. "One day this will all be under water. Shaughnessy will be a narrow peninsula. Most of it will be submerged, though." Lively worried words, half delighted by the idea of multi-million-dollar homes under water. Revolution by water. She doesn't disagree with Matthew. After all, God did it once before.

It is tempting to bring up the pastor's sermon, but she reminds herself that she is standing on God's promises. Nagging will not help, Katy is right about that.

She keeps busy. She reads at the library, hikes with other seniors, attends two Bible studies. Evenings she allows herself some TV. If she did what she felt like doing, it would be on all the time, and that would depress her. That she had become the kind of person who always has the TV on.

Still, sometimes there are interesting programs. She prefers factual shows about history or nature, marvelling at the organized migration of monarch butterflies. She watches an advertisement for a flashlight fifty times more powerful than a regular one. A man in military fatigues explains that it can withstand the weight of a Humvee. The flashlight is shown wedged beneath a thick wheel, then immersed in a pot of boiling water, resplendently intact. When pointed at intruders it blinds them. Useful for a senior who lives alone.

She calls the 1-800 number, but the conversation is so robotic that she's not sure she is talking to a real person, despite the woman's slow American speech. We have a special offer of two for thirty dollars plus shipping and handling. Can we offer you our special offer of four for fifty dollars plus shipping and handling? Today only, for a limited time, we have a special offer of six for sixty dollars.

Just one flashlight, please. The woman on the other end hardly hears her. It is like talking to her children.

Already Katy has flown to Jakarta, Sydney, Sao Paolo, and Omaha. No Matthew in church yet.

When she imagines her daughter's life, she sees Katy high above the earth in business class, squinting furiously at her laptop and waving away offers of sushi and champagne. As a reluctant immigrant, she never expected her children to zip around the world. Once she ended up in Vancouver, it was a relief to sleep in her own bed nightly.

Matthew is more like her. They can agree that when you live in Vancouver, why go anywhere else?

But the Matthew sermon series is over. He missed it.

When the package with the flashlight arrives, it is bigger than she expected. Inside are two flashlights. The second one fills her with a rage she has not felt in a long time. She hears the call-centre manager tell employees, Charge the old ladies whatever you like! With their bad hearing and wobbly voices, they will doubt themselves. And if they don't, they won't want to limp to the post office to return the extra product.

Younger people act like they know everything, when it's the elderly who are full of secret knowledge. Strong because they seem weak. The meek who shall inherit the earth.

The cost of returning the flashlight could be more than its value. And first she will have to call the robots to file her complaint. They will pretend not to understand her.

She calls Matthew, tells him about the second flashlight. Does he want it?

Matthew already has a flashlight. This is a special flashlight, she explains. It can blind intruders. Crow would alert him, Matthew says. Tootsie is half deaf, but Crow's hearing is so sharp he's almost psychic. He would save Matthew. Only Jesus can do that, she thinks. Matthew does not understand why she bought the flashlight and asks, "It's not just pandering to scared people?"

On Sunday the pastor surveys Christ's parables. She admires how articulate he is, how he talks about "unpacking an idea" or throws in lawyerly phrases like "pertains to." She has always admired intelligent men.

Had her second husband stayed in Poland, he would have been a lawyer. Life as an immigrant hemmed him in. He did not enjoy his work as a superintendent, dealing with complaints about noisy or smelly neighbors, or worse, tenants making stupid costly mistakes, running a bath and then forgetting about it. How could someone forget they were running a bath? He returned home fed up with humanity.

She does not know how long she did not know. He never told her. Matthew claims he cannot remember when it began.

What she knows is that when she learned about it, she did not leave immediately. She prayed, asking the Lord for guidance. After all, she was married. As a Christian she believed in the commitment she'd made at the altar. She made excuses, too. If only he could find work he liked, he would not be so angry. Matthew enraged him. Her second husband never touched Katy, whom he adored, because he expected so little from a girl. But Matthew he expected more from.

She waited on the Lord. She tried to make her husband happier and to keep his angry words away from Matthew. When she intervened, his anger switched off suddenly, for a time. He wanted to do better and needed her, and she needed him for the way he annihilated her at night, the way they forgot the world together.

When she finally left, he made no protest. She broke off all contact, even though she would have liked to talk sometimes. He died two years ago. She told Matthew about his death, thinking it would bring some relief, but around that time he went back on the drugs.

She doesn't believe that hell is flames and lizards. It is a place beyond human imagining, of loneliness and confusion. Confusion worst of all. While heaven sparkles with clarity.

According to God's Word, her second husband is in hell. The man who married a woman with two children and made terrible mistakes. Still, she cannot convince herself that he deserves an eternity of confusion and loneliness.

19

The young woman sitting beside her smiles at her, and she realizes that she is crying. The Holy Spirit is doing His work. Here she wanted Matthew to change his life when her own remains so faulty — the selfishness, the guilt. She wants her heart wiped clean. Only then will Matthew hear her words.

She fasts and prays, resisting the urge to call Matthew.

She has never seen Matthew high, only afterwards, when he was tired and aloof. When she imagines him high, he is always outside, in Chinatown, sitting on a sidewalk, wearing dirty jeans. Even though his jeans are always washed, and she knows he must have been high in each of the small apartments where he has lived. In her mind he is on the sidewalk, indifferent to passing shoes. Filthy. He has given up on life, unlike his mother who tried so hard to make one. It's awful to think about, though the first moments of giving up must feel exhilarating. No more struggle. Just not caring in your dirty jeans.

Sometimes when she prays she looks at the mountains. They are not God, but emblems of His glory, specks in a vaster reality that humans cannot see. At such moments, the mountains soar with meaning.

Sometimes her eye drifts to the peak of one mountain, and she pictures a small patch of it. How windy it must be, how cold and pure. No people to muck it up, only an occasional hawk. The hawk lands in the snow and listens to the wind. Then the hawk flies away. A moment that doesn't mean anything. The opposite of God's glory. A peculiar relief.

She wonders if God minds these thoughts. He hasn't said anything on the subject.

She is looking at a mountain peak when Matthew calls, his voice gasping. Something about a heart. She thinks of her first husband's heart problems, which Matthew must have inherited. She thinks of the super-drug, what it must do to hearts.

Hang up and I'll call 911, she tells him.

No, he cries, with an assertiveness that makes her pause.

Did you take a drug?

No, he wails.

She assures him she loves him, that she will not judge him. I just want you to live. Now she is wailing.

I won't die, he says. I wish I could but I won't.

The heart, it becomes clear, is not Matthew's but Crow's. Crow had a heart defect. Impossible to know until it was too late.

She tries to conceal her relief from Matthew. She calls Crow's death a terrible thing. So sudden. Not to have known until now. How painful not to know.

She wonders how much the visit to the vet cost. Matthew makes just enough to pay rent on his basement apartment and for other basics.

Such grief for a dog. She cannot imagine so much devastation at her own death. Beneath the sorrow, she suspects, will be a tiny feeling of release. No more phone calls every two days. No more invitations to church.

Their relationship began forty years ago, in radiant harmony, the two of them soft blind flesh, herself half asleep and Matthew frankly needy. He adored her breast, her milk, her — it was all the same. She didn't mind not being a person to her infant. He turned her into both less and more than a person, both a foodstuff and a god. How could the rest of life match such perfection? Everything after would be a letdown.

She spends the rest of the day with Matthew and cooks a stew that interests only Tootsie. His boss gives him three days off, and his landlord lets him bury Crow in the backyard. Matthew spends much of the afternoon digging in a half-frozen corner by a laurel bush.

She considers when to invite him to church. The loss of Crow might remind him of humans' essential need for God's guidance. But everything is too raw. Without Crow, something in Matthew has been amputated. Tootsie's wriggling efforts to comfort are like a flea's acrobatics for a sad elephant. So she stands on God's promises. She has no choice.

Sometimes she wonders how she can still love her second husband. Something in her must be rotten, or gravely weak. He was a man disappointed by life. The abuse was mostly verbal. She never attributed a bruise to him, though it was hard to know because Matthew got so many small injuries from skateboarding. Matthew never said anything. Perhaps he saw how she loved his stepfather.

Her own father was not a nice man. Life was not easy for him, an ethnic German among Czech nationalists. They were expelled at the end of the war to a country that was supposed to be home but was mostly rubble. She never felt at home in Germany. She found the people in town secretive and judgmental, and Berlin was not any better, so after nearly two decades she left. At least if she didn't feel at home in Canada, there would be an obvious reason.

Life in Canada was easier, but not. You could get endless peanut butter and free chicken carcasses, but with each achievement—a job, marriage, children—came new, subtle discomforts.

The absent daughter, the lost son. She was blessed to have a one-bedroom condo, but all she could see was that useless extra flashlight that someone thought she'd be stupid enough to keep.

If Jesus returned now, none of it would matter. The clutter and the confusion, it would all be gone. The mountains would rejoice and the floods clap their hands, as King David prophesied. Clapping floods sound disastrous, certainly Matthew would think so, but in the Bible they're not. In the Bible floods clap to angelic trumpets making a joyful noise unto the Lord, all of them like a masterpiece by Mozart and Beethoven and Freddie Mercury wailing and sweating over the piano — she loved his music before she found Jesus, and still does, despite her scruples — a sound so glorious that it would make every body vibrate; it would turn everyone who listened into instruments themselves, you wouldn't be your petty self anymore but something else, joy and beauty and goodness.

She calls Matthew after his shift. How was work?

Fine.

How is Tootsie?

Fine.

Should I come over to make supper? Will you be alright?

No. Yes.

Once Matthew starts adjusting to Crow's absence, she will invite him to church. She prays on it. She tells Jesus she wants to be a good mother. She doesn't understand how something that felt intuitive in the beginning has become impossible.

Don't act so calm, Jesus tells her. *Be honest with Matthew.*

She is delighted by the clarity Jesus brings to the situation. The simplicity of His solution. Like shining a powerful flashlight into the darkness.

When she calls Matthew the next day she launches right in. "Please come to church this Sunday, for the sake of your old mother."

"Okay," he says, as casually as if she'd asked him to move her couch.

She worries he will oversleep, that he said okay only to get her off his back. He likes to sleep late.

She watches the mountains as she finishes her coffee, pushing away the image of the meaningless hawk because it is Sunday, a day when her thoughts should glorify God. Especially today. She remembers the Bible verse, *How lovely on the mountains are the feet of him who brings good news.* She imagines sandalled feet tramping down Mount Seymour.

In the church foyer she finds Matthew on a bench, forearms on his knees, head bowed.

She points out the busy church café and imagines Matthew working there one day. A professional and a spiritual opportunity, all in one. Their coffee is better, too.

During the worship service, Matthew doesn't sing, but at least he stands and looks around. Katy would be sitting and smirking.

The pastor's sermon is about the criminals crucified alongside Christ. How the first man mocked Jesus, asking why He didn't save himself if He was the son of God.

Matthew fidgets, uncrossing and recrossing his legs. Other times he is very still, arms on his knees, gazing at his shoes. She checks that he's awake, and he always is. He seems to hear the pastor's words.

The second criminal rebukes the first. Christ is blameless, he says, and asks Jesus to remember him. Jesus tells the man, *Today you will be with me in paradise.*

The pastor calls people to the front of the church to make their lives right with God. Matthew uncrosses his legs and rests both feet on the floor, as if testing its solidity. When she looks over at him, his eyes are glistening like an angel's, the lostness gone, replaced by the open heart of a child.

She doesn't hear from Matthew the next day. She wonders if turning his life over to Christ means they'll talk more often. But her son is still his own person, she reminds herself, though now he's Jesus's son too.

She savours the memory of Matthew walking to the front of the church, gives a small laugh to recall her incredulity as he stood before the congregation and accepted Christ into his heart. A miracle.

Afterwards they sat together in the church café, and she felt so close to him. Not since her first husband died had she felt that close to Matthew.

Matthew's miracle puts everything in perspective. When she sees the extra useless flashlight, she feels not rage but tenderness. Probably the robot lady on the phone needed commission money to support her family. She must live in a part of America where jobs are hard to come by.

How powerful Matthew's testimony will be. A man off the rails for half his life, lost but now found. Surely his story will bring others to Christ.

One day Katy will come around. When she sees how powerfully Christ has changed her brother, she will realize there is more to life than success. It will not happen soon, Katy is too proud, though wouldn't it be amazing if all their hearts were right with God when Christ returns? What rejoicing then.

On Tuesday's hike she does not engage anyone in a long conversation. She overhears chats about someone's trip to Portugal and someone else's knee trouble. None of the hikers is saved, and she imagines telling them about Matthew. They do not know about his history with drugs. But if she told them the truth, some of them might come to know the Lord too.

At home she finds a message from Katy. After half a ring Katy picks up and says, "Matthew is with me."

"Where are you?" She thought Katy was in Omaha again.

Katy is in her condo. She cut her business trip short. She has been trying to book a rehab program. It looks like private is the only option.

For a moment, she wonders how Katy could have a drug problem and still fly around the world giving advice. When Katy clarifies, she contemplates whether her son has a double. Was the person who came to church two days ago an imposter? Jesus said that demons can impersonate ghosts. Maybe they can impersonate people, too.

"Matthew isn't at the café?" she asks. That is all she can think to say. In her mind, Matthew is working his shift, faithfully serving bad coffee.

"Matthew no longer works there." Katy speaks briskly, as if summarizing a business report. After Crow's death, Matthew didn't show up to work. He got back on drugs. He got fired. More drugs. A phone call to his ex. Yesterday he grew suicidal. That's when he called Katy.

"Doesn't he remember accepting Jesus into his heart? Ask him."

She hears Katy speak to Matthew, then silence. Of guilt or forgetfulness? She cannot imagine the state of her son's brain. She has a vision of dirty pudding.

Finally, his slow distant words. He was high.

The whole thing a sham, a joke.

Katy is talking to her. Something about Burma. They are heading out for lunch at a Burmese restaurant. The tea salad is amazing. Does she want to join them?

Is Katy asking if she is hungry? No, she is not hungry, but she will join them, yes.

Katy lowers her voice into the phone. "No drama, okay? No praying, please."

"Don't worry," she says. "I won't pray."

The mountains are venomous. If Christ dipped a sandal onto Mount Seymour, or yanked her up to heaven now, she would yowl, *No!*

Jesus did not tell her that Matthew was high. Jesus who knows everything. What must her rejoicing have sounded like to Him? An old woman celebrating a prank by the devil.

She is stunned to find her apartment intact, purse and keys on the entryway table. The stitching of her jacket somehow not rent. Instead of sackcloth and ashes, it'll be tea salad and polished glass, all the pretenses of pleasure.

She focuses on her shoes, moves one foot forward, then the other. She is still a fit woman, she reminds herself, not a big TV watcher, not a scooter user.

Outside the weather has changed. The sun has burst open the tulips, it is like early summer. A block down, pedestrians hurry along the main road.

She imagines the world without her. How people will rush down the sidewalk as usual, jackets flapping, coffee cups in hand, how today and yesterday and tomorrow will be of a piece, for them, more or less stressful but basically the same.

Katy would say that she is simply an old woman who wanted something spectacular to happen before she dies. A grand finale to make it all mean something.

She should have taken a cab. Even walking downhill has become an effort. She has become the limping old lady the call-centre manager prophesied.

Ahead is the second-hand store, window cluttered with bent plastic purses and fake silk pajamas. She leans against the window. Her heart feels tight. She can no longer tell if it is her physical or spiritual heart, the two are so entangled. She lets herself slide down to the pavement and tries to remember the symptoms of a heart attack. She knew them when her first husband died.

People stride by. She must look free-spirited, like the teenagers who sit anywhere and shriek at each other for no reason.

A young woman asks if she is okay. The woman—a girl, really—has the worried face of the innocent.

She tries to reassure the girl. "I am not an addict," she explains. She places a hand on the pavement to prop herself up.

A middle-aged man has joined them. He and the girl confer. There is talk of a medical condition. She tells the man what she told the girl, who takes out a phone. Neither of them listens. It is like being a new immigrant all over again.

The pavement beneath her palm is almost warm, its dirt like dust. Ashes to ashes. She thinks of how Jesus wrote words in the dirt, symbols so powerful they calmed an angry crowd. What does she want to tell the girl and the man? She pushes her palm into the dirt. It does not mean anything. It is just dirt. Sunlight bears down on her face and she closes her eyes.

The siren begins as a thin rope of sound. As it weaves through the city, its wail grows powerful and even festive, like something

Freddie Mercury might have sung along to. Did Freddie hear from God during his last days alive? When the siren winds up an octave and overwhelms the traffic down the road, she can hear in the distance a new note emerge, a more expansive pulsation, as the mountains rejoice and the floods clap their hands.

matsutake

For nearly a week, the young couple in the RV next door had kept to themselves. They'd said little more than hi, declining Ivan's offer of palachinky, even when he joked that Sonia made the best palachinky on Manitoulin Island. Ivan wondered if they were offended by the Jesus fish on his and Sonia's bumper. Sonia decided they must be from Toronto, or some big city.

At lunchtime on Tuesday, the young couple's RV erupted in metallic squeals, then went silent. "Sounds like the alternator," said Ivan, as Sonia spooned cucumber salad onto his plate. They munched on salami sandwiches and peered through the lace curtain, until Ivan brushed the corners of his mouth and stepped outside.

The young man had raised the RV's hood and was studying his phone. His wife stood at a distance on a limestone boulder, her face to the water.

When Ivan offered to take a look at the RV, the young man moved aside. As Ivan examined the alternator, the young man spoke. His voice was muffled, like he hadn't used it much. Their CAA membership had expired, he'd forgotten to renew it. They'd been in Mexico for a while. Now they were at the remotest point of the island. "I'm an idiot," he croaked.

"Where did you go in Mexico?" said Ivan.

The young man mumbled something about Mazatlán. His voice grew less mumbly as he named states in the southeastern U.S.

"What an adventure," said Ivan.

By then Sonia had joined them. "We spent March in South Carolina," she said. "Near Charleston the wisteria were out. I asked Ivan, why did we immigrate to Canada? But Ivan likes the snow."

"If we hadn't immigrated to Canada, we would never have met," he said. It was their social routine, Ivan playing the mild-mannered pedant. He smelled the overheated wires of the alternator, and the serpentine belt was in rough shape too, whitened by wear. The young man couldn't tell the alternator from the air filter and pecked at his phone to look up towing companies.

"Where are you from?" Sonia asked him.

"Vancouver."

"A beautiful city. But expensive."

"Yeah, we needed a break."

"Good for you," said Sonia. "I wish we'd discovered the RV life when we were your age."

Ivan offered to take a closer look at the alternator. Maybe the rectifier or bearings needed to be replaced. Or the young man could call a tow truck. How much it would cost to tow an RV from a remote location, Ivan couldn't imagine.

"Are you a mechanic?" asked the young man.

"No, just a retired teacher who likes to fix things. I repaired our alternator. It's not too complicated."

"Ivan has fixed all our vehicles, including a '91 Jamboree we drove for twenty-five years. It ran like a Swiss watch."

"I can give you a boost," said Ivan, "but it probably won't last to the nearest garage."

"Let me talk to my wife," said the young man.

They finished lunch, leaving the door open. "It's getting chilly," said Sonia. Outside, the poplar shrubs that surged up between rocky crevices had turned yellow, and the water was choppy beside the squat lighthouse. Besides the two RVs only one tent remained.

"How could they not renew their CAA membership?" said Sonia.

"We've forgotten what it's like to be young and stressed out," said Ivan.

"They're RVing like us. How stressed can they be? And they're not that young, either."

Ivan couldn't guess the age of younger adults anymore. Anyone under forty was dazzling.

The young man put Ivan in mind of a struggling student. Early in his career, Ivan had been impatient with the kids who failed. Why can't you take your life more seriously, he wanted to ask them. It won't get easier later.

But in his fifties, he began to find the failures endearing. Their honest bewilderment when they screwed up, again. Their surprise at the consequences of the screw-up. It seemed hardly their own fault, but an illustration of Original Sin or whatever fate was. These days, Ivan chalked up fate to physics, particles knocking each other around, sometimes in a way you liked and sometimes not, and sometimes in a way you found to like, later on.

Sonia had cleared the table and brought a plate of apple cake.

The screen door rattled when the young man knocked on it. His wife stood behind him. She had large blue stricken eyes.

"Come in!" cried Sonia. She told Ivan to unfold extra chairs, even though it was evident the young couple would have preferred simply to talk through the screen door.

"We don't want to impose on you," said the young man. He finally introduced himself and his wife. Ryan and Tessa.

"Welcome!" said Sonia.

Towing alone would cost fifteen hundred dollars, Ryan told them, and the repair was another thousand at least.

"The alternator isn't more than a few hundred," said Ivan. "You can buy it online and I'll install it. No charge."

"That's incredibly generous of you," said Ryan. He sounded dismayed.

"I enjoy the work. It's like solving a puzzle."

Tessa gave a pained smile. "It's just that we're supposed to be in Toronto tonight. Our friends are expecting us."

There was no way they'd be in Toronto that evening, unless they abandoned the vehicle. "It's up to you," Ivan said and reached for a piece of cake.

"Have some," said Sonia as she passed out napkins. "You know, RVers are like family. We look out for each other." She talked about another couple they had met, Judy and Paul. Judy and Paul's RV had conked out in the middle of the Badlands at the height of summer. They didn't have power for the AC and the vehicle was heating up. "They stayed with us until the tow truck arrived. Now we travel with them each year."

"How long will it take to fix?" asked Ryan.

"A couple hours. It's getting the part here that I don't know about. But you can expedite shipping."

"We should call our friends," said Tessa.

"If the alternator arrives tomorrow, you can be in Toronto by Thursday," said Ivan.

"Take some cake with you," said Sonia.

That evening, Sonia read aloud from the book of Ruth. It was a change from the book of Judges, with its litany of Israelites displeasing God and each other. At points it wasn't clear who was wronging whom. Sometimes Ivan closed his eyes, letting the cycles of violence and festivity wash over him. Sonia dug into the minutiae. "Remember, the Benjaminites were the ones who raped the visitors, so God is restoring the balance."

God brought order to human chaos. Ivan could appreciate that.

Ruth was easier to follow. In a foreign land, Naomi loses her husband and both her adult sons. She decides to return home and urges her daughters-in-law to find new husbands. One daughter leaves but Ruth refuses, following Naomi back to her hometown of Judah. Naomi is so changed by her tragedies that old neighbours don't recognize her. But Ruth gives Naomi something to live for.

"It's beautiful the way Naomi looks out for Ruth," said Sonia.

Ivan agreed.

"That Tessa seems so unhappy," said Sonia.

"I think she just wants to see her friends," said Ivan.

"I wouldn't have guessed that she and Ryan are RVers. You'd think they'd be more flexible. They really went to Mexico?"

"That's what Ryan said."

When they prayed before bed, Sonia spoke a few words about the young couple. "Tessa especially, Lord. Give her Your joy unspeakable."

Wednesday it rained. With the rocks and water draped in gray, and the white noise against the roof, Ivan was lulled into an afternoon nap, e-reader in hand. Sonia researched renting an RV in the Holy Land, the alert patter of her computer mouse playing against the rain, until she declared that Israel had no RVs at all. Not even the most basic fifteen-foot camper appeared to exist within its borders.

"It's a small country," said Ivan.

"But there's so much to see. And the hotels are expensive." Sonia clicked the mouse resolutely. "In heaven, I want an RV!"

"With a kitchen island made of sapphire and a flat-screen TV that broadcasts God's glory twenty-four seven," said Ivan.

Sonia gave him a sidelong frown. Again he'd taken the joke too far, like when he suggested she name her RV blog Holy Rollers. "In heaven our desires will be transformed." She spoke the words crisply, the way he imagined she had as a Sunday school teacher.

"Everywhere in heaven will be home," said Ivan. His standard excuse for his irony was having grown up in communist Czechoslovakia. As a boy, Ivan listened to his mother sing communist anthems while the cooperative farm next door failed. One afternoon, rain pounded the hay to mush — whoever was supposed to move it to the barn didn't bother — and his mother stood at the window and sang, *We will command the rain when to fall and the wind when to blow!*

Sonia had grown up in a communist country too, but Tito's Yugoslavia had done better than Czechoslovakia, at least in the fifties. Sonia's family was better connected, too. By the time things got ugly in Yugoslavia, she was long gone. From afar, she prayed for her family.

"Maybe we could rent an RV in Egypt and drive from there," said Sonia.

"We haven't even driven in Europe."

"Do you feel like visiting your relatives?"

"Very funny."

Ivan's brother lived in the house where they and their father had been born. Milos spent much of his retirement stringing glass beads onto necklaces and watching dubbed Hollywood movies. He liked to point out that the family had lived in town since the eighteenth century, and after a few beers was liable to rail against migrants, even though none lived there.

When Ivan told Milos that he and Sonia were going to RV full time, Milos said, "But where will you live?"

"In the RV. It has everything. Washroom, kitchen, a big bed, even a washing machine."

"What about a bathtub?"

"When is the last time you took a bath?"

Ivan's life sounded as pointless to Milos as Milos's did to Ivan. Milos loved his potato plot and cherry tree. When Ivan asked him who bought the necklaces—thick glittering ropes, the fashion of eighty years ago—Milos said: "Our beads are better quality than what the Chinese slap out. The Indians, the Brazilians, even the Indians in the Amazon buy our beads for their ritual outfits." He called Ivan's RV "your gypsy wagon." Milos hated gypsies even more than migrants.

Ivan loved being in motion, like Sonia. They loved that more often RVers asked *Where have you been?* instead of *Where are you from?* On the road, their accents and distant histories hardly mattered.

Sonia's laptop screen was visible as she worked on a blog entry, while Ivan read a book of popular essays by an Italian physicist. The physicist described reality as a fidgety swarm of particles. Reality was made not of things but of interactions, of movement and change. Ivan could get behind that. He liked how the essays invited him to see life on a different scale. The coarse rain and the shifting clouds; the agglomerating marks on the screen of Sonia's laptop, and his own eyeballs twitching down the screen of his e-reader.

He was reading about probability and randomness when Sonia said, "We should invite them for supper."

"I don't think they want to spend time with us."

"But it's a miserable day. And their situation. We're the only other RV here. It would be rude not to invite them."

She warmed up sarma, chopped vegetables for the salad, and set the table for four. When the oven dinged, she stepped out into the rain. Soon she returned with Ryan and Tessa. "We're down to tortilla chips and brie," said Ryan. Even Tessa gave thanks.

"Ivan says I buy too much food," said Sonia. "But you never know when you'll need it."

"We have a five-year supply of honey somewhere," said Ivan. "Don't worry, tomorrow we can get groceries."

Ryan and Tessa gaped at the cabbage rolls and cheese pie and salad. When Ryan picked up a fork, Sonia said, "Please. First we say grace."

Ivan thanked God for another day of freedom and health. After so many years of saying grace, each prayer had an algorithmic quality. Next was a grateful remark about that particular day. Ivan thanked God for Ryan and Tessa's company. From there, he acknowledged that God's will reigned supreme. Final remarks focused on the food, Sonia's gift.

He was winding down the prayer when Sonia murmured, "And the alternator."

"Yes, please bring the alternator quickly, Lord, so Ryan and Tessa can get to Toronto and visit their friends soon."

When he opened his eyes, Tessa was staring at him with her stricken gaze. It made Ivan want to ask *What did I do?*

But soon they were talking about RVing.

"Out of ninety-two nights in the U.S., we stayed in a park only twenty days," said Ryan.

"We've boondocked in a bunch of Walmart parking lots," said Sonia. "Nobody troubled us. I wrote about it."

"Sonia has a blog," said Ivan.

"Just some tips and stories and photos. The Walmart post got nearly eleven hundred views. Google *living the dream with Sonia.*"

"You don't ever miss staying in one place?" asked Ryan.

"Not yet," said Sonia. "We have communities. We go to the same park in Mexico each winter. Sometimes I miss our church, but there's a good one down there."

"How long have you been on the road?" Ivan asked Tessa.

"Since last September," she said.

"Over a year," said Ryan.

"We're looking into going full time." Tessa's face had grown rosy with the food, and her eyes were not really stricken, Ivan realized, just large.

"Young people can do that now," said Sonia. She described to Ivan the interior of Tessa and Ryan's RV, the robin's-egg blue kitchen cabinets with brass pulls, the wallpaper with gingko leaves. "It feels roomy."

"Our apartment wasn't much bigger," said Tessa.

Ryan gave a laugh. "It was more than twice as big."

"But can you watch the sun rise over a herd of bison while you sip fresh coffee?" asked Sonia. "I think it's great. There are so many possibilities now, with technology and everything."

Tessa had returned to work part time. She wrote emails for hotels throughout North America. Ryan had been in IT support and was still looking for work.

"It's a process!" said Sonia. "We have friends who work at an Amazon warehouse four months each year. They make enough to travel for the rest of the year. No more living to work. Now if only the rain would stop."

"Tomorrow the mushrooms will be good," observed Ivan.

"What do you mean?" said Ryan.

"Mushrooms come out after rainfall, and late September is prime mushroom season."

"We found a maitake last week," said Sonia. "It filled my lap!" She offered more sarma and salad. "Ivan grew up hunting mushrooms."

"Sonia's better at it than I am," said Ivan. "She finds the sneaky ones."

"The sneaky ones are the best."

"Sometimes," said Ivan.

"Ivan likes to correct me because he misses teaching," said Sonia.

"Sonia's the sharp one," said Ivan. "Nothing escapes her." And when Tessa smiled at last, it occurred to Ivan that Sonia had been right to invite the young couple after all.

Thursday it was still raining. Sonia completed a blog entry about Misery Bay, which Ivan proofread. He uploaded photos of the alvar landscape, flat limestone riven with cracks, like a prehistoric parking lot abandoned by fickle extraterrestrials. Not that Sonia saw it that way. She wrote about the lessons of God's creation: the fullness of life, even in a shallow, challenging landscape. Here, juniper slinked and burgeoned along the rock, plants digested insects, and the alternating extremes of dryness and flooding enticed many butterflies and birds. Hardship could beget riches.

Ivan, Ryan, and Tessa would wait until later in the day to head out for groceries. The drive was an hour each way, and they hoped the rain would stop by then. They also hoped the alternator would arrive; the park office was open for deliveries. Ivan could install it early on Friday morning and the couple could be in Toronto that night.

After lunch Ivan dipped back into the physicist's essays. Compared with computer science, physics was full of slippery paradoxes. As a teacher, he had taught students to define an operation as precisely as possible, in order to extinguish assumptions and ambiguity. All disagreement is a function of insufficient definition, he used to say.

He was annoyed when a chemistry teacher remarked, "I wouldn't have pegged you as religious. I mean, you teach science, and we're not talking social sciences." Ivan knew nothing about sociology or psychology but pretended to be amused by the joke. They were at a staff party, people were drinking, it was not a time to expect careful statements. Yet Ivan found the mental habits of computer scientists not so different from those of believers. Both valued clarity. Both sought a single, optimal answer.

The chemistry teacher must have sensed Ivan's reservations, or maybe the fact that Ivan didn't drink ruined the mood. "Well, real scientists don't teach high school, eh?" he said, before setting off for a refill.

Sonia woke Ivan from his nap at three. It was still raining as he headed to Ryan and Tessa's RV. When Ryan opened the door, Ivan glimpsed the blue kitchen, its counter crowded with bottles and bowls.

"Tessa went for a walk," said Ryan. "The two of us should just go."

In Ivan's pick-up, the tires pushed easily over the wet gravel, as they skirted the edge of a quarry. Beyond it, white pines crowded in on either side, fluffy and hypnotic. When they reached paved road, Ivan finally spoke. "Any news of the alternator?"

"Not really," said Ryan. The latest update indicated that the package was out for delivery by a guy named Nasim. "Nasim is out in this wilderness, somewhere." Ryan turned to the bush whipping past his window. "Part of me just wants to leave the monster behind."

Ivan conceded that RVs brought their share of frustrations. "What kind of IT work did you do in Vancouver?" he asked.

"For an actuarial firm. It paid the bills, and we could hike or ski thirty minutes from where we lived. The restaurants were great too."

Ivan agreed that Vancouver had many amenities.

"What did you teach?" asked Ryan.

"Computer science, back in the Stone Age."

The pick-up passed a broad misty bay to the north. On clear days, the upper shore of Lake Huron was visible.

"Do you have any opinions about the idea that reality is an AI simulation?" said Ryan.

Ten years ago Ivan might have gone on the defensive. He still had plenty of energy, but felt his mind disentangling from controversies; these days, he preferred descriptions to arguments.

"I'm not sure what it would change. I suppose it supports the idea of a higher power in control." Ten years ago, he would have brought up God more explicitly.

"It definitely puts a new spin on individual freedom."

"Even in an RV," joked Ivan.

An oncoming pick-up hurtled past them. It was the second vehicle they'd seen and soon they were alone again, the engine humming at their feet.

"To be honest," said Ryan, "the RV life doesn't feel so free to me. The first couple of months were good, but now it just feels like an escape."

Ivan conceded that tastes varied.

"But you and your wife," said Ryan, "I mean, if you'd been doing this in your mid-thirties, how would that have felt?"

"Hard to say." Ivan observed the parallax of the road, the gravel to his left whipping by, while the distant asphalt approached more gradually. "I couldn't have been a teacher."

"Most people crave stability by their mid-thirties, that's what I think. You want to build something. Then if you get tired of it, you can go on adventures, but you always have a home base to return to. Don't you agree?"

Ivan focused on the steadier distance and said, "An immigrant might not be the best person to ask."

Ryan gave a laugh. Through the passenger window he watched the speeding vegetation. "Why did you leave?"

"Life in Czechoslovakia was a dead end. Talk about a bad simulation. You got a job and potatoes for life in exchange for your freedom. In the early seventies, it felt like communism would last forever."

Ivan could understand Ryan's craving for stability. When he'd arrived in Toronto, the city was busier than Prague, but dreary. He found a job at an electronics store and struggled to keep up with the casual conversation of his coworkers. Some customers complained about his accent. Then a coworker invited him to church. There was coffee after the service, conversation with friendly, patient people who did not judge his English or complain about silly things or get drunk. Stable people. As he studied the Bible, much of it made sense. It was not the secrets of a priestly caste, but practical guidelines for living, devised over many hundreds of years. Compared with the pretenses of communism, the Bible was colossally useful.

When he met Sonia one Sunday after the service, there was God's answer. She was new to Canada and, even with her broken English, opinionated (about the quality of Canadian yogurt, about Anglo-Saxon smiles) and rather glamorous. She wore more makeup in those days, precise red lips and smudged mascara that made her eyes appear alternately indignant and naïve. When he spoke Czech, she answered in Serbian. On the day he told her he loved her, it was in Czech, and she understood.

Ivan realized that Ryan was waiting for an answer. "I wanted stability too when I was younger."

"We thought the RV would help us focus on our marriage. We'd do new things together. That's what couples are supposed to do, right?"

"Yes." Ivan wasn't sure what Ryan wanted him to say.

"If we hadn't, our marriage might have ended by now." Ryan returned his gaze to the side window. "It might still end, I don't know."

Ivan checked the speedometer and made sure not to accelerate or slow down. Maintaining a steady speed felt important. Then he spoke. "It's not easy, marriage."

He hoped the words sounded sincere. In fact marriage with Sonia had been amazingly easy. To be sure there were disappointments — their childlessness above all — but their hearts broke together. In time, Sonia decided that it was God's will. She threw herself into childcare at the church and became a godmother to three children.

In the first decades of marriage, he'd imputed their harmonious relationship to God's will. Now he ascribed it to temperamental compatibility and to the clarity of their roles as a Christian husband and wife: he the breadwinner, she the homemaker. It was what they both wanted. Sonia had been relieved to stop working. She loved making a home for them, down to the complicated baking and sewing.

"The thing is," said Ryan, "it's not Tessa's fault. We lost a baby. She was eleven months old."

How awful, said Ivan. He almost filled the silence by speaking of his and Sonia's grief at never having children. All the miscarriages, and the stillbirth at twenty-two weeks. Sonia had insisted on a funeral.

"It's been nearly two years since Penny died," said Ryan. "We're Skyping with a therapist, but not much has changed. Tessa sees RVing as a new start, and I feel like we're just running away. RVing wasn't supposed to last more than half a year." The green sidelines spilled past, and Ivan realized he was speeding. "I mean, we built something in Vancouver. Our family and friends are there."

Ivan said that he could see Ryan's point of view.

"But am I going to be the guy who walks out on his grieving wife and ruins her RV dreams? Tessa wouldn't RV on her own."

Ryan apologized for blabbing, and Ivan said the situation sounded difficult.

Ivan wished he could bring clarity to Ryan's predicament, that he could pinpoint a wobbly definition that might have precipitated marital disharmony. Both Ryan and Tessa were relatively young, both were capable of change. The future held possibilities neither could fathom. Particles in motion, the swerve from probability to novelty.

Because in the absence of abuse, one should stay. Ivan still believed that. If you had to finesse the truth or keep silent about certain subjects so be it. Marriage was like communism that way.

And in the scheme of an adult life, two years of marital difficulty wasn't so long. It was three percent of an average adulthood. It's not always going to be like this, he wanted to say, as one might to a suicidal teenager. What he said was, "You might still have happy times ahead."

Ryan gave a strangled laugh and turned to the passenger window. Ivan had the impression he might pull the door handle and jump out of the moving truck, but Ryan apologized again. "I shouldn't have said anything."

Ivan said no, over and over. "I appreciate your honesty."

"But your beliefs are different." He didn't say, You can't understand because you're evangelical, but the implication was clear. Ivan felt the gulf between them. He wanted to tell Ryan that they were more alike than it appeared, and bring the same intensity of disclosure to the conversation. The last time he'd spoken frankly about himself was over a year ago, with another man, sitting by an outdoor fire past midnight, near Odessa, Texas.

"You know," said Ivan, "I don't believe in God anymore."

46

Ryan didn't turn away from the passenger window. Had he heard Ivan's words? Ivan almost repeated them when Ryan said, "What does your wife think of that?" His voice was polite.

"She doesn't know."

"Yeah, I remember you prayed before we ate."

"If she knew, it would break her heart."

There was a time when he'd considered telling Sonia. He'd played out a few scenarios. At first Sonia would be puzzled. She would explain and coax. For a time, she might leave him alone and turn inward — reading the Bible, praying, fasting. She would pray more than she did now, and it would be for him. She would ask what she'd done wrong, pestering him, or she would despair. The two of them crammed in the gypsy wagon. It would be hell.

"How do you know that?" asked Ryan.

"How do I know what?"

"That it would break her heart?"

Ivan smiled at the younger man's skepticism. It was like talking with a precocious student. "I don't know for sure," he said. "But we have been married for thirty-eight years, and I've made a calculation that there is a high probability" — his articulation grew clipped when he was amused — "that it would disrupt our marriage significantly."

"How long have you not believed in God?"

Ivan pretended to count. "Eight years."

"And you never hinted anything? You don't trust your wife not to freak out?"

"I suppose I like things the way they are."

"But your wife is happy."

"Yes."

He and Sonia prayed four times a day and read the Bible each

47

evening. He liked the Bible. It was a historical document about human civilization and folly.

"How do you know she doesn't know?" said Ryan

"If Sonia knew, she'd think I'm going to hell. That would stir her to action."

"You never thought of divorce?"

"No."

Maybe if he'd lost his faith earlier he would have divorced. Had he been Ryan's age, he might have left. But he'd been fifty-seven. He and Sonia had built a life together. And sometimes his loss of faith felt like a small thing. Of course, it wouldn't be small to her.

"I'd request your discretion on this matter," said Ivan.

"No problem," said Ryan, with such an absence of judgment that Ivan almost mourned again the child he and Sonia never had. Even listening to the problems of the young was a treat.

The grocery store was bigger than Ryan expected, and he was pleased to find a brand of granola from Salt Spring Island.

That evening, Sonia read aloud from the opening of the first book of Samuel. After Ruth's happy ending in marriage, the book of Samuel began with Hannah's grief. It was Sonia's turn to read. *I am a woman of a sorrowful spirit,* said Sonia, as Hannah laments her barrenness to the priest Eli.

Even more than twenty years after their own struggles, Ivan felt a small apprehension, wondering how Hannah's affliction sounded to Sonia. He almost suggested they skip ahead to the book of Psalms. But listening to Sonia read, Ivan dropped into the story, the odd comedy of the priest Eli thinking that Hannah is drunk when she prays, the mishap of interpreting heartache as dissipation. Even the priest wasn't good at reading people. Ivan picked up an apple from the bowl on the table and began to pare it with the mushroom knife he kept in his pocket, carving the peel into a single streamer.

At the start of chapter two, when Hannah finally has a child and declares that her heart rejoices, Sonia said, "You know, my heart can rejoice too, even without a child." She recalled her past sadness. How God had warned her against bitterness, which would ruin their marriage. "God's will turned out better than I could have imagined."

Ivan thought about the human power of rationalization and was grateful for it. He was grateful to the god he couldn't believe in for keeping his wife content.

"I just wish I'd known that at forty," said Sonia. "I wanted to be Hannah, or Sarah. If Sarah could have a baby at ninety, why not me at forty-five? Forty-five was half of ninety, and modern times were half as miraculous as biblical times I figured. I held on for a long time."

Ivan offered an apple slice to Sonia, who shook her head. He thought of the naïveté of middle age. The feeling that yes, life is finite, but you still have plenty of time to be hopeful or bitter.

"You know, Tessa and Ryan lost a baby."

"I knew it," said Sonia. "I knew something was wrong."

"A little girl, eleven months old."

Sonia gave a pained moan. "It wasn't a stillbirth."

"No." He snapped the knife closed and placed the browning apple on the table.

"We must pray for them."

"You can't say anything."

In bed in the dark, Sonia's fingers found the decades-long knot in Ivan's neck and massaged it. She knew all his tender points, his ticklish earlobe and the cloudy birthmark beneath his right buttock. Yet his mind was a secret innermost muscle, a coy snail. Centuries ago, priests had tortured heretics to unlock its contents.

"All that driving," she murmured.

Ryan's question returned to him then. *How do you know she doesn't know?* There had been moments when Ivan suspected that Sonia suspected. Or had questions, at least. Why was he so reserved in church? In their early years together, he lifted a hand to heaven during worship. Now he didn't. She never asked why.

Just that week she'd used his e-reader and observed that he didn't read Christian books anymore.

"I don't read fiction anymore," he'd said.

"But there's nonfiction too," said Sonia.

"The Bible is enough for me."

Could Sonia ever wiggle into a new theology, the way their friend Hank had? Hank's son no longer believed in God. Now Hank no longer believed in hell. He said things like, "Who am I to say how God will judge?" Privately Sonia told Ivan, "God's Word makes clear what happens to unbelievers."

Another time she said, "Better no child than a godless one."

Ivan had lost his faith by then. He couldn't pinpoint exactly when it happened. At first he'd thought it was a spiritual dry spell. He continued to pray and attend church, and even spoke with Sonia about it early on, reassuring her soon after that the phase had passed. In truth he was still waiting for something internal to shift, for God to feel present and necessary again. In that time, key concepts — hell, a personal God, Christ's return — fell away. He felt very calm when he realized that a fairly massive reconfiguration had taken place inside him. It was a cataclysm with the force of a hiccup.

A change both huge and tiny. A physicist would grasp that

it was both. Losing faith was like a revolution and a change of preference, God both an ousted tsar and a condiment Ivan no longer enjoyed, having experienced more simply the flavours of life, already so rich. He didn't need anything extra. Anything extra was cloying, dishonest.

Of course in Sonia's mind, it would be Ivan who was dishonest. He wondered if their minds were wired differently. Her mind craved clarity and closure, stability and permanence. He craved clarity too, but not at the expense of truth, and he was fascinated by change and the complexities it begot. A paradox made his mind fizz pleasantly, and even ambivalence did, sometimes, and what was marriage but an invitation to ambivalence, though if he was truthful with himself he preferred to adore Sonia.

He could remember his other mind and heart, the one that had accepted Christ. After the brittle ironies of communism, it had been a relief to profess a sincere belief and live among a new class of people who had decoded the rules for life.

Could Sonia accept him as a non-believer? What would the past eight years of their life together look like to her, if she knew he'd been pretending, playing along? A delusion, a mirage.

Years ago, during a game of Scrabble, he'd thought he had the letters for MARRIAGE. The word LOVING was already on the board, and he planned to use the G — he could imagine Sonia photographing the intersection of LOVING and MARRIAGE and posting it online — but as he placed the tiles on the board, he realized he only had letters for MIRAGE. Even now, English spelling sometimes confused him.

If Sonia knew how he felt, would she want to read the Bible with him, even if he protested that he enjoyed it? Would she want to pray with him?

He wouldn't mind praying less. Sometimes prayer felt like a fiction he was spinning about their marriage. In his prayers, their life together was about freedom and purpose rather than constraint and incomprehension. A figment. Living the dream with Sonia.

Friday Sonia stepped out early. As Ivan dried himself in the bathroom, she told him from the other side of the door, "Tessa and I are going to look for mushrooms." He found muesli soaking on the table.

The new alternator had arrived and Ivan planned to complete the installation by lunch. If Ryan and Tessa felt up to an eight-hour drive, they could be in Toronto that night. "We'll play it by ear," said Tessa, which made Sonia remark to Ivan that at last the young couple sounded like true RVers.

But after the new alternator was installed, the RV gave a faint cough and still didn't start.

Ivan checked the battery and the fuses, the ignition switch and the starter, and finally the fuel filter.

Why hadn't he thought of the fuel filter? It needed to be changed more often than most newbies expected. Ten years ago he would have remembered the fuel filter. He would have been more vigilant and investigated other potential problems.

Delivery of the new fuel filter would delay them another day, more likely two. Even if it arrived tomorrow it would arrive late. Ryan and Tessa wouldn't get to Toronto until Sunday at the earliest. The campsite was costing them each day.

Ivan felt like an old man. Trapped in the bubble of his own dimming perceptions, he'd assumed his first hypothesis was right. It was like being young again, except without hope for future improvement.

He bought the fuel filter online without telling Ryan. He paid for it and decided to compensate Ryan and Tessa for the extra campsite time, maybe for the whole week.

He was too rattled to tell Ryan immediately. Had Ryan and Tessa paid for a tow truck they would be in Toronto now. Ivan could have cried out to God for guidance then, as he sat before his laptop and stared out the window, where the yellow leaves of the poplars flapped flimsily.

Piercing laughter drifted from the forest. It was Tessa. She carried their mushroom basket, which overflowed with grubby, milky specimens. "We found matsutakes," cried Sonia. She opened the door. "Can you believe it? Some chanterelles too."

Over lunch, the state of Tessa and Ryan's RV came up briefly. "I'm working on it," said Ivan, and their enchanted faces displayed no doubt. He was mortified by their faith in his competence. He wanted to tell them, You shouldn't have trusted an old man.

"I don't know how Sonia found them," said Tessa, as they ate the grilled matsutakes with rice and soft-boiled eggs. "They were nearly all hidden beneath pine needles. I wish I could see like that."

"You have to be a little curious," said Sonia. "You see a crack in the ground and wonder, maybe something tasty is tucked in there."

"You looked psychic to me."

"Not at all! I was simply curious, relaxed, not expecting much, like I'm just going for a walk, no big deal. But I have faith, too, that something good is out there." Eventually you walked right into the miracle.

"What do you think?" Tessa asked Ryan.

Ryan said the matsutakes tasted interesting.

"Ryan is a foodie whose favourite restaurant is Wendy's," joked Tessa.

"You don't think they're a little dank?" he said.

"They remind me of Vancouver," said Tessa. "The Douglas firs in Lynn Valley."

"Usually matsutakes grow in the Northwest," said Sonia.

"Count on Sonia to find them in the most improbable spot," said Ivan.

"You can take some to dry," said Sonia. "They're good in soups."

"But you found them," said Tessa.

"But you're leaving!" said Sonia. "We'll find more."

Ivan thought about how much longer Tessa and Ryan would be stuck on the island.

"Looking for mushrooms is meditative," said Tessa. "I need to get back to meditating."

"You never worry about poisoning?" asked Ryan.

"No," said Sonia. "The important thing is a positive identification. If you have even a tiny doubt that it's edible, leave it alone. No room for doubt!"

"The matsutake does have a poisonous lookalike, *Amanita smithiana*," said Ivan. After his screw-up with the fuel filter, he felt the need to know something, even at the expense of his guests' peace of mind. "But don't worry, we double checked each one."

"What's that Czech saying?" Sonia asked Ivan.

"All mushrooms are edible, some only once."

"Ivan taught me everything."

"My father liked to go into the forest on Sunday mornings. He sent me into the thicker areas adults couldn't reach."

Ivan thought of Sonia in the woods, discovering riches in

crumbling soil. Sonia was perceptive. She would have noticed the fuel filter. "Where did you find them?"

"Near the quarry," said Sonia. "The land is damaged over there. Mushrooms like damaged places, I was telling Tessa."

"The first thing to grow after the bombing of Hiroshima was a matsutake," said Ivan, and everyone paused to think about life creeping back after the end of the world. Charred, pulverized dirt as far as the eye can see, and then a glint of white, like a fragment of bone, but on closer inspection tender and damp, a new snout poking up. It was easy to project hope onto mushrooms, or curiosity or shyness, whereas it was simply life doing what it did, the perpetual swerve towards change.

"I love how mushrooms create new life out of death," said Sonia. "It's a lesson for us all."

Ivan worried that Sonia might start talking about Christ's resurrection or, worse yet, the dead baby. "The largest organism in the world is a fungus," he said. "Somewhere in Oregon." Talking about Jesus would be nearly as bad as talking about the dead baby. He saw how non-believers responded to Sonia's Jesus talk. The tight smile and the misty gaze. The politeness that hid disbelief, not at God but at her. *You really expect to change what I think?*

"Let me do the dishes," said Tessa.

"We can do them together," said Sonia. "I'll show you the secret dishrack Ivan made."

"Shall we take a look at the alternator?" Ivan asked Ryan. Even if Ryan knew nothing about mechanics, he would figure out soon enough that something was wrong. Better to tell him the truth. In a week Ivan's error would hardly matter. It wasn't the end of the world.

"She's a bully," said Tessa.

They were on a thin forest path shaggy with cedar and spruce. Tessa strode ahead of him, breathing heavily, almost jogging. Impossible to stay inside the RV, even with Ivan no longer poking at it.

Tessa seemed to have forgiven Ryan for telling Ivan about Penny, and on some level Ryan could understand Ivan blabbing to his wife. What did an old couple have to talk about from one day to the next? But that Sonia would tell Tessa that God had a plan for her, that everything was part of God's *plan*, even the tragedies, even losing Penny, this boggled any reasonable mind. Then Sonia's surprise at Tessa's outrage, Sonia's teary reminiscence about wanting a child so badly, expecting Tessa to commiserate while still insisting that God's plan was best.

There had been something like an apology, heavily disguised as an explanation. I only meant. I hoped that.

"I don't want her praying for us."

"She can pray for our RV," said Ryan.

"No, not anything of ours. It's condescending." Tessa slowed down and half turned around. "Are you going to get religion? Because I'm not sure I can live with that." Tessa gave him a frown, but it was jokey.

If Tessa weren't reeling from Sonia's words, Ryan might have stayed with the topic of what they could each live with.

"What if they fucked with our alternator?" said Tessa. "To buy time to convert us? It's just us and them here, pretty much, in the middle of nowhere."

"Deep in the woods with the evangelical zombies," said Ryan. "Brains! Brains!" He raised his arms and grabbed at Tessa's shoulders. She ducked and he darted after her, pulling her in. He hadn't felt her whole body since they'd reached the island. Most of their time had been spent giving each other space in the tiny RV on the forgotten edge of the world. Even before the island, the RV had been killing his libido. What had once been excitingly cozy, like making love in a tent, became shabby, like doing it in a car because you had no better options.

He buried his face in her neck. They were nearly the same height, and while he would have preferred to be taller, there were moments when he liked how physically matched they were. Like playmates.

"We could just go back to Vancouver," he said into her neck.

She stiffened. "What would we do there?"

"What we did before. Was it so bad?"

She extricated herself and took out her phone. "We have a cell signal. We could just call a tow truck and stay in Little Current for the night."

"If Ivan fixes the fuel filter, we save another six hundred dollars. We don't have that kind of money to spare. Ivan said he'd pay for our extra time out here."

"From Tuesday or from today?"

"I'm sure we can negotiate something. He's trying. He's not like his wife."

In bed that night, Tessa pressed her mouth hard against Ryan's. Soon she was on top of him and finding her own hectic pace. When they found a rhythm together, she cried out so loudly that Ryan wondered if Ivan and Sonia could hear. The window was open a crack.

Afterwards, they listened to the last of the crickets. Tessa sighed peaceably and said, "Screw God's plan."

"Ivan doesn't actually believe in God," said Ryan. "He used to, but now he just pretends for his wife's sake."

Tessa gave a pleased yelp. "That's kind of sweet. I mean it's sick, but sweet too."

"Isn't it just sad?" said Ryan.

"Holy fucked-up wedlock," sighed Tessa. "Holy fucked-up dirty wedlock." She tugged Ryan's balls and groaned into his ear.

Tessa was on the pill, though they planned to try again. When she would be ready was unclear. She was thirty-six. Ryan hoped a baby would make her miss a sedentary lifestyle. He didn't want them to become a lone couple seeking the thrills of novel landscapes to feel alive.

Tessa still blamed herself. *We didn't protect her. We don't deserve another kid.* At the daycare, Penny had been put down for a nap. Tessa arrived to find a daycare worker whose name she'd forgotten performing CPR incorrectly. The exact cause of death was never ascertained.

Tessa believed they should have found a better daycare, less crowded, with a higher worker-to-child ratio. In the middle of Vancouver this was tough but not impossible. Or they should have borrowed money so Tessa could stay home with Penny until she was two. They could have moved to a cheaper apartment.

Tessa had been a chill mother. Before Penny was born, Tessa dipped into a couple of the books that Ryan had bought and decided they'd figure it out once the baby arrived. She was impatient for Penny to be born. On the night she went into labour, she eased herself into the Uber and said, "Let's get this party started."

A few weeks after Penny's birth, they settled into a routine of Sunday breakfast at a café. Often Penny slept as they filled themselves with wholesome foods, thick slices of sourdough with poached eggs and vegan banh mi, focused on each other. Do you want something else? How do you feel? It's like a very long mild hangover, isn't it? This is crazy, we have a baby. This is NOT A PET.

There were even jokes about Tessa's poor track record with pets, the guinea pig who died of a cold, or was it starvation? A cold, Tessa insisted, and how was she supposed to know that colds could be fatal to guinea pigs?

After Penny's death, Vancouver became intolerable. The joggers with good posture and bouncing ponytails, the righteous cyclists knifing down the hill, the people buying bright, innovative salads, everyone keeping it together. Of course there were also the people falling apart, people with addictions. Where once they had confounded Ryan, now they scared him.

It took a while to realize the city was a problem. If he and Tessa had left Vancouver sooner, had taken a break rather than tried to keep going, Tessa might have healed faster, might have been ready by now to return to real life.

Tessa kissed him before turning away. "I can't wait to get out of here. At this point, any city would do."

Ryan felt the duvet pull as she tucked it beneath her chin. "Even Vancouver?"

"Sure."

Ivan would install the fuel filter as soon as it arrived tomorrow, so they could set out early on Saturday. Eight hours to Toronto, and then what? Maybe her friends would persuade Tessa to settle somewhere, if not Vancouver then Toronto or nearby, somewhere cheaper like Hamilton, though could he bear to live there? Living four provinces away from home was almost as depressing as running away from your problems.

Before breakfast, Ivan went for a walk. Along the limestone shore, water sloshed against a shelf of rock, smoothing out as the lake grew deeper. Ivan took in its huge mellow scale and attempted to erase the past forty-eight hours from his mind. His neck was still sore from the final repair on Tessa and Ryan's RV. He'd tried to keep his distance from them and limit remarks to practical matters. That was after he'd apologized to Ryan, Tessa having vanished, out on an interminable hike, or was she hiding in the RV? At the apology Ryan said, "We just want to get out of here and see our friends."

Ivan was still angry at Sonia when he remembered the conversation Thursday evening. They were reading the third chapter of Samuel, where God calls audibly to the boy and reveals a prophesy against the priest Eli. It was a prophesy to make the ears of everyone tingle, God said. Maybe if God had told him something to make his own ears tingle, Ivan mused, he would still be a Christian.

Sonia had said, "Samuel didn't want to tell God's message to Eli, but he did." She talked about how sometimes God's truth was difficult to hear. How God's perspective was challenging to digest, so much bigger than our own. "God's bigger picture," she called it.

That's when she told Ivan about her words to Tessa, as the two women washed dishes after the matsutake feast. "I wanted to help her see God's bigger picture, that her suffering is not meaningless." Sonia was ready for skepticism or confusion from Tessa, but not the impression that Tessa was about to brain her with the serving bowl she was drying.

"You couldn't keep this idea to yourself?" Ivan asked Sonia.

"She was so unhappy."

"She looked happy enough to me." Ivan thought to himself,

No, *you* felt unhappy about her dead baby and needed to comfort yourself.

"It was an opportunity to witness," said Sonia.

Technically, a Christian couldn't object. "It was poorly timed," said Ivan, "and you promised me you wouldn't say anything."

"It was a private conversation, just us women. I would never have brought it up among the four of us." Sonia compressed her lips. "It would have been easier to say nothing, but the Lord put it on my heart to speak up."

Ivan was staggered by Sonia's lack of empathy. "But she doesn't *believe* in God. Telling her that her dead baby is part of God's plan is like if I told you that the fairies of Misery Bay decided we'll never have children. It would mean nothing to you. It would be insulting."

"God is not a fairy."

"It's an analogy, my dear." Ivan felt very tired. Had Sonia's belief in God made her stupid, or had she always been stupid? Even before he'd lost his faith, there had been moments of bewilderment at Sonia's mind. She believed the world to be ten thousand years old, while he had always emphasized the Bible verse about a day for God being like a thousand human days, the word *thousand* a metaphor for many, an acknowledgement that humans and God operated on different time scales. The fact that their RV now sat on land that harboured fossils from hundreds of millions of years ago had no impact on her mind.

Still, he'd thought that he mostly accepted Sonia's beliefs, as long as they applied only to the two of them. He wasn't even so annoyed when she talked about Christ to their non-Christian RV friends — older, forbearing folks, many of them Americans accustomed to Jesus talk, who usually smiled and changed the topic.

But when Sonia tried to impose her beliefs on a young person who was suffering, and whose husband might leave her, then he experienced — what was it? Rage?

"You broke a promise," he said.

"You're right." Sonia's eyes returned to the Bible in her lap, and Ivan thought she might start to read the next chapter. "But God's ways are higher than man's." Sonia swallowed and her gaze grew scattered, jumping from the Bible to the kitchen to the framed, cross-stitched sampler that read, *As for me and my RV, we will serve the Lord.* "If you knew what she called me" — Sonia looked to the window, half covered by the lace curtain and half bare, reflecting the cramped interior — "I won't repeat it."

A mass of epithets bloomed in Ivan's mind. A meddling bitch. A heartless imbecile. An idiot an idiot an idiot.

Along the limestone shore, the transparent water continued to slosh peaceably as it had for nearly half a billion years. A place where the first fungi crept onto land, before the fruiting plants and the ferns, and long before the animals. He and Sonia delighted in nature together, up to a point. She was uninterested in its prehistory, the giant sea scorpions and the jawless eels.

For the first time in years, the thought of leaving Sonia returned. He would never respect Sonia's mind, that was a fact. He'd had this thought eight years ago, but now it took on a newly dreary finality.

He imagined telling Sonia the truth. The past eight years together a lie. It would be a devastating conversation, but also a relief, even a satisfaction. You think your God tells you everything you need to know, but he doesn't, see?

For a time she might try to coax him back to the faith, but eventually the firm boundaries of her mind would shut him out.

On the other hand, perhaps the revelation would provoke in her a spiritual crisis. Perhaps she would lose her God too. Then he'd be happy, but would she want him? The man who forced her to see the brutal truth.

Or she would become a greater zealot. More likely that.

Twenty years ago, once it was clear they would never have children, and the war in Yugoslavia was nearly over, she'd wanted to move back to her hometown and preach. What would I do there? Ivan had asked. I have a good job in Canada and don't speak your language. You understand it well enough, Sonia had said. She believed God would provide. Fortunately he was the head of the household and had the final say.

He wished he could simply adore her generosity and immoderate cheekbones and nimble, clever fingers. Often she was more perceptive than he. She saw the needs of others, whereas he assumed people were fine, until the crisis was obvious.

And she was the one who found the most precious mushrooms, ready to be delighted by them.

It was close to eight-thirty, and he turned back to the RV. Sonia didn't like when he was late for meals, and he didn't feel up to an argument. That could come later, once Tessa and Ryan were gone.

Meanwhile, Ivan would take his cue from nature, the steady rocks and the rhythmic water and the trees going sallow and bald without protest. Change was part of life, and he and Sonia were due for a change. Not divorce necessarily, but an elucidation, a reckoning. One time he'd described physicists' vision of reality to Sonia, emphasizing its dynamism in contrast with the insipid stability of eternity. Sonia was unimpressed. "But that's how God sees the universe," she said. "Physicists just want to see like

God does." To her mind, their overly complicated explanations were futile and self-indulgent. Someone already had the answers because He'd made them. She pitied physicists their fragmentary insights. Maybe it was God's joke on us, she said, quoting Solomon. *God has set eternity in the hearts of men; yet they cannot fathom what God has done from beginning to end.*

Ivan stood in front of the door to the RV and straightened his back, as he'd done many times before stepping into a classroom. Already from outside, the RV was aromatic. On the dining table were a big chanterelle frittata and a bigger bowl of fruit salad. Sonia was rolling palachinky.

"Help me and set the table," she said. "Tessa and Ryan will join us for breakfast."

"Really," said Ivan.

"I just spoke to Tessa and apologized. This time I really apologized." Early that morning, God had revealed to Sonia the enormity of her error. Sonia had been selfish to project her own suffering onto Tessa, God said. She'd talked when she should have listened. She had been proud rather than humble. Sonia needed to humble herself and apologize sincerely. "Tessa accepted my apology."

Ivan found it hard to believe that Tessa was reconciled with Sonia. Maybe she was being polite. You couldn't tell with some Canadians. But Tessa could have politely declined breakfast. She and Ryan were leaving that morning, after all. The four of them would never meet again.

Did Tessa want some kind of last word or revenge? What had Sonia said to her, precisely?

"They have a long day ahead," said Sonia. "They need a good breakfast." Her hands trembled as she rolled a palachinka, jam erupting from its edges. Usually her palachinky were neat, their edges tucked in. Sonia smacked the palachinka onto the serving plate. Jam oozed as she dug her fingers in.

"Can I help?" said Ivan. The last time he'd made food was when Sonia had shingles.

"I don't know," said Sonia.

"What's wrong?" he said, but when he saw her face he knew. The strange thing was that Sonia looked ashamed.

Her voice was a whisper. She flinched when she uttered the word *atheist.* "You told her husband."

"Ryan must have misunderstood." The words were instantaneous. Conviction surged within Ivan, panic extinguished hesitation. It was like diving into rapids to save a man overboard, except it wasn't heroic, because if he'd had to stab the man to death he would have. Anything to stop the panic. "I told Ryan about my period of doubt, years ago, remember?"

"I didn't believe her at first." Sonia stared down at the misshapen palachinka. "Now I'm not so sure."

"They're unhappy," said Ivan, "and the unhappy sow discord. Ryan is thinking of leaving the marriage." He put his arms around Sonia, kissed her cheekbone and then the frizzy wave on the side of her head.

Ivan kept talking, quoting Christ's counsel. Bless those who curse you, pray for those who mistreat you. If someone takes your coat, do not withhold your shirt.

"I would give Tessa my shirt!" said Sonia.

"I don't think they'd like our clothes." He squeezed Sonia's shoulders.

"Her tops have all those complicated straps," said Sonia, and they laughed. Ivan would have liked to keep laughing forever, together on a sunny day, the RV filled with good smells, but Sonia said, "You'll tell them the truth?"

"Of course."

Ivan unfolded the chairs for their guests and hummed the tune that went with the words, *Do not let your hearts be troubled, do not be afraid*, mostly for Sonia but a little for himself.

Because Ryan would understand. When Ivan professed his belief in God, he would look like a shabby old liar. Not that Ryan's opinion mattered much. The question was whether Sonia would buy the lie. If she didn't, she'd begin the mission to bring him back to Jesus. There would be long irrelevant conversations. Sonia might fast and pray. Or she might despair and become depressed, he'd seen it before. Either way, hell.

He wants to draw out the moment before the lie, pretend the feast is only for Sonia and himself. The fruit salad glittering, the palachinky golden: this is as close to heaven as he'll ever get. Here is eternity, a bright fall day when the birds linger on shore before flying out over the ruffled water.

Tessa and Ryan are at the door, and already Sonia has invited them in. His own mouth has creased into a smile as the guests seat themselves.

For a time, he watches the chopped plums in the fruit salad, dark and gold, in the flickering shade of the poplar — simple physics — until Sonia says, "Ivan, please pray."

He thanks the God he doesn't believe in for the beautiful day.

Per the formula, he thanks God for health and the privilege to live in a free country.

He begins to speak of Tessa and Ryan's drive to Toronto. If he still believed, he would think that Satan is tempting him to allude to the young couple's marital trouble. He might say,

Lord, bless and strengthen this young, struggling marriage. At the words, Tessa might dash out of the RV never to return. A change probable but not certain, because randomness is always in play.

His lips are on autopilot. He plans to download a Christian book in the next couple days. In the next month, he will lift a hand to heaven at a church service. He won't do it all at once, because Sonia is no fool. She sees what others miss.

When he asks God to protect Ryan and Tessa on the drive to Toronto, there is a restless shuffle across the table. Ivan has a panicked doubt that one of his thoughts has slipped from his mouth. The words of a bumbling old man. He is not sure he can pull off the lie and preserve the marriage he wants to keep easy.

He opens his eyes a crack. Ryan's eyes are closed, his face loose. But Tessa's eyes are open. She is looking at Sonia, whose eyes are also open, watching Ivan as his lips move. He nearly chokes. Sonia's gaze is neutral. She could be noticing a crack in the soil that harbours a mushroom.

The last time Sonia watched as he prayed, so far as Ivan knows, their marriage was in its early days. Back then, addressing the Creator was one of the most intimate things they did together. A third presence saturated their marriage, its hopes and frustrations and instincts. The things he'd wanted to do to Sonia, and sometimes did, between Amen and the first forkful. The things he'd loved sharing with God, too.

He feels a rush of love, whether for Sonia or for the God he once knew, he cannot tell. "Lord, bless our marriages," he says, because he wants to affirm what he and Sonia have — mainly for Sonia's sake, but also for Tessa and Ryan's — to demonstrate what marriage can be after many years, the care and faith it requires.

Both Sonia and Tessa are watching him now, as if they knew his lie long before he told Ryan. "Keep our marriages strong, my Lord," says Ivan, and Sonia smiles, because for the first time in eight years he means every word.

fearfully and wonderfully

The preacher called us beautiful and prayed for our future husbands. He asked God to keep us gentle because gentleness was the greatest power of all. Think of Christ the lamb, washing the disciples' feet. A godly wife could win over even the most difficult man.

I tried to imagine myself as a godly wife. My wifely self did not tell ghost stories or obsess about her pimples. Each morning in the washroom mirror I checked for new eruptions, evidence of some hot corruption deep inside me.

When the preacher instructed us to examine our hearts, I bowed my head and asked God to give me the right kind of heart. I was a lukewarm Christian, unable to thrill at Christ's sacrifice for humankind. Lukewarm Christians made God want to puke, He said so in the Bible. *Because you are lukewarm, and neither cold nor hot, I will vomit you out.*

Beyond the open windows of the worship pavilion, the evening forest throbbed with crickets, and I envied their lack of eternal souls. In that final summer of Senior Girls, within the reassuring routines of Bible camp — volleyball and worship, archery and Bible study — I worried that my soul was cosmically defective. When the horn of a train sounded, I imagined the dark machine rocketing to godless New York City.

Then the preacher invited us to repent, and I knew I needed to apologize to Tanya. Her head was bowed in the first row.

I wondered what she had to repent for. Tanya was the opposite of lukewarm, hot for Christ, praying daily for her foster parents, hoping to bring them to the Lord, and for her birth mother too. More than once she'd said, "I forgive her." Already at twelve, Tanya appeared to be preparing her testimony, the stirring tale of a personal crisis that climaxes in spiritual transformation, a happy ending with God's help. That summer I hoped she might help me draft a testimony of my own.

A week earlier, at the Bible-verse memorization contest, I had wanted to win the prize, which was a teen girl's Bible with pages to colour and journal on. My own Bible left me cold, the words on the pages like flattened bugs.

Tanya had signed up for the contest too, as had my friend Esther. We stood with the other competitors at the front of the worship pavilion, on either side of the splintery cross. We ran through the easy verses, about God so loving the world and confessing with your mouth that Jesus is Lord. When a girl bungled a verse, the judge read it aloud and the girl departed to sit with the audience. I recited, "For what shall it profit a man, if he shall gain the whole world and lose his own soul?" The worldly man's sad, empty life was obvious, though part of me wondered what it would be like to gain the whole world for a day. I had a muddled vision of shopping sprees, Satanic rituals, and communism; and music videos, lots of music videos.

Tanya said, "I praise you because I am fearfully and wonderfully made. Your works are wonderful. I know that full well." It was the verse every preacher read when condemning abortion.

Soon after meeting me, Tanya had confided that she'd nearly been aborted. "She's lying," Esther had said, believing that Tanya just wanted attention, but to me Tanya seemed miraculous, like a plane crash survivor, a blessed, wily fetus who made it out alive. Surely God had a purpose for her life.

Another girl recited the verse from Ecclesiastes about nothing new under the sun, but garbled it. She was out, as was the girl who tried to follow up Genesis 1:1 with Genesis 1:2, and the girl who tried to recite the parable of the wise and the foolish virgins. In it, ten virgins await a bridegroom whose ETA is unknown. All they know is that it will be at night. Five virgins remember to put oil in their lamps, while another five do not. When the bridegroom's arrival is imminent, the foolish virgins ask the wise ones to share their oil.

By this point the girl had botched her recitation, but I remembered the rest of the story. The wise virgins refuse, saying they do not have enough, and advise the foolish virgins to buy some oil themselves. When they are out shopping, the bridegroom arrives and takes the wise virgins to the wedding feast.

"And the door was shut." The foolish virgins pound on the door, begging the bridegroom to unlock it. He tells them, *I do not know you.*

That summer the bridegroom's words troubled me. His absolute coldness to the foolish virgins, when he too had been delayed. Nor could I understand why the wise virgins refused to share, if not their oil, then their lamps. Light is easily shared, as Jesus himself said. *Let your light so shine before men.*

The Prodigal Son had received lavish forgiveness, offered a new robe and a fatted calf. But the foolish girls would have no feast.

When Esther's turn came, she declaimed, "A wife of noble character who can find? She is worth far more than rubies." The verse was common on inspirational plaques, and I hoped that Esther was running out of verses too.

The only verse I could think of was "Jesus wept," the shortest verse in the Bible. When I uttered it, Esther gave a honk of laughter.

Tanya spoke up. The verse was not spiritually edifying, she said.

It shows us Christ's humanity, answered the judge.

It's not even a full sentence, said Tanya.

But it is, said the judge.

When Tanya recited "Take no part in the unfruitful works of darkness," she looked at me. Earlier that week, I had been caught telling a story about a terrorized babysitter to a huddled group of campers. When our counsellor found us, she asked, "Girls, do horror stories glorify the Lord?" Esther thought that Tanya had tipped her off.

Esther recited another verse about the wife of noble character. With her ski-jump nose and clear white skin, Esther appeared a plausible future candidate for the role of noble wife. She looked like the girl in our manual on Christian charm, a Barbie without boobs, a ready smile on her face — unlike mine, and unlike Tanya's, with her lip-compressing earnestness, to say nothing of her breasts and a feature the manual referred to as "snake hips."

That round I was out and went to sit with the audience.

"For to me, to live is Christ, and to die is gain," said Tanya. She said it like she meant it.

Esther was on a roll. She knew the verse about the noble wife awakening before the servants, and the ones about her working a distaff and planting a vineyard. The judge scanned her Bible to check that Esther got each word right, as I thought of my own mother, a wife who spent much of her time praying on a narrow futon in the basement, an activity she called "spiritual warfare" and that my father called "resting." When I tried to imagine what kind of wife I would be one day, the idea conjured freshly-baked cookies and balls of used tissue.

"With man it is impossible, but with God all things are possible," said Tanya.

And the rest? asked the judge.

Tanya had missed the opening words about Jesus looking at the disciples. She was out, and Esther won. The judge asked Esther to recite the rest of the chapter, until "Give her the reward she has earned, and let her works bring her praise at the city gate!" After a round of applause, Esther was awarded the teen Bible. That evening she explained that her missionary grandma paid her a dime for every memorized verse. By then she'd sold the Bible for ten dollars and bought out the tuck shop's supply of Hot Lips, which stained her teeth pink and made her every word redolent of cinnamon.

At supper Esther wasn't hungry, nor was Tanya, who sat hunched over my copy of the year's Christian bestseller. It was a gothic novel about an American town beset by demons, who infiltrate primarily through the college via secular ideas like feminism and self-esteem. Soon enough, self-esteem leads to false accusations of rape and molestation, and later to suicidal impulses. A thin stack of pages remained as Tanya read the final showdown between good and evil, where angels bright as comets rout the demons, who flap leathery wings and gasp sulphurously.

Esther flashed her pink teeth and said, "Tanya, have you read all the books of the Bible?"

Tanya looked up, dazed, and said yes.

"Habakkuk?"

"Yes."

"Leviticus?"

"Yes."

"Even the rules about cattle and whatever?"

"Yes."

"What about Song of Songs?"

Tanya's eyes went back to the novel. "Yes Esther, I've read Song of Songs."

"And what did you think?"

Tanya kept her eyes on the book. "It's a parable about Christ's love for the church."

"But what did *you* think?"

"Most of it went over my head."

"Maybe it's time to reread it," said Esther. "Nothing wrong with reading the Word of God. Have you read it, Beth?"

I didn't think so. It's short and easy to miss. Our pastor never brought it up.

"Have you read it, Esther?" I asked. Esther loved answering her own questions.

"Of course I have," she smiled.

When dessert was wheeled out (fruit salad, again), she said

to me, "Let's go." We went to the cabin, where Esther found Tanya's Bible and sat on her thin sleeping bag, reviewing Tanya's annotations. Many verses in Psalms were underlined, including *See how numerous are my enemies and how fiercely they hate me!*

Lying on Tanya's sleeping bag, I stared at the upper bunk. When a train sounded its horn, I punched Esther's shoulder — our secret reminder that we would visit the tracks one night.

In a stern preacher's voice, Esther read, "The Song of Songs, which is Solomon's!"

She continued in a melting voice. "Let him kiss me with the kisses of his mouth; for thy love is better than wine. Because of the savour of thy good ointments, thy name is as ointment poured forth, therefore do the virgins love thee."

Thy good ointments! we hooted.

Were the virgins in the Song of Songs foolish or wise? More likely foolish, except that they were at the bridegroom's party, so it was confusing. At twelve, the word *virgin* conjured that other v-word, its botched anagram. This new awareness marked me as a virgin, even if sex remained an abstraction glimpsed in nude paintings from centuries ago, its sumptuousness as foreign as dining on stuffed pheasant. Still, God must have thought that some sex education was a good idea, because He'd included it in His Word. Meanwhile, I waited with trepidation for my mother to bring up the subject, but fortunately she was busy with the spiritual warfare.

Esther skimmed a page and said, "Okay, here. Your breasts are like two fawns, like twin fawns of a gazelle that browse among the lilies."

"Is a gazelle a bird?"

75

"You need to watch more *Animal Kingdom*, Beth. It's like a deer with horns. They're graceful is the point."

The image was more bewildering than the locusts of Revelation, with their lions' teeth and women's hair.

"Honeycomb . . . spikenard . . . okay." Esther turned the page. "How beautiful you are and how pleasing, O love, with your delights! Your stature is like that of the palm, and your breasts like clusters of fruit. I said, 'I will climb the palm tree; I will take hold of its fruit.'"

The line was as hilarious and appalling as a dirty joke. Impossible to hear it and not see the avid grope. For the rest of the day, it was a refrain. One of us said, "I will climb the palm tree," and the other replied, "I will take hold of its fruit!"

Sometimes all Esther said was "I will climb . . ." and we fell into a torment of laughter.

It was funniest around Tanya. She'd finished the Christian bestseller and was hanging around us more. "You climb trees?" she said.

"That's what campers do," said Esther.

"Where are the fruit trees?" said Tanya, and Esther's cheeks grew bloated and bright.

"There are blackberry bushes," I said.

"Fruit!" sang Esther. "Fruit! Fruit! Fruit!" She went into an ecstasy of imaginary fruit tasting, her cinnamon lips opening and closing like an ardent fish's.

"Stop it," said Tanya.

"You need to read the Bible more," said Esther.

During the evening service, Tanya leafed through her Bible and figured it out. After that, the line was even funnier.

So the day after the preacher's visit, I looked for Tanya. I found her watching a tetherball game and asked to speak with her privately. "Jesus told me He'd send you," she said.

She led me through a copse of sugar maples towards the beach, as the tetherball's thunks grew faint. We skirted a marshy patch thick with lilies and dragonflies, and reached a granite boulder tucked behind a white pine half toppled into the water, with low boughs that canopied us.

"I like to pray here," said Tanya, squatting in the dappled shade, as the water of our small lake puckered with tiny ripples beneath a cloudless sky. "You need to be careful, Beth. There are demons here."

In the July sunshine, I tried to imagine demons all around us, flapping their leathery wings and scrunching their reptilian faces. What came to mind was the water snake I had seen earlier that week, a rubbery whip with a dainty, alert face, which it held high above the water.

"You're under attack, you and Esther."

"What?"

"The joke about the Song of Songs."

I apologized again, said it was awful and stupid and that I hoped she'd forgive me.

"But it's not really you, it's the demons." There was a deeper pattern, she would explain. At her foster family's house, she'd found a photo in her Bible. Someone had planted it there. "Of naked people, doing things." She was sure that it was her foster father, Mr. Barry. "He thinks I read the Bible too much."

She'd hidden the photo in her closet (and prayed over her Bible to cleanse it). The next day the photo was gone. "It was a group, like six people."

"Gross." That was all I said. At twelve I expected evil to be sensational, like the Satanic covens down in California drinking babies' blood, or the Whore of Babylon in glittering purple, drunk on the blood of the Saints. Or like the sulphur-breathing demons with leathery wings in the Christian bestseller. I didn't know that evil could be confusing at first, that it could make you think, *What?*

The photo had been planted in the Song of Songs. The demons had started to work through Mr. Barry and were continuing through me and Esther. Did I understand now?

The pattern was horrifying and irrefutable. I had become an agent of the demons. The sun filtering through the pine boughs, the barely ruffled water of our camp's small monsterless lake, all were props hiding a ghastlier reality.

When Tanya said "Let's pray," I took her hands and closed my eyes. As she prayed for God's guidance, a mood of solidarity descended on us. God would protect Tanya and give her the wisdom to act. She wasn't a victim anymore, because God was in control.

My words joined Tanya's, as I prayed more ardently than I had in years. When the prayer was over, it occurred to me that helping Tanya could reignite my lukewarm heart. The convergence felt providential.

When she promised me to secrecy I agreed. "You know, it's normal to suffer for the sake of the gospel," she said.

Years later, my cluelessness would be difficult to fathom. How did I not insist that we tell an adult? Despite the church's silences around sexual abuse during those years, the camp would have notified Child Protection Services. The fact that Mr. Barry was not a born-again Christian would have made it easy.

Praying about the abuse made it feel like we had connected with a deeper reality. We had uncovered the demonic root and brought it to the all-powerful Creator; surely a more effective strategy than relying on imperfect institutions. It didn't occur to me that praying privately was a way of keeping quiet — exactly what we, as girls, were supposed to do.

When Tanya vowed to bring Mr. Barry to Jesus one day, I admired her determination worthy of a wise virgin.

The second-to-last night of camp, Esther and I met outside the girls' washroom. We passed darkened cabins and the worship pavilion, where the EXIT sign glowed red. Somewhere a counsellor was making the rounds, and as gravel crackled beneath our runners and we neared the dining hall, we listened for alien footsteps.

"Where are you going?" someone shout-whispered from a dark corner of the dining-hall porch.

"To the washroom," said Esther too quickly.

The washrooms were long behind us, and the person laughed at Esther. It was Tanya.

"We're heading to the tracks," I said, and invited her.

We passed the dining hall and the gloomy tuck shop, the cooks' cabins too. At the edge of camp was the director's cottage, lights on. We slowed our pace to quiet our steps.

Then we were inside a completer darkness, feeling our way along a pale strip of road. The trees obscured the stars, and around us crickets pulsed in the bushes.

At a clearing, the sky surged above our heads, and a belief from years ago returned to me — that the stars were heaven's bright light escaping through tiny holes in a dark firmament;

that God could tear down the dark curtain in a single flourish, like a matador, and reveal heaven's glory. A revelation to ignite my lukewarm heart.

The moon was barely half full, but substantial, a chunk of light. When a star slipped and disappeared, I said, "Isn't a person supposed to die when a star falls?"

"That's superstition," said Tanya, and for once Esther agreed with her.

The road widened at the train tracks. To our left, a granite hump obscured a bend in the tracks. On the right, the tracks ran straight. When I switched on the flashlight, it revealed little more than a shadowy jumble of timber and stones, and I turned it off.

"When does the train come?" asked Tanya.

"Midnight," said Esther, and I wondered how she knew. In the parable of the wise and foolish virgins, the bridegroom's imminent arrival is announced at midnight.

The rails held some of the day's warmth, and we huddled on them. Tanya kept slapping her ankles.

"Tell us a story, Beth," said Esther.

"Not now," I said.

"Why not?"

"You know."

"I don't!"

To make light of dark things, as if they were only thrilling fictions, could not please Jesus.

"It's demons that tempt you to desire ghost stories," said Tanya. "They're with us right now." She let this idea sink in, as I swatted away a mosquito. "Remember, Satan doesn't want us to believe he's real."

"Okay, then it's Truth or Dare," said Esther.

There was a crumbling of rocks as Tanya stood up. "I'm going for a walk."

"Where?" said Esther.

"Down the tracks." Already Tanya was walking away, her tread rhythmic with righteousness.

"At least take the flashlight," I said. It was my dad's, with a wide reflector and a handle. "If you hear us call you, switch it on, okay?"

I figured that Tanya could be the wise virgin, while Esther and I would be the foolish ones. We'd enjoy the darkness and have a little party, no bridegroom required. Plus, with her looks and missionary-granny pedigree, Esther always seemed like a wise virgin, even when she broke the rules.

"Story time!" she said.

There was the story about an inmate escaped from an insane asylum who tries to murder a teen girl locked in a car on a country road. In a moment of guilt, I drew on elements from the Christian bestseller. The inmate is possessed by demons that waft inside through the car's air vents.

I could feel Esther losing interest and was figuring out what else the girl could do besides pray, when she said, "Look!"

The granite boulder was bright. For a moment we felt caught, our soft rapt bodies on the tracks, blind to the oncoming reckoning.

We slid down into the stony ditch beside the tracks and were stopped by a wall of blackberry bushes.

"Train!" we shouted in Tanya's direction. By now it was audible and bright, a single night-extinguishing light.

"What if she doesn't hear us?" I asked.

"She has to see it!" said Esther.

When the train hurtled darkly past our noses, each windowless car hulking and relentless, Esther gripped my hand.

The train was pure mechanism, steel and momentum, its physics non-negotiable. It was not spiritual or symbolic but a fact. In its presence I felt myself fearfully and wonderfully made. How easy to sidle closer to the machine, to invite steel to crash into bone and be blasted into the bushes. To be alive one moment and not alive the next. Just like that.

Esther was screaming, giddy shrieks delighted by their terror. I joined, and the sound became a new frequency as impersonal as the train.

The experience moved me more than the songs about God's awesomeness. The things of this world — trains and voices and clasped hands — enthralled me. I didn't want an afterlife. I would not have stated the feeling so directly at twelve, but years later I saw how the train at Bible camp planted in me one seed of the end of my faith.

As the caboose sped away, my thoughts returned to Tanya.

We called her name — my own voice reedy, Esther's a bellow. I was sure that any moment we would see the bright distinct dot of my dad's flashlight, but the tracks remained dark.

Esther and I began to walk in the direction Tanya had taken. Minutes ago it had seemed impossible that she could fail to notice the train, but now I thought about how inward she became when she prayed.

"You stay here," said Esther, "and I'll walk."

"Why?"

"Someone needs to be here in case she returns. Maybe there's another path back."

The loose crumble of stones beneath Esther's feet went on

for a long time, and then it was just me and the crickets and a whippoorwill with its deranged little plaint. There were tiny cracklings in the blackberry bushes, and deeper in the woods a sound like chattering teeth. I thought of Tanya praying alone on the tracks. If I hadn't told ghost stories, she would be with us now, and none of this would be happening.

I had let the demons win. When I asked God's forgiveness, my *Thank you, Jesus* sounded weak. Jesus wouldn't buy it, and neither would the demons.

I repeated the words more emphatically, like the characters in the Christian bestseller would. Confident, handsome people who made the demons shriek for mercy. As I prayed, my fingertips investigated a new zit forming near my temple.

My fingertips halted when I felt a new presence nearby. Not God, who was everywhere, but something more situated, deep in the blackberry bushes.

I cycled through some Bible verses. *Yea though I walk through the valley of the shadow of death I will fear no evil!* If only I knew more verses. *Jesus wept* was useless here.

When I got to *For me to live is Christ, and to die is gain*, I stopped. I didn't want to die. As I hesitated, a chuckle slinked from the bushes. It wasn't the mechanical chattering teeth but intelligent, with the accent of a malicious observer.

I felt around for a stone with a sharp edge and thought of running back to camp. But I couldn't outrun a demon. And if the thing in the bushes was a bear or a man, I probably wouldn't outrun it either.

Alone on the tracks, I experienced the sinner's wretchedness that the preacher had talked about. The recognition of one's own folly that only God can heal.

When Esther returned without Tanya, I grabbed her hands. I begged God's forgiveness for the ghost stories and for bullying Tanya. "Transform my wretchedness into righteousness!" I cried out, and "We rejoice with trembling!"

"Are you okay?" asked Esther.

"Yes!" I felt my need for God at last, and could almost see heaven pulse behind the dark curtain, the stars the light of God's love, the whole a cosmic blanket that encompassed us all, including Tanya, wherever she was. After the sinner's wretchedness, I was buoyant with relief. God was in control. He would bring Tanya back.

Esther was mad at Tanya. As we walked back to the cabin, I told her about the demonic chuckle in the blackberry bushes, and she said, "I bet it was her. Tomorrow she'll be covered in scratches."

At breakfast Tanya was absent. I stared at the pile of puffed rice in my bowl and stroked a pimple with gloomy fingers while Esther poured herself a second bowl. Amazingly, she'd slept, despite Tanya's empty bed. Meanwhile I'd spent most of the night supplicating God for Tanya's protection, listening for footsteps outside. In the bathroom mirror that morning, my face pale and newly mottled, I thought about how evil was ugly.

At Bible study, Tanya materialized. I stared at the back of her steadfast head as at a ghost, while we sang about making a joyful noise unto the Lord.

From then on she avoided us, though I saw her long enough to confirm that she bore no visible scratches. On the last day, when everyone else was packing, Tanya's small pleather suitcase was already zipped shut on her bare mattress. Tanya herself was nowhere to be seen.

I found her on the praying rock. She didn't look up when I stood beside her and said, "Where's my flashlight?"

A mellow breeze stirred the boughs of the white pine. The day was nearly cloudless again, except for a few streaks on the horizon.

"Something happened," she said.

I reminded her that the flashlight was my dad's.

That night on the tracks, Tanya had been ready to succumb to the devil. She'd had such hopes for Bible camp, expecting God to offer a solution to Mr. Barry, but nothing had changed. She couldn't go back to that house.

She sat on the tracks and watched the train annihilate the darkness. It was easy not to move, as glimmering strands thickened into ropes. It was easy to let yourself be swallowed by the light.

She'd hooked her fingers deep inside her ears and apologized to Jesus for not being stronger. She hoped He'd understand.

A comet plunged in front of the train. It seared her eyeballs, and she dropped into darkness. She wondered if she was hurtling through outer space on her way to heaven. But she could hear the train's wheels against the tracks and feel stones poke into her spine.

In the thundering darkness, she believed herself to be in an intermediate stage of existence, just before death. She'd heard of people injured so seriously they felt no pain.

Then she was alone with the bright-dark sky, the little gasping stars that harboured other worlds. And God spoke to her. He reminded her that He'd saved her from being aborted and still had many plans for her.

"It was an angel, Beth. An angel pushed me off the tracks just in time."

Here was a testimony, the kind of story you'd tell at the front of the church to inspire others in their faith. It also echoed the Christian bestseller. A pretty elaborate excuse for losing a flashlight, I thought.

"Do you believe me?"

Soon we'd be on the bus back to the city, where Tanya would return to her foster family. The idea made me think of God puking. I suppose part of me wanted to believe Tanya's story, because if it was true, then God was in control, and she would be okay.

"Yes."

Tanya's voice dropped. "God sees your doubt, Beth. You know what He says about the lukewarm."

Her echo of my secret anxiety made my face tingle, and I said, "What about Esther?" Surely Esther was as lukewarm as I.

Tanya's gaze trained to the narrow clouds on the horizon. "God will humble her one day. She'll repent."

I tried to imagine Esther repenting, but it was easier to imagine Christ surfing one of those narrow clouds. Almost everything Tanya said was made up, I decided, a story in her head.

On the bus back to the city, she sat five rows ahead of us, alone. I watched the back of her head and reflected on the pitiful state of my testimony.

When I told Esther about the angel, I waited for her to laugh. But all Esther said was, "Did she say anything about me?"

I hesitated before answering, "That one day you'll repent."

"Whatever." Esther turned her face to the window, and I wondered who was wise, who was foolish, and who was the most foolish of all.

the righteous engulfed by his love

The first time Carl invited him to church, Ben laughed. The third time, Carl's tongue had nearly drawn itself along the length of Ben's erection. Ben called Carl a bastard and with a huff of laughter agreed to attend, as Carl's tongue sidled back into place. In bed, tomorrow felt unreal, and Ben half liked the idea of sitting on a hard, plain bench, sore and sated.

In fact, the church had plush individual seats, like a movie theatre. The stage supported a sprawling band that included a fiddle player along with six youthful singers, two of whom wore fedoras.

When the drums started up, everyone stood as if for the national anthem. Carl leaned towards Ben and said, "I'm so glad you're here." Had they not been in church, surely he would have squeezed Ben's hand, but soon Carl was lost in the music, crooning the words *consume me, break me,* as a woman with a dove tattooed on her nape lifted her hands. The infantile reaching of adults irritated Ben, as did the alternately bouncy and soothing songs that promised ecstasy or security. Why all this appealed to Carl — who was smart enough to be an internist — Ben could not understand.

He never imagined he'd go for a religious guy. Not that he and Carl were together — it had been barely three months — but his interest in other men was waning. Maybe it was the approach of forty, the organism slowing down.

Ben spent the first part of the sermon trying to guess the pastor's age. He was willing to bet mid-forties, though the pastor, named Jer, could have passed for a decade younger. As Pastor Jer spoke fervently about Christ riding a donkey, the truth of what Ben was witnessing unfolded slowly and inescapably, like a banner unfurling on the enormous screen behind the stage, announcing to all: Pastor Jer is gay.

How could Ben know? He trusted his inner algorithm the way Carl trusted his god. "Gut feelings are algorithms for making decisions," he once told Carl.

"Sure, but don't we do more with our feelings than make decisions?" Carl had asked.

"Like what?"

Carl's reply was vague, something about transformative experiences. Because fundamentally life was a series of decisions, each person a dot in a maze, deciding whether to turn right or left.

Ben wanted the service to be over so he could tell Carl about the pastor. "He's for real!" cried Pastor Jer, talking about what an authentic guy Christ was. How he scattered the moneychangers from the temple and fazed the chief priests with no-BS answers. Christ the populist hero. Pastor Jer didn't say it outright, but the subtext was clear. And yet Pastor Jer's style was urban elite, an expensively threadbare henley and gray tapered jeans with gratuitous diagonal stitching — chinos were out of the question — so the effect was confusing.

When the pastor talked about how faith can send a mountain crashing into the sea, Ben took out his phone and contemplated a graph showing how much the ice caps had melted since 2011. He felt embarrassed for Carl, and was surprised when after the service Carl asked if he'd like to meet Pastor Jer, who was in the foyer glad-handing congregants.

"He looks busy," said Ben. Smiling throngs surrounded the pastor so thickly that Ben couldn't be sure whether the man was indeed wearing a motorcycle jacket.

Over lunch, Carl gushed that the church was a community. *Church* was the wrong word for what Pastor Jer had helped to create. When Carl went for a mouthful of udon, Ben finally said, "You didn't tell me your minister is gay."

The bar area was dim, and Carl remained in profile as he chewed unhurriedly before giving Ben a crooked, sidelong smile. "Are you trying to make a joke?"

"No, I'm serious. He's obviously gay."

"He also obviously has a wife and three children. And he's not a minister."

"Well" — Ben shared a laugh with himself — "some men have families with women, but they're gay."

"If you've never slept with a man, how are you gay?" said Carl.

"Because you want to. Besides, how do you know he hasn't slept with a man?"

"It's very unlikely." Carl laid his chopsticks on the bowl, as if embarking on a two-minute hunger strike.

"Even if he's never slept with a guy, he can still, deep down, be gay." Ben made a show of enjoying his eel filet. He was disappointed in Carl. A doctor should be able to entertain a hypothesis without sulking.

"How can you know that?" Carl said. Ben almost laughed at the absurdity of Carl playing skeptic. Carl's resistance was denial — Carl who, when first introduced at the hospital, had intuited what few people did, that Ben was gay, and proceeded to launch a series of looks and remarks that slid from collegial to friendly to flirtatious, with a salsa-like agility that Ben could hardly keep up with.

Finally Ben said, "Even if I can't know for sure, let's call it a compelling hypothesis, based on two decades of data." He smiled at Carl. Even sulking over his udon, Carl was adorable. Ben imagined Carl aged by fifteen years, pouchy, paunchy, less fetchingly furred. He wished Carl weren't attractive. It was infuriating that a hot, smart, successful man could be so deluded.

"In any case," said Carl, as if to conclude the debate, "the church wouldn't be as big if Pastor Jer were gay. We just hit the four thousand mark. Unofficially it's more like six."

At last it was out — a truth Ben had long suspected — that Carl was a self-hating gay man. For a time, Ben watched Carl's blank temple, as it pulsed with each clamp of his chewing jaw.

"How are you okay with that?" Ben asked. "How can you, a gay man, attend a church full of people who would reject a gay minister?"

"Pastor Jer is hugely gifted and would still have a congregation if he were gay, but some people wouldn't be comfortable with it. It's just a fact."

"Do people at church know that you're gay?"

"The ones close to me do."

"Pastor Jer?"

"I think so. Davin came a few times, but it was too loud for him. He preferred the Quaker services, which I could never get into. All that silence, interrupted by someone expressing gratitude for the bean salad at the potluck. How is that inspiring?"

How is Pastor Jer inspiring? Ben wanted to reply. Instead he said, "Does Jer support you?"

"Of course he does. Didn't you see what a warm person he is?"

"I mean does he support your gayness."

"He doesn't support it or oppose it. It's my business. It's between God and me."

"So he doesn't support it. And some of those nice people who sit beside you think you're a dirty faggot." Ben plowed the rice across his plate, capturing as many grains as possible, not dropping a single one. In med school he'd considered becoming a surgeon.

Carl's face had grown rosy and humid; even his hair appeared curlier. He looked like a child. "You know, Ben, my gayness is just one part of me. It's not all of who I am. Sometimes it doesn't even feel primary."

"It feels pretty fucking primary to me."

"Our culture overplays sexual identity, makes it a big deal. Why isn't it comparable to being—I don't know—a really devoted hockey fan?"

"It's what you yearn for."

Carl talked about how Jer's church had helped him realize that his sexuality wasn't the whole truth about himself. "My primary identity is as a Christian. Those are my values." The Saskatoon church Carl had grown up in condemned homosexuality. Only

91

when he arrived in Toronto for med school did Carl even realize he was gay. He discovered Pastor Jer's church then too. While Jer never endorsed Carl's sexuality, he was more interested in other aspects of Carl's life. What could have been an unbearable burden became a small vice, like smoking.

"Okay, so if gayness is just a tiny part of a person, as you say, why would the people at church care if your minister were gay?" The comparison to smoking annoyed Ben, lumping him in with the needy, bedraggled figures who stood in the rain outside the hospital.

"I never said I'm consistent." Carl's voice was quiet. He seemed to have given up. It was as if he had written a sign that read *Kick me,* and awkwardly but successfully taped it onto his own back.

They went for a walk, soon parting when Carl said he needed a nap. Ben didn't jokily angle for a nap invitation and wondered if this was their first fight, or the end.

At home, Ben googled the pastor. Besides the sermon videos with up to nineteen thousand views, Pastor Jer was in an issue of *Toronto Life,* standing between a community-health leader and a philanthropic restauranteur with a septum piercing. The article described him as a leader of Christianity 2.0. His motto was *Let's have a conversation.*

Ben watched video clips on mute, looking for data points to send Carl. The pastor's skin glowed, implying Kiehl's as much as holiness. His eyebrows were groomed. Overall, the level of self-care was high and not perfunctory, not just because he was in the public eye. The man liked nice clothes with natural fibres and handcrafted details, half Zen half punk, though for the previous year's Easter sermon he'd worn a floral shirt that might be from Paul Smith. The pastor definitely worked out.

Of course, plenty of straight men worked out and liked nice clothes. The three children didn't mean much either. Yet the pastor did not appear miserable. Could someone live a lie and be happy? The pastor must have a pleasant life. He could be bi, but even then would be ignoring some essential part of himself. Or maybe he wasn't ignoring it. Who knew what the pastor did in private?

Many times Ben had been unsure if a man was gay, especially in his youth. Now he was more experienced and the initial, powerful impression remained. When he tried to reverse it, when he tried to see the vase instead of the profiles, as in those optical illusions, he was left with incoherent squiggles. Either the figure was radiantly clear or it collapsed.

Ben took a break from the screen's fifteen tabs and stood by the window. In moments of stress, he liked to watch the cars and pedestrians twenty-two floors down, their haste reduced to a crawl, as hypnotic as a lava lamp. The ant farm, he called it.

Why did the pastor's sexuality preoccupy him? It came down to Carl, of course, and how Pastor Jer's church supported Carl's lesser idea of himself, his unwitting self-hatred. Ben hated to see Carl hate himself. On some level, he hated Carl for hating himself. How wrong to hate yourself, how cowardly.

If Carl didn't hate himself — if he were a different kind of Christian, or no Christian at all — the two of them might have a shot. Ben had not been in a relationship since his late twenties, and it had lasted hardly three years. Now finally, when he grasped the appeal of a stable relationship, the sweetness of its routines, it was being taken away.

He planned to email Carl with his case about the pastor. Probably it would not have much effect, though something might stick. After that, he would likely break things off. Or maybe Carl would beat him to it.

The week was busy with follow-up cases, plus an uptick in flu complications, surprising for late March. But mostly it was the chronic stuff. A patient with Crohn's told Ben that all supermarket food was nutritionally void. The man spoke of lemons without vitamin C, carrots without beta carotene. "Then what makes them orange?" Ben asked, and the man muttered something about artificial dyes, like in meat.

Mrs. Harootunian came in for her follow up, and he repeated his advice to walk twenty minutes each morning. "You'll be less tired, I promise."

"I tried the walks. It doesn't do anything. I just walk and am tired."

"We ran all the tests we can," he said. "The diabetes is under control."

"This city is ugly. So flat. And in the valley, the pleasant space, they put a freeway."

He wrote her a prescription for vitamin B12.

On Thursday he finished early. He walked past the hospital's statue of the sacred heart of Jesus, its gaze imbecilic. He hadn't sent Carl the email, and Carl had skipped their usual midweek text. He began to think of Carl in the past tense, imagining telling a future beau about the evangelical guy who gave amazing head.

Saturday he checked who was in the neighborhood. Maybe he would find Carl online. They were not exclusive, though Carl claimed he didn't like the app.

Ben scrolled down, then back up. The first guy he messaged liked hikes and darkroom fun. The second guy asked if they could meet at Nordstrom.

Can we meet near Nordstrom instead? Ben typed. He suggested a café and closed the app, leaving his phone on the kitchen counter. He went for a jog.

When he returned, Ben found a message from Carl and exhaled the word *yes.*

The Easter service began with a re-enactment of Christ's crucifixion on the giant screen. It reminded Ben of the heavy-metal videos of his childhood. A crimson montage of a cross on a cliff followed by a shuddering ultrasound of a heart, muscles churning, shadowy blood pushing through arteries. A blurry page from the Bible was intercut with a dark red EKG line that dimmed into blackness, as a wall-shaking bass declared, *Nails on the wrists put pressure on the median nerves.*

When the bass described how the Roman soldier's sword pierced the pericardium—and so Christ died of a broken heart— Ben cackled inwardly at the canny layering of scientific and emotional language. A broken heart, how quaint.

He had stopped wondering what Carl thought of it all. Carl's mind was a black box, with outputs that Ben mostly appreciated. He was surprised when Carl had apologized for his grumpiness the previous week, saying "Maybe Pastor Jer is bi, who cares." That morning, still in bed—Ben emerging from some underwater dream after a pre-dawn entanglement—when Carl draped an arm around him and announced that it was Easter, the most important day of the year for Christians, and would Ben consider joining him at church, Ben said sure, to Carl's and his own surprise.

Over breakfast he began to regret it as Carl went on about how the music pastor had worked for Mirvish Productions.

On the darkened stage, dancers crept dolefully after Christ's heart stopped. Ben pressed his knee against Carl's, and Carl returned the pressure briefly before retreating. Even in the dark, Carl kept up appearances. Ben could have told him to fuck off then, stood up and marched out of the church, or better still grabbed Carl and started kissing him, until he succumbed and stopped pretending to be a good little Christian. When the lights came on, everyone would see the truth.

As it was, the service had been going on for nearly forty minutes with no sign of Pastor Jer. "Did your preacher take the day off?" Ben hissed into Carl's ear. The stage had grown brighter, and the dancers now leapt, hip-hop style, as the screen cycled through a montage of Christ's faces, from agonized to radiant. One thing the son of God had going for him was that he was always fuckable, an eight at least. Either he was young and hot, or dead, like Kurt Cobain. The glamour of it, including the suffering. Especially the suffering, the gory injustice. No chronic conditions, no Jesus with diabetes struggling with nerve pain and gluey vision and erectile dysfunction, scratching his arms because of the eruptive xanthomatosis spattering their lengths, all because he made some bad decisions. That's human suffering.

Against the backdrop of Christ's huge, hot face, the pastor appeared finally, wearing shades of pale gray. Ben tried to see him as a straight man, seeking out any hint of the obtuseness straight white men often had. Within the totalitarian regimes of children, even the most unneurotic gay kid had experienced the realization that they were not like most of the others, and carried the memory within themselves. The memory of being a freak.

That time was long over, fortunately. If anything, it had made possible Ben's capacity for detachment and wit. In some men, it became camp. Did the pastor have anything like that?

Pastor Jer was as excited by Easter morning as a child by Christmas. He talked about Mary Magdalene's delight when the resurrected God called her name, unlike Thomas, who insisted on placing a finger into the Lord's wounds. Thomas the unimaginative, handsy empiricist. The story was familiar enough from Ben's childhood, when he attended a Lutheran church on occasion, until his rationality and sexuality made themselves known.

The more Ben looked for data points that were not simply clichés, the more elusive they became. At best he could say there was a higher-than-average probability the pastor was gay.

Carl was right. Ben couldn't know that pastor Jer was gay. All Ben had was a hunch, a belief.

He wished he could pull a Thomas, stick his finger inside the fact and know the answer. He felt the corners of his mouth tighten at the thought of sticking his finger inside Pastor Jer's "fact." If only. Thomas was a proto-scientist, a crude early version who had it easier than any real scientist. One specimen, one trial, then the answer settled for eternity.

Granted, closer contact with the specimen would help answer some questions. If Ben could make eye contact with Pastor Jer, for instance, he would know more about the man. Not enough for an answer, but something.

When after yet another song the lights grew bright and people began to stand, Ben asked, "Will Pastor Jer be in the foyer again?" Carl said he thought so.

If Carl had any suspicion about Ben's motive, he didn't show it, which made Ben wonder if Carl thought he might convert one day. The idea was hilarious, albeit useful. As they squeezed through the crowd towards the pastor, Ben tried to imagine himself as a born-again Christian. Some of these smiling people would become his friends. Would he smile more too? What else would change? No more snide remarks, no more dirty mind. He would be lobotomized.

Even though Pastor Jer was a little taller than Ben, up close he appeared slight, like Hollywood actors do, as he laughed and hugged congregants, or simply rested a hand on the shoulder of a young man wearing a beanie, then of a young woman with a keffiyeh around her neck. Ben wiped his palm against his pant-leg. Jer was superbly at ease, the cool kid who's also nice, the powerbroker uninterested in power tripping.

When Carl introduced Ben, surely the pastor could tell he was no mere friend, though that is what Carl infuriatingly called him. Soon the distance between the pastor and Ben was bridged by a warm, strong palm, his own still damp, yet Pastor Jer did not pull away, if anything he seemed drawn to Ben's hesitation, seemed to care about Ben instantaneously. Even after releasing Ben's hand, the pastor's gaze enveloped him, not only in its unblinking duration but in joyous amazement that Ben was standing before him, after a service he hadn't really wanted to attend — surely the pastor could tell — all of which meant more than either of them could know.

Had they been at a bar, the pastor would have been flirting, but they weren't at a bar.

It was Ben's turn to speak. He said he found the service thought provoking, and gave the pastor a playful smile.

98

"I hope we can keep provoking you," said Pastor Jer, "in the best possible way." Might the pastor flirt with visitors to draw them in? What exactly did they teach at pastor school?

Even after experiencing Pastor Jer's enveloping gaze, there was no way to know. Ben felt a connection with the man, but the man connected with everyone. If he wanted to test his hypothesis, Ben realized, he would have to fuck Pastor Jer himself.

Work consumed him that week, though between endless cases of cardiovascular disease he sometimes thought of the pastor. Wednesday night he was on call. A COPD case was sorted out by phone, and close to midnight he lay in bed, mind cycling between whether he should have reminded a flaky resident to check on a patient with sepsis and how to get closer to Pastor Jer. Could he get the pastor's attention by fabricating a spiritual crisis? The lapsed Lutheran who realizes he has a Jesus-shaped hole in his heart? But why would this problem require Pastor Jer's private attention? The church website invited prayer requests via text and DM, promising that their "squad" took on any problem.

At least Pastor Jer's email address was on the website. The man was open to all, or at least his assistant was. Part of the difficulty figuring out how to get closer to Jer was that Ben kept imagining already being close to him. A hand claiming a thigh, then the crackling, mutual recognition.

Ben had never slept with a man of the cloth to his knowledge. He'd slept with a married guy in his reckless youth. If there was better sex than with Carl, it was the first time with the married guy: after deciding against it and avoiding him, finally the capitulation, the mutual melting, no more pretending; at last the truth that annihilated all scruples.

Of course, afterwards the scruples arrived, even as the wife remained an abstraction. But he saw how upset the married guy was. Had he met the wife, he would have told her, *Trust me, your husband loves you, he just wants to fuck me.* The words would have been heartfelt, if ignorant. Was the husband's guilt a symptom of love or was it just guilt? How much of marital love was guilt?

Aside from that, Ben was struck by how decent his own life was. Most people were no longer shocked by gay sex, or at least pretended not to be, except the religious people, bless them. A preacher would be his hottest lay yet.

At three in the morning, he went to the hospital. The sepsis case had worsened, the patient's speech slurring. Then a heart rhythm anomaly arrived. On his way out, at close to five, the flaky resident asked if Carl could look at a young woman with abdominal pain and difficulty swallowing.

"Solids or liquids?"

"I didn't ask," said the resident, who used the most rudimentary diagnostic flow charts, which devolved into whimsical rivulets of speculation or simply dried up.

Ben asked the young woman about her recent food and drink. A spicy margarita yesterday. She'd never had one. Could it be the spicy margarita? Maybe, he said, his mind scrolling down a list of possible causes, many in the same order as in the textbooks he'd studied over a decade ago. He reminded himself to maintain periodic eye contact and noticed that the edges of her irises were cloudy. An ancient textbook page flashed in his mind. Kayser-Fleischer rings, he was pretty sure. That would mean Wilson's disease. He'd never seen an actual case. She had no visible signs of jaundice, but he put in an order for a blood test.

The potentially rare case gave him a rush of energy which the cab ride home did not relieve. He watched the people twenty-two floors down and contemplated going for a walk. He couldn't remember the last time he'd felt so energized by work. Most cases were predictable, a reality he'd not anticipated in med school. He missed how absorbing work was back then. People paid money to be absorbed like that, played videogames in diapers or clung to cliffsides with bloody fingertips. Probably it was why some of them went to church.

At the ant farm, people were starting their day on a chilly, overcast morning. A statistical viewpoint, you could call it, comparing the proportion of those wearing hats to those without, those with briefcases to those with knapsacks, and he didn't have to care about any of them. A nice break from the Hippocratic oath, not to worry about doing no harm, to be an asshole even, because from the twenty-second floor people appeared inconsequential at best, even expendable.

This is what single shooters saw, didn't they? From an upper storey, everyone's the same, a squealing little target. And wasn't this how God was supposed to see people? Up in the clouds, looking down on a humanity that multiplied with metastatic rapidity. If this was God's vantage point, He must be an asshole sometimes.

He imagined sharing his theory with Carl or Pastor Jer. How do you know your God is good? With Pastor Jer it could be a playful provocation, while Carl would just feel hurt.

Was Carl even capable of telling Ben, You're an asshole? Carl seemed to enjoy Ben's profanity while recusing himself from any of his own. Fortunately, Carl didn't say golly or geez; for that matter he didn't have many moments of open dismay, and when he did, he said *wow*. Wow that guy is in a rush. Wow that policy is a terrible idea.

Ben went to bed with pleasant sensations of being an asshole washing over him. He hadn't changed the sheets since Carl's visit, and a dark helix of pubic hair rested near the pillow. After anyone else the sheets would be fresh, aside from his ex. You are truly an asshole, Elliot had said — reflectively, as if thinking aloud while Ben happened to be present. That was after Ben awoke one morning to realize he'd fallen out of love. The sequel was inevitable. He wasn't interested in "working on it." He had enough work at work.

He hoped he wouldn't have another dream about work. Sleep had never been a problem, but lately his dreams were set at the hospital, stupid dreams in which poorly designed software lost vital information. The work dreams had increased since the upgraded bed, the mattress devised by NASA and the Swedes, and swaddled in organic sateen. One way to tell that a guy was too young was if he was amazed by the bed. One boy had a full beard and looked nearly thirty, but turned out to be nineteen.

He thought of the young woman who might have Wilson's. She could have had the disease for years already. How easy to go through life ill and ignorant. Most people didn't know where their liver was, or what a gallbladder was for, though these days, who really understood what was going on inside anything, whether a person or a phone? Unless you were a specialist, inside was a mystery, run by elves.

He awoke in the milky light of a foggy noon as an idea slid into consciousness. What if he suggested to Pastor Jer that he might have Wilson's disease? Something rare and discreetly corrosive. If the pastor was too busy to wait at an Emergency Room, Ben would be happy to stop by his office for a preliminary exam. It wouldn't take more than five minutes, and Ben could give him paperwork for blood tests. What would happen from there, Ben couldn't map out exactly, but the conditions for physical contact would be in place.

Of course, there was also the risk that Ben wasn't Pastor Jer's type. But if the man was gay and repressing it, wouldn't he be more susceptible to the touch of a confident, attractive man? Ben remembered sitting on a bus beside his high-school crush, a track teammate, and shivering with desire. He'd wondered if it was possible to hyperventilate with longing. Had the boy placed a hand on Ben, the results would have been explosive.

If Pastor Jer wasn't gay, the touch wouldn't mean anything. Ben would feel the body's steady surface and know. Even if the body flinched — as it did for many patients — Ben could tell the difference. He got out of bed and began to draft an email to the pastor.

When Ben tried to imagine Carl's boyhood in Saskatoon, he saw grain elevators on flat yellow land.

"Did you drive a pick-up truck?" he asked Carl, half-jokingly. They were in Carl's bed, which was even nicer than his own, despite the superficial austerity of crumpled gray linen.

"No," Carl said.

"What did you do?"

Carl played rugby. There was a mall. He got drunk once. There was a girlfriend.

"How old were you when you knew?"

"Twenty-four."

"No, I mean when you knew you were gay."

"That's when I knew. I came out at twenty-six."

"I thought you said early twenties."

"I don't think so."

"And before twenty-four you had no idea."

"No."

"Not even with your girlfriend, you didn't have doubts?"

"Girls were pretty. They were nice to be around. I thought I was a late bloomer."

"Okay, but twenty-four. I thought it was twenty-one, and even then —"

On a church camping trip for young men, Carl learned that many struggled to stay pure with their girlfriends. Around the campfire, they bound the devil in the Lord's name and vowed to seek out open, well-lit places on dates. Witnessing their anxiety, Carl was grateful that he could hang out with his girlfriend in the basement, snuggling sometimes, and nothing more. He was grateful that his desire for her wasn't degrading. He was in awe of her prettiness, and thanked the Lord that virtue was so easy.

"What about boys," Ben asked. "How did they make you feel, on those church camping trips?"

"I liked them."

"I know you liked them." He slid a hand onto Carl's hip.

"Boys were sweet."

"Sweet?"

"Christian boys were."

"You make them sound hot."

"I do, don't I?" Carl gave a slow smile and leaned towards Ben.

"So before twenty-four you never had a crush. You never felt awkward around a boy."

"Sometimes, but I was shyer then. It felt like shyness."

Carl's words sounded like denial. Ben reminded himself that it wasn't Carl's fault he was born into a religious family. Plus, memory was imperfect. Maybe Carl remembered realizing he was gay at twenty-four, when in fact it was more like seventeen. He must have fantasized about boys.

"So your first crush on a dude was at twenty-four."

"There was one in university. I thought it was the devil tempting me, once I left home."

"In wicked Toronto," said Ben, and they laughed.

During med school, Carl visited a gay bookstore and saw a play at a gay theatre. Later, he watched porn at a film festival and found it both hot and jolly. But he never attended Pride, not even after telling his parents about his sexuality. That happened when he was thirty.

Not to know yourself like that. How was it possible? Thanks to his obliviousness, Carl had avoided the pain of high school. Ben almost envied him that, though he made up for it as an undergraduate, while Carl did not.

Could Pastor Jer be like the youthful Carl? Was it possible not to know you're gay until your forties? Presumably Jer had experienced sex only with his wife, which might be pleasant enough, and of course he must care about her and the life they had built. The life you've built. It could block out who you really are.

But from what Ben had heard, even the men who came out in midlife had known much earlier. They just didn't want to.

That week, Carl didn't invite Ben to church. Ben simply went. He tried mouthing a fragment of a bouncy song about the righteous rejoicing and God counting their heartbeats and the hairs on their heads. God must know the number of jelly beans in the jar too. God the canny calculator, the cosmic algorithm.

The pastor hadn't answered his email. Three and a half days and no answer. After forty-eight hours Ben had googled the admin assistant, a young woman named Isabel, distinguished by her lilac mullet. He imagined approaching her after the service, reminding her of the email, saying "This is serious." But Isabel was not in the auditorium, or maybe she was one of those people who changed their hair with the seasons. In the photo she was overtly pretty, which struck Ben as a further scrap of evidence. What straight man who wished to remain faithful would invite temptation by hiring so attractive an assistant, someone with whom he'd work privately, and who no doubt admired him? Maybe this was a form of Christian machismo, a bravado of virtue, as in, *Look how attractive my assistant is, and yet I remain faithful to my wife.* However, if Pastor Jer was more attracted to men, then Isabel's looks were no risk.

Pastor Jer must not have seen the message. If he had, surely he would have responded. How many people would be indifferent to a doctor informing them they might have a disease that, if untreated, leads to psychosis?

Ben settled into the plush seat and resisted reaching for his phone as Pastor Jer talked about renewal. April, the pain of it. The bear emerging from hibernation, weakened and starving. "He's in rough shape!" Jer exclaimed, and people — including Carl — nodded and felt sad for the bear. To stay in the cave, however cozy, meant death. Death was stagnation, the avoidance of pain.

The allegory was basic, the language slangy and earnest. Three Sundays had made it clear that each sermon had a formula, beginning with a jokey anecdote to disarm the congregation. (Today's was about Pastor Jer and his wife's ongoing snack debate — Jalapeno Doritos all the way!) Whatever Pastor Jer said, the congregation responded with delight. Pastor Jer could have said, *I am a shithead*, and the congregation would have applauded and echoed, *He is a shithead!*

Ben had never gone in for communities, not the gay one, not the medical one. He didn't understand people who volunteered for committees. He'd always been independent, maybe because he was an only child, maybe because of his parents' rankling codependence, which ended only when he left for university and they divorced, far too late.

Ben figured that if he stayed in shape and made himself useful and entertaining, he could keep his independence without getting lonely. He liked his customized life, the bespoke sneakers and the grand cru coffee pods, the weekly meal kit with an elongated baggie holding a single green onion to garnish the evening's updated bún bò huế, ready in under thirty minutes. The nice thing about being a doctor was that you were obviously useful, though the other day he'd joked to Carl that he couldn't wait until doctors were replaced by algorithms.

"You'd actually like that, wouldn't you?" said Carl.

"Why not?" He was half convinced.

"You don't think your patients would miss you?"

Ben thought of Mrs. Harootunian. "Not really, once they get used to the new system."

"But how can an algorithm care about a patient?"

"An algorithm doesn't need to care. That's our software. Frankly, I'm due for an upgrade."

Carl began to murmur a protest, and Ben continued, "The thing is, if the right data collection mechanisms are in place, an algorithm offers a more capacious view. That's all a patient needs."

"That's not what the research shows," said Carl.

"Why can't an algorithm's indifference be a plus? The patient doesn't have to worry about the algorithm judging them or being in a bad mood. The patient just interfaces with a vast analytic intelligence. It could feel like kindness."

It could even feel like God, Ben thought to himself, as Jer talked about God's all-knowing love. What was God but a primitive metaphor for whatever complex algorithm kept the universe humming along?

When the service ended, Carl wanted to leave. Ben would have liked to find Isabel, or approach Pastor Jer, but Carl marched through the foyer into the rain. By then the pastor was already mobbed. Even if he had seen Ben's message, it wasn't the right time to talk. Maybe Pastor Jer had googled Wilson's disease and looked into his own eye, seen nothing, and decided it was a prank. He must get dozens of messages from randos. In the pastor's eyes, Ben's message could look like spam. Special offer, not to be missed, unique funny game, I am alone, I wait for you.

Although Ben checked email on Sunday evening, Monday morning brought too many new messages, including one from Mrs. Harootunian. *I am exhausted,* she wrote. *I am going to have a breakdown.*

He sent her a referral to a psychiatrist. He wanted to add the words, *There is only so much that medicine can do. It cannot fix an unsatisfactory life.*

He knew that he was an impatient man. He tried not to show it at work, and as failings went, it didn't really bother him. Sometimes it felt like a covert virtue. He was busy and didn't understand people who weren't. Mrs. Harootunian did not work and had a one teenaged son who would soon be in university. What did she do all day?

He was thankful that work occupied him as he awaited the pastor's reply. He'd considered sending a follow-up message, but it might've weakened the impression he wished to convey, of a busy expert.

Dinner was a meal-kit steak with panzella, almost too convenient, and soon the dishwasher was swishing discreetly. Ben didn't have the focus to read or even to watch Netflix. He texted Carl. *Can I come by?*

When he arrived, Carl was watching a show about the universe.

"Is your apartment a mess again?" he asked Ben, whom he liked to tease for being both a slob and a snob, remarking on Ben's maltreated designer furniture, the LC4 chair covered in jackets and junk mail, the Togo sofa flecked with crumbs. It was one of the few subjects about which Carl was almost mean. If Carl were mean more often, one day Ben would fall for him completely, he suspected. As it was, Carl's niceness saved him from Ben's closer affection.

"I missed you," said Ben. The words felt truthful, as he leaned against Carl and they watched a baby levitate, the camera zooming in to reveal the molecular structure of its pinky toe. A galaxy curved into a mighty nipple, as the famous American astrophysicist spoke in his resonant, reasonable voice. The universe was exciting, but he never got hysterical about it.

If Pastor Jer were talking about the universe he'd probably hyperventilate. Man! he'd exclaim. He'd use words like *glorious* and *ginormous*.

When the astrophysicist walked along a volcanic landscape from four billion years ago, Ben said, "We're a fluke, a joke."

"Something can't be both a fluke and a joke," said Carl. "A joke is highly designed."

"A joke on our need for meaning, I mean. Too many people think everything happens for a reason, but people just make up reasons after the fact."

Onscreen the prehistoric earth belched and the astrophysicist took cover, calmly.

"Do you think I believe that everything happens for a reason?" said Carl.

"I don't know."

"Why don't you ask?"

Onscreen the astrophysicist walked through an ancient, columned building.

"Okay, do you?"

"I believe in flukes, Ben. Evolution too. I'm not a total moron because I believe in God." The astrophysicist opened a door to a room where trilobites glided along the ocean floor. "Anyway, God isn't some control freak."

"I was just saying that humans look for meaning in stupid places sometimes."

"They do indeed."

Carl seemed unbothered by human delusion. The harm it could do, then the mess and the regret. The patients who instead of taking their meds tapped their third eye daily, their occult notions.

The astrophysicist opened the door to another room where volcanos erupted. When the soot cleared, dusty dinosaur carcasses scattered the landscape, necks bent at despairing angles.

"You know," said Ben, "when my mother was pregnant with me, my aunt told her not to name me Philip. My mom liked the name. I was supposed to be a Philip."

"Okay."

"But my aunt said that men named Philip are usually gay, so my mom named me Ben."

"And that fixed everything," said Carl. They laughed, though Ben felt his throat contract at the absurd story.

"You didn't get Philip as a middle name?" asked Carl.

"Nope."

"Then you'd be super gay," said Carl.

"I'm already super gay, aren't I?" They grabbed each other, and like that, it didn't matter that they'd been arguing.

On Tuesday morning Ben saw that the pastor had sent him an email at 11:21 p.m. on Monday. He and Carl had been asleep by then, and now Carl was beside him at the counter, eating muesli and checking his own email.

The pastor had addressed him as *Dr.*, misspelling Ben's last name. He thanked Ben for his concern. *Can you stop by my office Wednesday at two?*

The next steps were clear. Wednesday at noon, Ben would experience food poisoning. An ill-advised chicken caesar. He would reschedule the afternoon patients for later on Thursday and Friday, even into Saturday morning, if necessary.

Carl was spooning his muesli, dark curls damp. Ben gave him a kiss and said he had to check on a patient.

The rest of the day the pastor was on his mind, like an acute case. Ben would begin with flattery and follow with flirtation. To complete the Wilson's "diagnosis" he would stare into the pastor's eyes. "Look straight ahead," he'd say, or better still, "Look at me." He was counting on those studies showing that if two people stared at each other for three minutes, they were more likely to fall in love. Not that Ben needed love. A little lust would do.

He was going to be a creep, for the sake of the truth.

Beyond that, things grew less clear. If he could get into the pastor's pants, he would tell Carl. Carl might break up with him or he might break up with Jesus. He and Carl would have a real shot then, the happiest ending of all.

At the pastor's office, Isabel appeared delighted to see Ben. Her hair was new, an ombré pageboy that swung as she ushered him into the pastor's office.

Pastor Jer sat behind a glass desk, staring at a thin expansive screen as he typed. He invited Ben to sit down and kept typing. On his right arm, an elaborate tattoo poked out from beneath his T-shirt sleeve, and above the V-neck a rakish smudge of chest hair was visible. "I'm wrapping up revisions for a keynote tomorrow," he said. "I fly out to LA today."

Behind the pastor, the wall was covered in framed images: a poster of Jesus in the tricolour style of Shepherd Fairey; posters from conferences — Breakthrough 2016, Revolution 2017, and lower down, Revolutions 1990. Other images were less dogmatic: a primitive-looking angel in primary colours; a print of a turquoise pool, the only sign of human presence a white spray of water above the pool's surface — Ben had seen it before but forgot the artist's name. Books along one wall, a shaggy Beni Ourain rug, and on it, by the window, a Barcelona daybed in cognac leather, probably a replica. Was the pastor a napper?

When Pastor Jer looked away from the screen at Ben, he said, "You're Carl's friend."

"I'm impressed you remember." Ben gave a millisecond wink, expecting the pastor to smile back or say something nice about Carl, but he didn't.

"So you think I'm sick."

"I don't know for sure," said Ben, "but it's worth checking out. Wilson's is serious. Undiagnosed, it takes a toll on the liver, the nervous system, the works."

"I know, I googled it."

"Great. Less talking for me to do." Ben gave another smile that got no reaction, so he asked some questions about abdominal pain and anxiety. To all of them, the pastor said no. Finally he said, "I looked at my eyes and didn't see anything."

"What colour are they?"

"Hazel."

"Hazel can be tricky," said Ben.

The pastor was too in control. In five minutes, Ben would be back on the sidewalk no wiser. He needed to get closer to the cool man across the expanse of glass. "I've never met a minister with a tattoo," he said.

At this the pastor smiled briefly. "Tattoos are useful. They're reminders of who you are." The pastor pushed up his sleeve, revealing a dark horse on its hind legs, and a bearded man crumpled beside it. "Did you go to church as a kid?"

"Sometimes, before I was a teen."

"Do you recognize this guy?"

If it wasn't Jesus or Moses, it could be anyone. Ben recalled some story about a talking donkey.

"Balam?" said the pastor. "No, think New Testament."

Ben felt like he was failing an important test. "Sorry, nothing's coming to mind."

"It's Paul before he was Paul, when he was Saul. Before he fell from that horse, he'd killed scores of Christians. The Bible says that he breathed murder."

But one day, on his way to murder more Christians, Saul was blinded by a bright light and fell from his horse. A voice asked him, *Why do you persecute me?* For three days he was blind. Saul was so traumatized that he ate and drank nothing.

The pastor sat back in his chair to let Saul's sad situation sink in.

When his sight was restored, Saul became a Christian. He did major work for Christ, spreading the gospel to the gentiles, writing nearly half the books in the New Testament. He changed so much that he changed his name.

"Christianity is about becoming your best self," the pastor said. "Becoming who *God* wants you to be" — he jabbed his fingers into his solar plexus — "not who you want to be." Because human desire led nowhere enduring.

You could bend desire to a righteous will. With a righteous will, you could pray for twenty-four hours straight, or fast for an entire week.

"No water for a week?" said Ben.

"Water's allowed, but that's it."

The body revolted, of course. Days two and three were the worst. But by day four your mind was clear. At night, dreams were vivid.

"Fasting takes you to your soul," said the pastor. "That's why mystics have done it for millennia. It's exhilarating to feel the body melt beneath the passion of a pure soul."

Was the pastor trying to convert him? It felt like a strange kind of seduction, away from desire. And yet the office was sensuous, the room of a man who desired fine sensations, not just the carpet but the daybed, which Ben saw was a very good replica, the metallic joints smooth and the leather so fine grained it shone.

Ben decided to play a polite Thomas. Couldn't a person take self-denial to an extreme? He'd seen a patient who had gone without water for four days. It wasn't pretty. Too much discipline didn't make most people happy. Most people weren't mystics.

"Of course professional supervision is necessary," said the pastor. "We are not always the best judges of our limits."

But with so much self-denial, how could a person be authentic? In the pastor's sermon, he'd called Christ an authentic man, passionate in his expressions.

"So you were paying attention to my sermon," said the pastor, finally giving Ben a smile.

The self you discovered when fasting was different than your desiring self, he explained, but just as authentic, more authentic. It was a self that existed beyond mere momentary feeling. A self filled with love that wanted nothing in return. "You must understand something of this, as a doctor."

"You overestimate my profession," said Ben.

"But this visit. You don't know me, yet you're taking time to check that I'm okay."

"Right." The word hung in the air, and Ben wondered if the pastor really thought he could convert Ben. "I should look at your eyes." He suggested moving to the daybed where the light was stronger.

"Didn't you say there's no problem?" said the pastor.

"Probably. But we want to be sure."

"Of course," said the pastor, remaining in his chair. Ben reached down to his knapsack for the ophthalmoscope.

The pastor seemed frozen, and Ben wondered if he was phobic of doctors. Ben complimented the daybed.

"I got a deal on it through a friend who sells antiques."

"It's the real thing?" said Ben, and when the pastor nodded, he said wow like Carl would. An image flashed in his mind, of the pastor languid with fasting, lying on his ten-thousand-dollar daybed. "I don't think I've ever sat on a real one."

"Go for it."

Ben pressed his hand into the yielding leather, easing himself onto it. "How do you not spend all day lying on this thing?" He patted the space beside him. "Let's take a look at your eyes, and I'll be on my way."

The pastor took in the floor between them. Finally he pushed himself up from the chair and walked slowly, as if injured, to where he towered over Ben. When he sat down, the leather gave a whispery groan.

"Great," said Ben. The skin near the pastor's neck was flushed, down to the clavicle and chest hair. The T-shirt was so thin that it revealed the contours of his deltoids. Ben could feel the heat emanating from the man.

"Okay, let's take a look at your eyes." He raised the ophthal-moscope, and the pastor grew still.

The pastor's iris was complexly freckled, reddish dust scattered on gray. The eye itself was owlishly impersonal, though the eyelashes quivered and the pupil shrank with the sensitivity of a sphincter before shifting downward.

"Try to look straight ahead," said Ben. The pastor had stopped breathing. He was staring at Ben's torso, face miserable. Ben felt the man's desire, and the familiar pleasing ache in the moment before anything happens. But he couldn't make a move. He couldn't be a proper asshole and disturb this man's life. Ben had the answer he wanted, but it was only for himself. It would make no sense to Carl.

Ben wanted out of the gorgeous office. He would announce that the pastor was healthy and excuse himself for interrupting a busy day, expressing relief that the man esteemed by his dear friend Carl was in good health. He would wish the pastor all the best with the keynote.

A pressure slid onto Ben's knee and rested there. It grew more defined, as fingers squeezed. The pastor's face was no longer miserable. It had grown intent and serene, as if the man were hearing a new message, and Ben the mere witness to his revelation.

For the first time in years, Ben couldn't sleep. If sex was about losing control, then what was sexier than the loss of control of someone desperate for it? Afterwards, as they lay on the daybed, Jer's eyes had glistened and he'd asked why transgression felt like grace. Ben had no answer, he wasn't even sure Jer was talking to him. He felt not triumphant but happy for Jer, that he had finally gotten what he wanted so badly, and glad that he, Ben, could be the one to give it.

The day was overcast and time grew vague. Jer sat up to squint at a clock.

"When's your flight?" Ben asked.

"In three hours." Jer searched for his boxers, giving Ben a final flash of his pale, muscular ass and now-demure cock. A small suitcase stood beside the door, and it occurred to Ben that Jer might have guessed Ben's intention and planned accordingly.

When Ben asked to stay in touch, Jer said, "Send an email."

"What about Isabel?"

Jer refused to give his cell number. "Don't write anything that Isabel couldn't see. I studied New Testament Greek for three years. I can read between the lines."

"So we're talking follow-up visits for the Wilson's?"

"I don't know." Jer buttoned his pants. Ben, still naked, picked up the daybed's tubular pillow from the floor, holding one end. He felt ready to play a demanding, intricate game like cricket. "I can promise total patient confidentiality," he said.

Jer looked up from his crotch, confused, and Ben remembered that the sex he took for granted was still novel for Jer, still tender and disorienting.

Jer returned to his desk and Ben dressed hastily. "I counsel individuals sometimes," said Jer. "Tuesdays or Wednesdays are good."

They decided on next Tuesday. Ben would take an extended lunch break.

If in Jer's presence Ben hadn't felt triumphant, that night alone in bed he did. He'd been right. Part of him wanted to proclaim the truth, watch the knowledge ripple through the congregation in their plush seats about the man they thought they knew. But a secret was almost better, a specialist's knowledge.

Jer's glistening eyes remained with Ben. Ben felt protective of the man, as if he had prised open a fist held tight for thirty years, had coaxed the fingers and admired the dark gem on the palm, speaking sweet, silly words to reassure Jer that what had been hidden out of shame was in fact delightful, and that the pastor loved him for it. Not that the pastor loved him, but that he loved what Ben had done for him.

On the night table, his phone lit up.

Are you awake?

He remembered that it was Wednesday night. He and Carl usually texted Wednesdays to confirm Saturday, though it was past midnight.

Sorry I'm late, Carl continued. *I was at a dinner.*

Ben left the phone on the table, despite half wanting to pick it up and type *Saturday's good and by the way your pastor is definitely into men.*

What would Carl say? The whole point of the seduction had been to tell Carl, to reveal that the church — or at least its leader — was living a lie. The man who peddled authenticity and helped Carl feel okay about his sexuality was in terrible denial. If Carl broke with the church, he would feel more than merely okay. Carl who had never attended a Pride parade.

But Ben felt no urgency to reveal the truth. Carl would be upset, and Ben didn't want to deal with it. Maybe Carl would be pissed at Ben. He needed to figure out how to tell Carl. Find people who fully accept you, he'd say, who don't merely tolerate you. Their tolerance is a sham, more for their own sakes than yours, so they can feel like good people with no hate in their hearts. Let's call a dick a dick.

Ben picked up the phone and reviewed the email thread with Jer, seeking a hint of what had been to come. He followed up on his previous reply. *Thanks for the inspiring conversation today. You gave me a lot to think about. :)* A smiley face felt too bland, so he revised it to a winky face.

What was it about Christian men? Differences could be sexy, but there was something about the discipline of devout Christians, more rigorous than seven years of medical training. The twenty-four-hour pray-a-thons, the fasting for a week. Your whole life, not just the professional, was evaluated by an all-knowing, hard-ass deity. The stakes were high.

During patient follow-ups for diabetes and COPD, memories of Jer flashed in Ben's mind. The glistening eyes and hard shoulders, the shapely forearms. Never before had Ben felt so drawn to a man's forearms.

On the weekend, Carl seemed tired until they went to bed. Looking at Carl, Ben thought of Jer. Physically they were different, Carl more compact, body hair denser. By comparison Jer was dry and elongated.

What Carl and Jer shared was an ignorance of their sexuality at different points in their lives.

Are you sure you didn't know sooner? he wanted to ask Carl. He wanted to understand Carl better, and Jer too. You must have known since you were a teen. Instead he said, "When you were a teenager, did you masturbate?"

"Sure," said Carl. He gave a long stretch that expressed either sexiness or sleepiness.

"What did you fantasize about?"

Carl smiled. "Not much."

"What do you mean, not much?"

"I tried fantasizing about marital sex. Sometimes I didn't fantasize at all."

"What do you mean, you didn't fantasize?" Carl's bed, a low platform, struck Ben in that moment as monastic.

"I just felt the sensations."

"That's impossible."

"No it's not, if you haven't seen porn. It's what our youth pastor taught."

"Your youth pastor taught you how to jerk off?"

Carl laughed. "No, he just reassured us that it was okay to touch yourself, as long as your thoughts were pure."

For a time, Carl had tried to masturbate as one might do push-ups, a purely physical exercise to release tension. He kept his eyes open and stared at the washroom's blank baseboard, moving a brisk hand. Release did not come.

He closed his eyes and allowed himself to visualize a back sloping into an ass. That wasn't a fantasy but an image. A fantasy was an immoral made-up story. An image could be in a biology textbook — it was a true fact, created by God.

The problem, he discovered, was how easily an image conjured a fantasy. The ass was a man's, atop a woman, husband and wife. Carl made sure to visualize the shining wedding bands, though the woman was a vague pedestal, less a body than a vaporous layer, sweetly forbearing. Soon all Carl saw was the bouncing scrotum.

Afterwards, Carl would remind himself what the youth pastor had said. Most, if not all, men masturbated at some point in their lives.

Ben mused on the pre-porn imagination. So inventive, like a lost boy scout who constructs a shelter from branches and leaves, who relishes squirrel meat in the absence of more toothsome options. Was Carl's religious background partly at the origin of his sexual talents? All those years of feeling the sensations, in the absence of high-octane fantasy.

"I'd like to join you at church tomorrow," Ben said. He could hardly wait to watch Jer preach since Wednesday.

The duvet heaved up as Carl propped himself on an elbow and said, "The Lord has put a question on my heart."

"What is it?" said Ben, trying not to smile. It felt physically impossible to enunciate the words, *What has the Lord put on your heart?* without bursting into laughter.

"Why are you coming to church?"

The laugh caught in Ben's throat. "It's thought provoking."

"Ben." Carl's voice was parental, disappointed and coaxing. "I can tell you don't want to be there."

"That's not true."

"You don't have to go to church for my sake."

"It's not for your sake."

"How am I supposed to believe that? That you'd go if it weren't for me?"

"You introduced me to the church, but I'm not going just for you. Trust me, I'm a selfish bastard."

"I'm glad to hear that," said Carl, as Ben slid a hand down his back. He felt a little sad to think that one day they would probably be over.

"Remember last week's sermon?" said Carl.

Ben's brain laboured to bring up the relevant terms. April. Renewal versus stagnation. The bear leaving hibernation. "Yeah, the bear," he said.

"Pastor Jer got me thinking about areas of stagnation in my life."

"Okay."

"And I thought about us."

Ben rested his hand on the divots of Carl's lower back, pressing his middle finger into the cleft between them.

"I wonder what we're doing. We've been hanging out since January. You said you missed me on Monday, but then hardly communicated until today."

"Well," said Ben, "we're doing this." He wrapped his fingers around Carl's cock, which was erect. How could Carl be hard and want a serious conversation? "And this." He sank his fingers into Carl's butt cheek.

"No, really," said Carl. "If that's all we're doing I should go back online."

The idea abashed Ben. "I care about you," he said, and it was true. Carl was easy to be with. They could talk about anything, work or science or even Ben's youth in Orangeville, when the world's rules were crude and irrational, when the most popular boy was simply the fastest runner. Until late high school, Ben was smaller than most boys. He excelled at math, a realm of unassailable proofs, where you could map out patterns and processes, and if you were smart enough, predict what came next. Back then he'd wished to live in a different place and time. He read about powerful mathematicians and developed a crush on Alan Turing. No one had cared how fast Turing ran. Men even had better haircuts then. He fantasized about Cambridge half a century earlier, despite Turing's tragic end. Still, he'd have preferred to be a secret fag in Cambridge than in Orangeville. Simply existing in Orangeville made the muscles of his own neck tighten and start to choke him.

Sunday morning Jer's hair was newly trimmed, almost shorn. Uncharacteristically, he wore a suit. No jokey anecdote began the sermon, which was about Saul.

Jer spoke of Saul's certainty, shaking his head. "He's so sure he's right."

Ben thought about the tattoo on Jer's bicep, of the man who went from very bad to very good. Did Jer feel like a murderer? Ben remembered the body beneath the suit, its dry hard heat, and the skin of Jer's shoulder, down to the drawn-out sigmoid of his forearm.

Ben wanted to know Jer better than the most devout congregant, better than Isabel, better than the wife. Did Jer fantasize about marital sex while secretly focusing on the guy, as Carl once had? Would Jer concede that Christ masturbated? Christ was a man, he wept and shat, he expelled the fluids men do. For a time, Ben imagined the son of God getting off, his mind a bright blank wall, the radiance of heaven itself.

Onstage, Jer kept talking about Saul and the light that felled him. How Saul tumbled from his horse into the hot dirt, face down. Only then could change begin.

"We do it a little different now," joked Jer, before dropping the smile. Two thousand years later, the process hadn't changed much. First you fell down before God. Then you became the person God wanted you to be.

Saul might have had a disorder of the inner ear, Ben mused. Or he just wasn't paying attention. It happened all the time: people felt they were in control the moment before the accident. As for blindness, the fall could have caused head trauma. Three days without food and water didn't help. Saul just needed a doctor.

When Jer called sinners to the front of the church for prayer, dozens came. Jer held a hand above their heads, walking along the stage's edge. Sometimes he squatted and touched a congregant's forehead, in the classic gesture of televangelists. Ben thought of the waggish news headlines. The Temptation of Ted. Porn Again.

Was Jer a joke? He didn't feel like one to Ben. Jer had begun as an experiment, and basically still was, albeit a very pleasurable one. But Ben was feeling Hippocratic, too. He wanted to help Jer explore an essential part of himself. He couldn't forget the incredulity of the glistening eyes, the amazed gulping of air.

Onstage, the singers crooned about God's relentless love. *You are a flood, engulf me.* The prayer squad assisted supplicants as they fell to the floor. Usually this happened after Jer touched a forehead.

Ben had asked Carl if he'd ever fallen like that. "No, I'm too uptight," Carl said. "Anyway, it's pretty old school. Most pastors don't touch you anymore." When Ben asked what Carl thought was going on physiologically when a person fell down, Carl conceded that it could involve some form of hypnosis.

The youthful singers purred about Jesus bringing down fire.

They had no idea. Ben hadn't had a big secret since Orangeville, nor could he recall feeling so curious about a man. The pastor's hidden layers and tensions were like a psychiatrist with borderline personality disorder. Maybe their affair — what else was it? — made Jer a better preacher. He couldn't quite think of Jer as a hypocrite. He could only think of the fallen man branded onto the arm, and the dry heat of the flesh beneath the sleeve.

Midafternoon on Monday, Ben saw the message. Jer had sent it late that morning.

Jer had to cancel. He apologized for *failing you last Wednesday*. He'd misled Ben and was in the process of making things right with God. He invited Ben to speak with a counsellor about any spiritual question he might have. The man he recommended had a PhD in biochemistry.

Jer was scared, obviously. Ben pitied him for choosing shame over self-acceptance. His expression of worry for Ben's soul rankled the most. Ben wanted to send a cryptic string of emojis — a piñata and a credit card, a banjo and a curling stone.

Fortunately Ben was busy, the chronically ill plentiful. Their afflictions did not require much thought. He explained the risk score to a male patient aged fifty-two who had high blood pressure and smoked. "If you stopped smoking your risk for a heart attack would go down by forty percent, from eighteen percent to eleven percent."

"Eleven doesn't sound much lower than eighteen," said the man.

Ben listed the latest smoking cessation options, while thinking, Go ahead and kill yourself if you love your denial so much.

He didn't answer Jer's message but checked email mindlessly, including midway through chopping a tomato. He tossed the shishito peppers in oil, grilled them, and added the miso-sake sauce. A well-defined operation. He thought cooking would relax him, and he would eat at last, but he refrigerated everything. The next day he barely had the patience to open the baggie of pre-sliced fennel for the gratin. As it baked he reread Jer's message, drafting replies in his head. *Isn't your God a god of love?*

He swallowed a forkful of dinner and went for a long walk, ending up at the church. In the parking lot, he found the window of Jer's office, on the third floor. He imagined the empty day bed behind the brick facade, his and Jer's molecules embedded into the leather.

Why did Jer change his mind on Monday? Did he see Ben at church and freak out? Was the winky face in Ben's email indiscreet?

Ben cancelled appointments Thursday and Friday. He called Carl and cancelled Saturday. "You got through the winter without getting sick," said Carl. He offered to bring soup, which Ben declined.

"Are you sure you're okay?" said Carl.

Ben stood by the window, facing the condo towers, a panorama of bland blue glass. "I can't eat," he said, and it was true.

He hadn't really eaten since Tuesday. A pair of condos wavered like watery tornadoes. "I just need some sleep."

Ben waited for Carl to say goodbye, but Carl started talking, saying he was sorry Ben was unwell, but Carl couldn't pretend that Ben's secretiveness wasn't a problem for him. Ben was evidently hiding something. Plus there was the history of Ben's erratic attachment, the neediness followed by stretches of silence. Ben seemed to want an extended fling, while Carl wanted something more. Their relationship, or whatever it was, wasn't working for him. Carl apologized again. "It's shitty timing — no, it's shitty of me. I should have brought it up sooner."

It felt especially shitty to lose not just Carl, but the newly swearing Carl. Ben sat by the window and felt nothing. Except for the lake lined by the freeway, he was surrounded by condos and shrunken squares of mashed sod. The CN Tower insisted on itself, aspirational and unimaginative. At its base lay the gargantuan Rogers Centre, a bloated mollusk. The city *was* ugly.

He'd hoped to get Jer to his condo one day. Carl would have been there, secretly. He would have seen the evidence. It was all supposed to have been for Carl's sake.

When Ben slept, he dreamed he was back on the daybed, naked with Jer. Ben clung to him, Jer motionless but tolerant, until a hand stroked Ben's head and he looked up to discover a taller version of Carl. Carl called him a shithead, tenderly, and Ben became aware of someone watching them from the glass desk. It was Mrs. Harootunian. Her hand rested on a large fennel bulb. Aren't you hungry? she said.

He awoke with sore eyeballs. In his throat, something like a hiccup. The last time he'd cried was before med school. Med school made many students cry, type As who screwed up, empaths whose patients died. Not even when he broke up with Elliot did he cry, a fact that surprised him, because he did feel sad. But Elliot was different because Elliot had wanted him.

Some part of Jer must want him, too. Jer's absolute silence must mark the intensity of his secret desire.

At least he wouldn't have to go to church anymore, neither for Jer's sake nor for Carl's. The soaring, manipulative music and the self-help platitudes, the pathetic attempts at hipness.

But Sunday morning he showered and found a clean button-down shirt. He placed a coffee pod in the machine and shook granola into a bowl. When he mixed in the dense Greek yogurt, the bowl slid over the counter's edge. He left the halved porcelain and slop on the floor and savoured his doppio. Carl would have called him a slob.

The congregation was singing when he arrived, and he found a seat near the back. Jer stood to the side of the stage, one hand clapped to his heart, the other lifted, as the young singers begged Christ to break them down with His love. When Ben spotted Carl's dark head near the stage, he felt a pang of longing. He imagined telling Carl that he'd slept with Jer. Carl would never believe him. The thought made Ben's throat start to choke him.

When the sermon began, Ben watched the distant figure in the fitted suit hold up an open Bible. With his shorter hair and the suit, Jer appeared as unreal as a hologram. The figure lifted a hand to signal that everyone should applaud, which they did. You think you know him, thought Ben, but you don't, not like I do. The hologram flickered across the stage.

If Ben could talk to him, then Jer would become real again. And if Carl were present, surely Jer's reaction would give something away.

Because it was Carl who really mattered. Yesterday's breakup had clarified that fact. Without Carl, Ben was bereft. If Ben exposed Jer in church, in front of everyone, would Carl believe him then? The idea activated Ben's inner flow chart as actions ramified into consequences. Like an unconventional course of treatment, it was risky but feasible.

When Jer called people to the front of the church for prayer, Ben stood. It was easy to walk down the sloping floor, a chute funnelling cattle.

At the front it was crowded, and Ben took a deep breath as he nudged past huddled shoulders, until he reached a young woman standing before the stage. Her chiffon blouse quivered as she sobbed. Everyone's head was bowed as Ben raised his own face to Jer. Surely Jer would see him.

Someone placed a hand on Ben's shoulder. A young man, hoodie stamped with the word *Courage!* introduced himself as Nizen.

When Nizen asked if he'd like prayer, Ben said, "I have been deceived."

"I'm so sorry to hear that. Can you tell me a bit more?"

"Ten days ago, your pastor and I had sex. Now he won't talk to me. He's pretending nothing happened."

"I see." For a time, Nizen seemed to listen to instructions from an invisible earpiece. Finally he said, "I'm here to pray with you, Ben. What is your need right now?"

"He's the one who needs prayer," Ben raised a finger towards Jer, "or some kind of help." Ben's throat began to close up again.

A second squad member materialized, an older guy, rangy and bald, in black jeans. "Can I join you two?" His accent sounded Australian. When Ben told him about the pastor, the man said,

"That's a serious allegation, Ben, but let's focus on the present. What is on your heart, at this very moment?"

"That's what's on my heart. That's it."

The Australian closed his eyes and said, "Thank you Lord, for bringing Ben to us today." Nizen's eyes also closed, and Jer stood at the opposite end of the stage, obviously avoiding Ben, moving a slow hand over people's heads, eyes closed as well, the perfect symbol. Turning a blind eye. Looking the other way.

The woman in chiffon blew her nose. Ben touched her shoulder and said, "I just told them that Pastor Jer and I fucked, and they want to pray about my feelings."

The drums started up and the woman shook her head — eyes wide above the tissue — as the youthful singers warbled their slogans. *His kingdom will come!*

Ben needed to get onto the stage. Jer was touching the forehead of some Bay Street–type, his closed eyes making it easier to wrest a mic. Ben needed only a few seconds at the mic.

He shrank beneath the Australian's and Nizen's hands and dodged past the chiffon woman, placing his hands on the stage. He braced his elbows and lifted himself up.

"Assistance needed!" called the Australian.

With an instantaneousness that felt supernatural, Ben was surrounded by powerful hands. They held him away from the stage, ready to expel him, no doubt, as they had all the skeptics since Thomas, because they couldn't bear the truth about their fragile idols.

"Ben," said Jer. He was kneeling on the stage, his face so close that Ben could see a razor nick along his jaw. Hands continued to press against Ben, but did not push him to the door.

Jer was still beautiful. "You fucker," said Ben. He'd lost Carl because of Jer. His throat closed up.

Jer brought a hand to Ben's forehead and said, "Your faith has made you whole."

Ben could feel the man's familiar dry heat. Above Ben's head the air pulsed, as if beaten by the wing of an immense bird. Everywhere voices spoke of love. *Love like a river. Engulf him with Your love.*

Someone must have turned up the lights. Ben was split open by light, sunk into a warm paralysis. Beneath his head, carpet. His throat rattled before it loosened. "Remember to breathe," said a familiar voice. Ben found himself inside a cocoon, where touch and sound enfolded him, as voices spoke in tones he hadn't heard since early childhood, outrageously tender. When Carl's voice thanked Jesus for Ben's repentance, Ben could not disagree, feeling himself within a vast sentient net, one that had tracked his past and numbered his heartbeats, and whose operations reached far into his future.

a history
of prayer

She is not afraid of the end, because Jesus will be there. That's what she tries to explain when Zdenka asks, "Who will take care of you?"

"Jesus."

"Jesus will wipe your ass?"

"If that's what I need. He'll find someone."

"You think your church friends will do that for you? In Canada?" Zdenka believes Canadians to be slippery and insincere, heartless smilers. Onscreen, the window behind her sister is dark; beside it, the squat brass pendulum wags indefatigably. Pavla bought that clock long ago, for herself, before she ever imagined she'd immigrate. Her own wall gleams white and bare on the snowy, overcast afternoon.

"God will give me a swift end. I'm praying for it."

Their father died of a heart attack, and Pavla enjoys butter greatly. When she heaps butter on toast or potatoes, she sometimes asks Jesus, *Let me die in my sleep.*

"You're nearly eighty, Pavla. You need a plan."

Onscreen, her face is doughier, a slack, uneven terrain. Zdenka looks much younger. With her spiky platinum hair and turquoise-lined eyes, Zdenka could be sixty. Pavla's absence of makeup used to give her a girlish appearance, until she hit her fifties and never learned to apply makeup in a flattering way. Would Zdenka worry less if she wore makeup and dyed her hair?

On the whole her health is excellent, and she walks daily.

"I'll be alright." She reminds Zdenka that the power of attorney is taken care of, and wishes she could convey the power of God, which is so much greater than any human law. How to persuade Zdenka that God's power — over the past four decades, on a new continent — has made possible some of her greatest adventures?

In the early days of her faith, the prayers were for babies. The first was Brandon, a preemie with arms like thin dry sausages. Born ten weeks early, Brandon had never opened his eyes. While changing his diaper one day, she asked Jesus to make Brandon strong and alert. "Jesus loves you, Brandon," she said, and the baby opened his bottomless eyes.

After that, she prayed for all the babies, even the healthy ones. When Zdenka asked if she didn't want a baby of her own, she said not really, and was surprised to discover it was true. By then her marriage had ended.

When Pavla moved to palliative care, she found her vocation. To the agitated, solitary gentleman whose contacts board was blank — no relatives could be found — and who ordered her to call his accountant, she said, "Don't worry, Sir, the Boss on High will sort it out." The man grew docile, and she spooned a bit of food into his mouth. To the lady who moaned for her Alva, she said, "Call on Jesus. All you have to say is, Please Jesus, come into my heart. You can even just think it." The woman closed her eyes and grew quiet.

The next day the nurse supervisor told her to stop praying for the patients.

She explained that she hadn't in fact prayed for them, and besides, Sruti sometimes told a patient that she'd remember them in her prayers.

"It's an expression," said the nurse supervisor. "It's not literal."

"Hindu prayers aren't literal?"

"Don't talk about God to the patients, okay? You're not a chaplain."

When she moistened the solitary gentleman's gums with a wet sponge, she thought of Christ on the cross, receiving the sponge of vinegar before his final breath, and said inwardly, *Give him your perfect peace, Oh Lord*. She hummed a happy song. Surely the nurse supervisor could not forbid that.

This is the day that the Lord has made,
We will rejoice and be glad in it.

Not being allowed to share the Good News was like being in communist Czechoslovakia, she complained to Jesus. He told her not to let bitterness grow in her heart, because there would be other opportunities for prayer, more than she could imagine. Prayer could take many forms, Jesus said, some unexpected. She had only to seek them.

Onscreen, eight little boxes of women. One woman lifts her palm in a high five to heaven. Other women clasp hands before their mouths and look down, others sit up with closed eyes, a panorama of white bangs and russet perms and creased chins, depending on webcam elevation.

"Lord," they pray, "place Your shield of protection around us."

"Keep our immune systems strong, Lord, for You are the Great Physician."

"Lord, as this new variant spreads, guide our leaders, give them the wisdom of Solomon."

Most are in southern Ontario, though Wendy is out in Abbotsford, BC. Even though it's seven a.m. for Wendy, she joins because she feels the Spirit's presence here. *The Spirit moves faster than the internet!* she likes to say, her very yellow hair, in the style of that starlet's shag, swinging around her weathered face.

"Paula, would you like to add a few words?"

Prayer begins with a big inhalation. When Pavla closes her eyes, she drops into a rosy darkness that takes her down to her throat and heart, where she waits. Then the first slow word — *Lord* — an opening up to the vastness around her. Often she has no idea what to say next.

The Bible supplies useful prompts. "Lord, You tell us in Second Timothy that You have given us a spirit not of fear, but of power and of love, and of a sound mind. Today, eight sound minds are gathered to hear Your voice."

(Amen! and a *whoop* from Wendy.)

"Because we wrestle not against flesh and blood . . . and viruses!"

(Chuckles and Amens.)

"But against the rulers of the darkness of this world!"

Repeating the Bible's words, she feels prophetic, like Isaiah but nicer. She doesn't want fire to rain down. She wants the prophet's fearless clarity of vision.

Long ago her father complained that she talked too much, but the Tuesday ladies love her words.

"Thank you, Paula!" they say.

"Paula our prayer warrior!"

Forty years ago, after leaving her husband, she sat in her new apartment on a cream sofa purchased on layaway. Her husband would have dismissed it as impractical, but she was done with the dark, gory velour of her marital apartment. Up on the eighth floor, she felt close to the clouds.

Despite her serene furnishings, she'd hardly slept those first two weeks. Her life felt as empty as her new apartment. It surprised her how emptiness could bring a bodily sensation of suffocation, when suffocation was in fact caused by an absence of space. How strange that the mind could create absurdities with no analogue in the real world. How it could become incoherent with repetition.

She'd feared becoming more fearful. *Little goose with goosebumps on her goosebumps* her family had called her since she could remember.

She hadn't left the apartment for nearly two weeks. Attempts to walk through her front door provoked vertigo and a racing heart, as if a crouched panther awaited her in the dim hallway. Her boss had already given her a warning, and she was down to oatmeal and bouillon cubes.

In daydreams she was back in the sooty village in the little mountains, stepping along the springy earth of the pine woods.

But she knew that if she returned home, it would be a bleakly predictable life, not as a nurse but at the bead factory, chopping glass straws until retirement. That was the best-case scenario. Probably they'd put her to work as a janitor because she'd defected. Her life a stray bead that had slipped from a table and rolled into a dusty corner.

On the television were gaudy cartoons and gloomy dramas. A blonde woman pleaded with her blonde husband to adopt a baby, and Pavla thought of her own husband. Maybe her health problems were a sign that she should reconcile with him. Yes he put her down, but their routines had been familiar, and she missed the company. She needed something familiar within her still-new life in Canada.

She switched the channel to a cooking show in which a woman sautéed onions with an unbearable absence of anguish. If she returned to her husband, she would have to leave the apartment to buy onions. She would come back home to chop and sauté them.

She changed the channel and stopped at a live broadcast that looked like a fundraiser. The man on the screen was absolutely thrilled! His suit was navy and his hair looked soft. A 1-800 number scrolled beneath him.

Nobody she knew smiled like that man. In Czechoslovakia, when adults smiled, their faces usually reverted rapidly to seriousness. The man on TV did not stop smiling. Was he embarrassed? Guilty?

He talked about the peace that Jesus brings to troubled hearts. *Be not afraid!* Christ told countless people.

Elsewhere in the studio, rows of people answered phones, the women in high-necked blouses, the men in suits, though a few wore polo shirts. Many of them also smiled, though some nodded solemnly as they listened.

The soft-haired man closed his eyes and clapped a hand to his heart. "Jesus," he said, "I invite You to come into my life. Take away all my sins. I receive You as Savior."

On that day, so many years ago, she repeated the last two sentences aloud. She almost expected to hear an echo when she spoke, so cavernous was her loneliness. But her voice was low with fatigue, her pronunciation laboured compared with the happy man's. *Tek avay.*

The happy man urged her to call the 1-800 number. The lady who answered had a husky voice with an accent similar to Britain's new prime minister. She said, *my dear Pavla.* They uttered the complete prayer together.

Afterwards, the lady with the British prime minister's voice congratulated her. She asked Pavla where she was from and called her brave.

"I say these words every day?" asked Pavla.

"Once is enough."

"What should I say every day?"

"Share with Jesus whatever is on your mind."

The statement made Pavla consider what was on her mind on an average day, whether she could put it into words, even in Czech. She would learn. She wanted to change what was on her mind, and it sounded like Jesus could help with that.

The lady also gave her the address of a nearby church, called New Life. Pavla liked those words.

As they said goodbye, the lady declared, "You're a new creature now," and Pavla thought of the leaping gargoyles on St Vitus Cathedral.

She didn't feel God's presence immediately. Sitting on the white sofa, she experienced curiosity about what else was possible for her in Canada.

That afternoon, she went out to buy groceries, heart racing in the dairy aisle as she contemplated Canada's vast selection of cheeses. At home she sautéed onions to make an omelette, and that night, after repeating the prayer she had spoken on the phone earlier that day, she slept.

"This summer when you visit," Zdenka says, "just stay. Jesus isn't going to wipe your ass, little beetle."

In fact it was exactly the kind of thing Jesus would do. He was the God who washed feet.

"What would I do in Drzkov?"

Sometimes Pavla misses the landscape of her hometown, the low cozy mountains and the pine woods, but she doesn't miss the people. How is she going to fit into a village of six hundred? She's a city person now.

"Tell me you're not a tiny bit worried, little goose," Zdenka says.

To Zdenka, Pavla will always be the anxious big sister who fretted about nuclear war and later followed her husband to Canada despite an unhappy marriage, too scared to make a life alone.

"Aren't you the little goose now?" she asks Zdenka and winks. When they smile, their cheeks bob up in the same way. She tries to imagine how she'd look if she pencilled her eyes blue.

"But really," says Zdenka. "Imagine there were no Jesus. What would you do?"

"I don't understand."

"There was a time when you didn't believe in a god. Remember what it was like."

All she can say is, "That was a different life."

"Don't you *ever* take a break from Jesus?"

"Why would I?"

What a huge loss it would be, not to remain connected with the Creator of All Things! To lose that connection would be like leaving behind a harmonious symphony performance to sit alone in a basement washroom and listen to a tap drip.

"At least you should take statins," Zdenka says. "Dad could have lived another decade if he'd been on them. I can't believe you were a nurse for almost thirty years."

Her friend Evelyn is on statins and they upset her stomach. Pavla tells Zdenka about the cake she made for Evelyn's birthday, luscious with whipped cream and sour cherries in kirsch. Evelyn couldn't finish a slice because of terrible indigestion from statins. If you can't enjoy your own birthday cake, what is old age for? Besides, she has seen death so many times. In most cases, the body shuts down. God created the body so that it knows how to die.

When they say goodbye, Zdenka adds, "It would be nice if we could have a conversation without Jesus. Next time, okay?"

Pavla says she will try.

"We're tired of living in fear," says Wendy. Her very yellow hair quivers.

"You can't take a man's millstone to pay his debts! He needs to make a living!" That's Joanne.

"The fact is that we are living in Revelation times." (Wendy again.)

Wendy is not vaccinated, though most of the Tuesday ladies keep their status private, like a pricey, unorthodox skincare regimen. Pavla cannot understand why. As a retired nurse she is accustomed to needles and masks.

One time she said, "A little piece of cloth on your face, how is that oppression?" She recalled Soviet tanks creeping down the streets of Prague.

"It's the principle!" said Wendy.

She prefers to get along with the Tuesday ladies. *Our Anna*, they call her, after the elderly prophetess who lived her final years in the temple at Jerusalem, praying day and night. She is at least a decade older than Joanne, the next oldest. The ladies know her stories, about the flasher and the mugger, the unscrupulous superintendent, the predatory GP.

Tomorrow Wendy leaves for Ottawa. She'll drive some fifty hours, all the way from Abbotsford. There is talk about Ottawa's medical experiments and tyranny.

Pavla is too tired to feel outraged. The older she gets, the less arguments interest her. Maybe the wisdom of old age is mostly fatigue.

When the Tuesday ladies ask her to pray, she focuses on the power of faith. Faith turns a tiny seed into a tree. "Let us be like the mustard seed, Oh Lord, which became a mighty tree where birds nested." She loves the image of a huge tree pulsing with birds and their songs. She thinks of the birch below her window, where in August the starlings gurgle rapturously.

When she finishes praying, the Tuesday ladies rejoice like starlings, and Wendy calls her *Paula our prayer maven!*

In the early days, she prayed haltingly. Some of the words were difficult to understand. Covenant, dispensation, sanctification.

After God cured her agoraphobia, He healed her teeth. That's when she really learned to pray. She'd needed a bridge she couldn't afford, and had just committed to give five hundred dollars to a mission in Soviet Moscow.

She looked up Bible verses about teeth in Strong's Concordance. *I have given you cleanness of teeth* (Amos 4:6). *Like a bad tooth and an unsteady foot is confidence in a faithless man* (Proverbs 25:19). The Bible did not have much to say about her dental situation.

She asked God how to find money for a bridge.

"You have enough money," God said.

Did He want her to use her credit card? Go into debt?

"No debt," said God.

She wondered if someone at church would give her money. When Floriana needed rent money, a secret donor left three months' worth with the church secretary. Floriana figured the donor overheard her pray at the front of the church. Floriana also had a little girl.

Pavla waited a week, then two weeks, with a clove pushed into her gum. Evenings she allowed herself a Tylenol. Tooth complications were part of growing older, she accepted that. Her first tooth had been removed when she was fifteen, without anaesthetic. She was lucky. A girl in her class had the wrong tooth removed by the same dentist.

Four Sundays in a row, she stood at the front of the church for prayer. On the fourth Sunday, on the bus home, she began to cry. Maybe she should have kept the money she'd given to the Muscovites. She'd imagined her five-hundred dollars buying secret suitcases of Bibles, hopeful communiqués to an oppressed people. What was a bit of metal and porcelain in her mouth by comparison?

And God said, "Go into the wilderness."

His words stopped her tears. Did God want her to travel to the far North? Or to the deserts of Israel?

Beyond the bus window, old four-storey apartments slid by, their windows curtained by tinfoil and grocery circulars, and in one instance by a blanket with a wolf howling at the moon. Then came the discount grocery and the car dealership, as the bus approached the parkway that cut along the ravine.

The ravine. As the bus whooshed past it, she pulled the yellow cord to request a stop.

She entered by a steep dirt path. In winter, the ravine was an arrangement of gray sticks and dry, broken grass. The main walkway was paved, and a couple with a dog smiled at her. Avoiding the pavement, she followed a winding frozen path towards the river, where black water roiled sluggish between banks crusted with snow, amid the parkway's low vibration. Brush and the lower elevation hid the parkway from sight. A plausible wilderness.

She had not planned on a walk, and the cold sidled around her pantyhosed legs and up her skirt. She balled her fingers within the palms of her gloves. For a time, the cold distracted her from the pain of her tooth, until the sensations mingled and made her feel vulnerable and foolish.

She asked God what to do.

"Look at the grass," God said.

Bleached reeds drooped beside shrunken burdock bushes. The ravine had none of the beauty of her hometown's forests silvered with snow. There were few conifers here.

"Keep looking at the grass."

She thought of the dead grass. She thought of her aching tooth. What was the connection?

"Why aren't you praying?" God said. He reminded her that Christ had withdrawn to the wilderness to pray.

She asked God to heal her tooth, or to help her find someone who could.

"That's a start," said God. "Go bigger."

She was in too much pain to think clearly. She tried to pray for the dental health of Torontonians, but couldn't bring herself to care. She prayed for the Muscovites. Some of them must have tooth problems, terrible ones. Maybe she would just get the tooth removed, even if her dentist claimed that it would ruin her smile.

Further down the river path, the trees were taller and bushier. She recognized the elephant skin of a beech among the maples, a rare European sight, and felt a little at home. Nearby were the flaming tips of a sumac bush, and within it, a human figure, a man in a long coat.

She stopped, considered turning around, and decided to keep walking. Showing fear felt imprudent. If the man stayed in the sumac, soon he would be behind her.

The man stepped out from the sumac wearing a rakish smile and opened his coat to reveal unzipped pants. She felt the familiar spiteful bloom of goosebumps. A woman who'd walked right into a trap, that's what she was. How had her life come to this moment? She felt abandoned by God.

It was the same feeling when, as a girl, she climbed down the side of a quarry to reach a raspberry bush bright with fruit, only to realize she couldn't climb back out. The slow recognition as sun-bleached limestone crumbled beneath her sandals; then the afternoon alone beneath the sun, skin growing sore, until a camping group walked by and threw her a rope.

In the ravine she could have screamed at God with frustration, except what is the point of screaming at someone absent? The only option is to scream at oneself.

"Remember what happened to My Son in the wilderness."

Somehow, God was back.

"Satan paid a visit." God's tone was calm and teacherly.

Satan was here. She could believe that.

"And there was a test, remember?"

The flasher's expression was jauntily defiant, delighted by her fear. An unclean spirit.

She was fed up with fear. She was finished with the little goose. Her tooth throbbed with rage.

She rebuked the unclean spirit in the man. She commanded it to leave *in the name of Jesus*. Soon she was speaking in tongues, uttering confident, perfectly pronounced syllables that echoed the Hebrew of hymns and the Greek of the New Testament. *Shaddai, Yeshua, diakrisis, nestis, nerititititi!* She felt like a Hebrew prophet in the wilderness.

The man regarded her with disgust. He turned away to button his pants, in a surprisingly modest gesture. Perhaps the unclean spirit had departed from him already.

"Jesus loves you!" she cried out, and he hurried away. Both energized and exhausted, she walked along the river and sang her favourite song. It was for children, but she didn't care. She was a child of God.

> *This is the day that the Lord has made,*
> *We will rejoice and be glad in it!*

Her tooth pain was still present, but less important. She told God that she trusted Him to take care of it.

"You passed the test," God said. "Go home and lie down."

Her bedroom was sparsely furnished. On either side of the low double bed were two small tables and that was all, except for a pothos sprawled along the high windowsill, a vivid, speckled garland. The window spanned the room, and the refracted northern daylight stunned her pupils, amid white walls and white bedding, the duvet cover a gift from Zdenka, softer than anything you could find in Canada.

And God said, "Remove the clove."

The pain radiated into her right cheek and ear. She felt close to her own decay beneath the graying popcorn ceiling. She felt alone again, very far away from Zdenka and anyone who mattered to her.

When she awoke, the window was twilit, haloing the pothos.

"Be still and know that I am God." The voice wafted from the vivid, speckled leaves. Perhaps the pain had caused a mild hallucination. Then again, God spoke to Moses from a bush.

The right side of her face still hurt. She let the pain be the pain.

All evening she lay there, aching as the sky went navy. She remembered the ravine, now a dark band running through the spangled, intricate city. In a couple of months, the trees would become a pale fluorescent green, then the deep green of summer, then red and brown, then bare again. In her mind she saw the trees as God must, from above and at cosmic speed, passed daily by thousands of people who skittered like fleas, each one swelling into adulthood and, in time, shrivelling down into perfect stillness.

She felt a bloom of goosebumps, new ones, not of fear but of astonishment. She was becoming a new creature. A new goose.

The next morning, the pain felt bearable. She decided to wait another week before making an appointment with the dentist.

For the rest of the winter, every evening after supper, she lay in bed and let God work on her teeth. Gravity pressed her into the bed, and she felt her breath draw as smoothly as a magician pulling silk from a sleeve. Sometimes the pothos breathed with her.

Seek and ye shall find.

When, in the final decade of the millennium, revival broke out in Toronto, stories circulated about people receiving gold fillings from God. She wasn't surprised. She visited the revival church a few times, but it was too far away. Besides, by then God had already healed her teeth.

Zdenka tells her about the bullfinch that visits the feeder daily, and a new family of house sparrows, their debates and maneuverings. Pavla recollects the sparrow that knew how to open the automatic door to the grocery store.

"They're in decline in Europe," says Zdenka. "Nobody really knows why."

"A sparrow doesn't fall without God knowing," says Pavla.

Zdenka looks away from the screen. Her voice goes flat. "Nothing I say really matters to you, does it?"

"What do you mean?"

"Last time we spoke, I asked you not to bring up God every time we talk."

"But He's part of who I am."

"It completely changes the mood of the conversation. I can't just talk to my sister, because God is always listening in." Zdenka compresses her fuchsia lips. "It's gotten worse lately."

"I don't know what to tell you."

"You know, you're right. Probably it wouldn't work if you moved back here. We would drive each other crazy."

The conversation ends, and she folds the laptop shut. She needs to go for a walk. She shrugs on her coat and leaves for the ravine. In winter, the fast fancy bikes are gone; the only people out walk dogs that snuffle the withered grass.

A sparrow perches on the stalk of a wild carrot, before another sparrow chases it away. She admires the wild carrot's bleached starry skeleton, among the subtler beauties Jesus points out. Jesus who spoke tenderly of ordinary things, like sparrows and wildflowers and trees, indifferent to heaven's gems. In the ravine, He taught her to enjoy the cracked bark of a red maple, which she pats. Patting that tree is a kind of prayer. After all, as Jesus reminds her, prayer can take many forms, some unexpected.

What a loss it would be, not to have that connection! How can her own sister want that for her?

She prays for Zdenka and asks God for wisdom in how to communicate. She'd thought her joy would be persuasive: that Zdenka would see that Pavla, even if she lives an unconventional life in a distant land, is full of joy.

On the narrow, frozen path to the river, she thanks Jesus that her legs are still strong. She tells Him that she is trusting Him about her future.

"Actually," replies Jesus, "don't assume I'll wipe your ass."

The river ripples dark green, almost black, under a cottony gray sky. Against the muffled rumble of parkway traffic, there is the sharp, intimate rustle of a few dry oak leaves still attached to a tree.

"What do You want me to do, Lord?"

In a white pine across the river, the sparrows squabble merrily. A sparrow doesn't fall without God knowing, but a sparrow also doesn't fall without another sparrow knowing, because they are always together.

Today Jesus keeps His distance.

Satan isn't here either. It's terrifying. To be alone, without a fiend to rebuke.

She is in the quarry again, except now she's old. "Guide me, Lord," she says. What she hears are a few wobbly words that express a truth long suppressed: that the end scares her.

The Tuesday ladies are excited today. Wendy's very yellow hair is toqued and bounces from inside a vehicle as she says, "It's been an amazing outpouring of generosity and love!"

There is a prolonged blast of low honks as Joanne's lips move. When the honking pauses, she becomes audible. "How many trucks are there?"

"Ten thousand!" Wendy laughs and explains that she is far from the main action, at the very end of Lyon Street.

Joanne remarks that the number sounds biblical.

There is talk of the Ottawa protest sparking a global movement. To Brussels, Canberra, Washington D.C., and beyond.

"The Spirit is so present here." Already a woman has been healed of chronic depression, and a man of acid reflux, no doctor required. Wendy describes how people gather daily at nine in the morning to pray.

"Did you meet the lady who brought a ram's horn?" asks Marguerite.

"What's it called?"

"A shofar."

More honking, and the fall of Jericho, that's what they're talking about, how the Israelites walked around Jericho's walls and conquered the city in a week. It is difficult to keep up with the speedy cacophony. If only Wendy would put herself on mute.

Marguerite's prayer rehearses the story of Jericho, the six labourious days walking around the city's perimeter. What a journey! On the seventh day, the priests blew the rams' horns and the people *shouted a great shout.*

The great shout of the people! And the walls of Jericho tumbled down!

She looks for the volume button. Her laptop bleeps at her as she presses different buttons while the Tuesday ladies rejoice.

Why do people talk so much?

Someone says her name. Marguerite is repeating her name and the word *pray*. It's her turn.

Pavla knows what to do. First the big inhalation, then *Lord* . . .

She waits for the Holy Spirit to proffer the next words.

"We ask . . ."

The winter sky is too bright. It is hard to focus.

"Your . . ."

Inside herself, a slackening. As if she has skin inside her body and it is buckling, like earth along the Don River.

". . . Peace."

Her mind wiped clean.

A long silence from the ladies. One — what's her name? — utters a clipped *Amen*, like she wants to swallow the word. The blast of a horn, and soon Wendy is talking about taking things one day at a time.

Pavla needs to lie down. In a single gesture, she raises her hand and shuts the laptop.

Her mind gone still, like a landscape after an earthquake.

The duvet cover soft beneath her fingers.

Beyond the window, flecks of snow drift sideways and glint in sunlight.

At the edge of her mind is a thought.
Something she once knew.

Seek.

The tune that goes with the words *This is the day.*
This is the day.
This is the day.

At the window, a vivid speckled garland
And along her nape, goosebumps.

be ye ready

He's ready to slay the manticore when his mom arrives to pick him up. "How could you forget? The pastor's family is waiting for us!" she says as he stuffs his feet into his sneakers, while Liam holds open the front door. He's never told Liam he's Christian. Because God is mostly something his mom needs, something private, like the box of tampons under the bathroom sink.

As the car crawls through rush-hour traffic, the manticore's brutal slouch replays in his mind. His mom talks about what an incredible blessing it is for the pastor to invite them (just them!) for supper, especially the pastor of such a big church. But now they're late, because Santi forgot his promise to be home by five.

He has a strategy, because manticores are rarer than dragons, and trickier too. Just when you've dodged a claw and are prepared to drive your sword between the monster's ribs, its stinger will be flying at you. Before the tip of your sword can graze the manticore's chest, the stinger will be deep inside your kidneys, pumping your doom.

"Santi? Pon atención tonight, okay? Try to focus. Please."

The pastor's house is east of the city, beyond the huddled high-rises and strip malls. Then patches of forest, yellow leaves that glow in the dusk, the strange bright evening of October, though dull compared with the landscapes of the game, its winter panoramas of jagged peaks and dark pines, where even the sharp dry grass is riveting.

He just acquired an elixir that grants extra speed. Following the ancient recipe on a moth-bitten page, he combined angelica, myrrh, a magical thistle, and the heart of a basilisk. He drank the flashing green broth without delay.

"Thank you, Lord Jesus," says his mom, as the car skates down an empty road beside a golf course. His mom's aged hatchback is almost not embarrassing there, unlike in the city, where it stalls at intersections or accelerates so slowly that cars behind them honk, while his mom calls out to Jesus for protection. He thinks they're still beside the golf course when the car swings to the right and a house heaves into view from behind a high clump of bushes.

After she turns off the ignition, his mom reaches over to squeeze his hand and thank Jesus again, before stepping out into the dark. Above the pastor's front door, an upside-down prism blazes.

When the pastor opens the door, he looks different than he does in church. In jeans and a blue-checked shirt, he could be the father of one of Santi's white classmates, though his teeth are dazzling.

In the vaulting foyer, Santi's mom apologizes for their lateness. "The spirit is willing, but the flesh is weak." She admires the marble floor and the oak staircase.

"We're blessed," says the pastor. He places a hand on Santi's shoulder and walks them deeper into the house. "It's pizza night!"

The kitchen is suffused by white light, as if illuminated by powerful crystals. At an island of cream-coloured stone, the pastor's wife smiles and chops mushrooms, surrounded by small bowls of toppings.

The pastor's son is there too. He initiates a high five, as if Santi has already joined the youth group, which he is supposed to, next year when he turns fourteen.

"Good timing, Santi," says the pastor's son. "Pizza is the best. The secret is Mom's sauce."

"Secret sauce!" sings the pastor's wife. She places a circle of dough before Santi.

He distributes the sauce, dabs the pale spots, then segments a ribbon of green pepper to outline a manticore, the sinuous back tapering to a stinger, but the result is a crippled rat. Already the pastor's son has placed his own pizza in the oven and says, "Let me know when you're done."

Before Santi first played *Fiend Hunter III: World Gone Wrong* at Liam's, he used to draw sneakers. His mind was steadied by the smooth, graduated curve of the toe and the intricacy of the laces. Sneakers were powerful and serene.

A slice of green pepper becomes a sole. Grated cheese criss-crosses into laces.

"A shoe," says the pastor's son. "Awesome."

"Is that enough toppings?" asks his mom.

The pastor's daughter enters the kitchen. Her hair is short and ruffled, and she wears a sweatshirt with the outline of a plump fly. When Santi pushes the bowl of cheese to her, she says, "No thank you."

155

Everyone else sits at the table, waiting for her and Santi's pizzas to finish baking. The pastor and his mom talk about the state of the world.

"So much corruption and uncertainty," says his mom.

"At least there's Jerusalem," says the pastor.

"Yes, Jerusalem!"

"Remember what the Lord says: In the last days, I will pour out My spirit upon all flesh."

His mom's face gladdens beneath the lights. "And your sons and your daughters shall prophesy, and your young men shall see visions — eh, Santi?"

Santi feels his head nod as he stares down at the stone counter, which reflects a radiant blob of light. When he looks away, the radiant blob follows his gaze to the night beyond the window.

"And your old men shall dream dreams, eh Dad?" says the pastor's son.

"Can't wait!" says the pastor.

"Blood and fire and billows of smoke," murmurs the pastor's daughter, standing beside Santi. "The sun will be turned to darkness and the moon to blood, before the coming of our Lord, our Father." She gives him a sad smile and whispers "Be ye ready," when the oven timer beeps.

At the table, they hold hands and close their eyes. Santi's hands are swallowed by the pastor's dry meaty palm and his mom's cooler damp fingers. The pastor thanks God for their visit and asks for guidance, though why guidance is needed to eat pizza eludes Santi. He recalls a video about the grip strength of chimpanzees and wonders how long the pastor could withstand a chimp's grip.

Compared with the professor, the pastor's words are mild

156

and dull. The professor calls the world a slaughterhouse of doom. Life is a tragedy—he says so in his book. Only when you discover the rules and apply them do you become a man.

"Go ahead, Santi," says his mom. Everyone is chewing.

His mom studies the sweatshirt of the pastor's daughter. Beneath the plump fly are the words *Save the Rusty-patched*. "What is the rusty-patched?"

"A bee that's endangered. They used to be abundant. Now extirpation is imminent."

"Lexie has a heart for God's creation," says the pastor's wife.

"She got solar panels for her seventeenth birthday," says the pastor's son. "Or more like, *we* got solar panels." He gives his sister a wink.

"This house is too big," says the pastor's daughter.

"Lexie," says the pastor's wife.

"Why are the bees dying?" The words feel gravelly in Santi's throat.

"Neonicotinoids in pesticides are a major cause. Loss of habitat, too. Without pollinators we wouldn't have most of the ingredients for this pizza." Lexie speaks quickly, an outpouring of facts about corn monoculture, bee immune systems, and the importance of hedgerows. "So much life will just *end*."

In the game, there's a landscape blighted by the Sorcerer's curse. The crops are withered, the peasants' huts mottled by mildew, abandoned by even the bubonic rats.

"Lexie has been protesting at the golf course next door," says the pastor's wife. "She wants them to switch to organic pesticides. That's why she was late."

"I'm not even protesting the lawns, which trash biodiversity." Lexie tears off a piece of crust.

"We changed from grass to clover a couple summers ago," says the pastor. "Much easier to maintain."

"It's not too cold now, to protest outside?" asks Santi's mom.

"People are still golfing," says Lexie.

"We can pray about it," says Santi's mom. She folds her napkin into a tight little square and tucks it beneath her plate. "Later we can have some prayer."

"There's no rush," says the pastor.

Santi thinks about life ending, the withered plants and the piles of stiff bees. His face grows prickly.

Soon his mom and the pastor's wife are talking about green smoothies. "So much good energy," says his mom. She looks down at Santi's jiggling knee.

"I see you drawing in church all the time, Santi," says Lexie.

"It's a hobby he has," says his mother. "I pray it is for God's glory."

The last time he drew in church, a demon materialized in his Bible. The pastor had been talking about wrestling powers of darkness and Santi drew the demon without thinking, it was just something his hand did. Beneath the horns, eyes bulging in opposite directions and a scrawny, gulping neck. A tumorous Adam's apple, skeletal ribs, and a tiny drooping dick. Before he realized what he'd done, his mom's coral fingernail had dug into his hand, followed by a hiss of words. "Santi, what is this?"

"Nothing." He closed the Bible fast.

At the end of the service, his mom walked to the front of the church for prayer. The pastor's wife prayed with her, and probably that's when they talked about his demon.

In the crystalline kitchen, Lexie says, "You love beauty, Santi." Her voice is matter of fact, eyes unblinking. She looks like Alma the elf apothecaress, and he feels his face grow prickly again.

"Excuse me," he says and stands up. As he walks away, the pastor calls out, "The powder room is to the left."

He overshoots and ends up in the laundry room, then back-tracks and overhears the pastor's wife say, "Sometimes medication can be godly."

"But the side effects," says his mom.

He locks the door and lowers the toilet seat cover, sitting on it and drawing his chest down to his knees.

He and his mom used to do yoga together. At first he didn't see the point of sticking your butt to heaven while your wrists ached, but it made her happy. That was when they still snuggled and watched *Dr. Poon: Exotic Animal Vet*. He'd planned to buy her a house like the pastor's where they'd live together. He still wants to buy her a house one day.

Then she stopped the yoga, just when he'd started to enjoy it. Yoga was demonic, she said, and apologized. She was always apologizing for things that didn't matter. Like the professor's book, a gift she regretted when Santi told her that the professor insisted everyone has chaos inside them. "I thought it was about getting organized," she said.

A towel hangs from the rack, and he folds it on the floor against the wall. Kneeling, he roots the top of his head onto the towel, clasps his hands around the back of his head, and launches his right foot upward, joined by the left.

Then comes the peppery cascade of blood to the head, as the upside-down world sharpens into view. A bug's world of small, forgotten things. It calms him to stare at a curly shred of translucent plastic beneath the vanity. Otherwise the pastor's floor is spotless. Probably they have a maid, someone like his mom when she first arrived in Canada.

There's a knock on the door. "Santi?" says the pastor's son. "Everything okay in there, buddy?"

"Yes." The word comes out squashed.

"We're having dessert. Sundaes. Come join us."

"Alright," croaks Santi.

"Awesome."

He returns the towel to the rack, fluffing the fibres to wipe out the imprint from his head.

In the hallway, his mother's voice carries. ". . . when his father left."

"You don't know where he is?" says the pastor's wife, and the pastor's son cries out, "Santi, help yourself!" On the kitchen island are pints of ice cream and jars of toppings. Ten eyes are on him, like the holy monster in the book of Revelation. It sings *Holy Holy Holy* to praise God, but it's terrifying, an eyeball-covered lion worse than any manticore.

At the table his mom murmurs, "Todo bien?"

He mashes sprinkles into his ice cream, while the pastor and his mom talk about finding God's purpose for your life. "What exactly did you do?" asks his mom. "When did you know for sure?"

"It took a lot of prayer," says the pastor.

The conversation is obviously for Santi — his mom has been getting on his case to find God's purpose — but all he can hear are the words *when his father left.*

In kindergarten, in one picture after another, he drew his father, a smiling man with orange hair. Usually his father was driving a truck. Later, he stood on an oil rig.

There had been a job in Alberta. At first his mom said it was taking longer than expected. Later on she said, "I don't know" and looked tired. Then first grade began and she found Jesus.

When Santi asked about his father, she said he was dead. She said he went on a hike and never came back. She said there's a park almost as big as Costa Rica up there.

One time when she found him crying, she said, "Jesus is your daddy now." But Jesus looks like a girl with a beard, a soft-haired loser.

"Why don't we pray?" says the pastor. The ice-cream bowls are empty.

A choreography commences, as Lexie and the pastor's wife stand behind his mother, while the pastor and his son stand on either side of Santi, pressing a hand onto his shoulders.

"Lord," says the pastor, "You remind us in Your Word that we can be *trans*formed and renew our minds when we place our trust in You."

Santi lowers his head as if to dodge a punch, and for a while the pastor prays for his mom.

Then the pastor says, "Lord, You know how precious a son is. You're a father. We ask You to give Santi Your peace that passeth understanding, the power to focus and pay attention."

It becomes clear why he and his mom have been invited for supper. The pizza, the sundae. They are not for her.

"Lord, we bind the spirit of ADHD." The pastor's voice is low and firm. Any demons are to leave Santi at once. The pastor lists some demons. The demon of distraction. The demon of anxiety.

"Release him!" cries the pastor's son, gripping Santi's shoulder.

Santi remembers sitting on his father's shoulders, his chin resting on the sandy reddish hair and his arms wrapped around the forehead. His father walked beside a shallow river where the pebbles winked.

With the pastor's family crowded around him, asking God to fix him, he feels himself float away, and briefly glimpses himself from above, until a voice declares, "Lord, how can your creatures *not* be distressed in this world?" The voice is Lexie's.

The pastor's son gives a subdued *Amen.*

"Protect Santi in this damaged world. Protect Beatriz too, and all Your creatures, the loggerhead shrike and the little brown bat, the woodland vole and the American eel."

Lexie's hand touches his upper arm as the list goes on. "The Persius duskywing, the pale-bellied frost lichen, the Shumard oak, *Your martyrs O Lord.*"

Santi thinks of Alma the elf apothecaress and her solstice elixir, which grants the power to vanish for thirty seconds. As Lexie lists other endangered creatures, she gives his arm a little shake. The Jefferson salamander, the Acadian flycatcher, the river darter.

His chair scrapes against the floor, and then his feet are in motion, across the kitchen's stony expanse.

"Santi!" cries his mother.

She repeats his name and the pastor says, "Let him go."

He makes sure to slam the bathroom door, but from the outside. In the foyer he grabs his shoes and jacket. Beside the front door is a keypad, where a tiny red light blinks. "Please Lord," he breathes, as he pushes down the handle, because sometimes God helps him when it really matters.

The door makes a low sucking sound and clicks behind him, and he slips away from the shining prism overhead to the dark side of the house, where he squeezes into his sneakers and jacket.

In the pastor's backyard his feet are loud on the stiff grass, then thunderous on dry leaves. He stops to listen for a door opening or someone calling his name. The kitchen lights blaze from afar. He turns towards the golf course and nearly runs into the fence. His toes fit into the interlocking wires, one two three. On the other side, the ground smacks into the soles of his sneakers.

The lawn of the fairway is spongy, unreal. If he runs the length of the golf course, he'll get back to the main road and eventually to the city. No way he's going back to the pastor's house. No way he's going home, either. Maybe Liam's mom will let him stay. *I was forced into an exorcism for my ADHD. My mom believes in demons. She lied to me. She lies about everything. I don't feel safe.*

A pale moon hangs steady over a patch of forest. The moon's light grants him a long, nimble shadow, his own skilled avatar. Soon enough the pastor will send out a car. The forest is his only choice, a broad clump except for one faraway tree near the main road, peaked like a wizard's cap.

In the woods, he feels his way through fallen leaves, as one twig then another flicks against his face. A spiderweb stops him briefly, but he keeps moving, hands pushing away branches, limbs in alert slow motion, the wizard tree a beacon in his mind. If he were in the game, he'd use the panther philter for night vision.

Without the company of his shadow, sounds sharpen, mostly his own charged breath, though the crickets are out, even in October, and their throbbing refrain fills the forest. In the denser darkness, the exorcism surges back into his mind—the pastor's grip on his shoulder and his mother's voice pleading with God to fix her son.

His throat convulses and he vomits, sprinkles and green pepper scraping his throat. It dampens his jacket, and he is a small child again, alone in the woods. He tries to visualize the wizard tree, a serene beacon, and says, "Please, Lord."

In the dark forest, the invisible feels real. Here God feels realer than in the bright noisy church. He doubles his pace towards the wizard tree.

Next thing his shoulder is twisted against the ground. For a time, all he can do is try to breathe, beneath branches that lattice the sky, where a few stars tremble.

"What do You *want*?" The sound of his own whimpering voice makes him even angrier at God.

He imagines lying there until the cold claims him, though it is not cold enough yet. He'll be found alive first. The dusty leaves beneath his palm are useless — no magical thistles grow here — and the throbbing of his shoulder grows bearable as he clutches it. Nothing seems to be broken.

If he were seriously hurt, then his mother would care. She and the pastor would be sorry.

High above his head, the dry treetops shift in the wind. A sound like the rush of many waters, an intricate and shifting arrangement of forces. When a stronger gust arrives, the forest crackles, as if with the approach of fire.

The sun will be turned to darkness and the moon to blood, before the coming of our Lord, our Father.

The end of the world. It's awful, but it's when he was born. There are facts he must accept. The exorcism, his father come back to life: they are all part of the End, a new level in God's game. It is more demanding than anything at Liam's.

The thought makes him very calm. Usually Santi is hungry for excitement, but now he sees how calmness can be more appealing.

Amid the velvety pulsations of crickets, the forest is both peaceful and electric. There is a fluster of leaves, then a scrabble along bark. Santi takes in everything. One day he will draw this darkness filled with life. Because tonight he is covered in eyes like the monster in the book of Revelation that sings *Holy Holy Holy*. A monster not terrifying but intensely awake. Santi has never felt so alert in his life, not even while playing Liam's game. It is as if he has swallowed ten elixirs, as if he is surrounded by twenty manticores and ready for them all, because an immense focus has descended upon him, a peace that passeth understanding.

for what shall it profit a man?

I could not believe that Esther was happy, despite her beautiful children and her thanks to the Lord. Everything was a blessing. The boys' skill at building a chicken coop that spring, the girls' care of the chickens, her husband's small church; even his job as a janitor was a blessing, though Esther spoke little of her own success. When I brought it up, she called it *the Lord's provision for the family.*

"No but your work is brilliant," I said as Martha, her eldest, came onto the deck and handed me a cup of iced tea. The clay cup was Esther's creation and had its own intimate landscape, of tender distortions and secretive dimples.

"She's right," said Martha, but Esther looked away to the forest beyond the garden.

"You should heed your daughter," I joked. "Why don't you join us, Martha?"

I hoped Martha's presence might change the subject from blessings to something more interesting, but Esther turned the talk to my own life, where she discovered ample blessings as well. My PhD in art history was a blessing, and so was my work at a global management consulting firm, where I parlayed skills once devoted to sixteenth-century Dutch painting into streamlining supply chains for the largest supermarket in Argentina. (Esther skipped over my fruitless struggle to find a tenure-track job, as well as my absence from church for the past two decades.)

The blessing talk was a way to express enthusiasm, I reminded myself, while Esther gushed about how far I'd gone, and travelling so much too.

"Well, I'm back in Toronto," I said, "and still haven't been to Japan like you have." I wanted Esther to acknowledge her old life, even briefly, when she had been magnificently reckless and given me permission to leave the faith.

"You were in Japan?" Martha asked her mother.

It hadn't occurred to me that Esther might not have spoken to her children about Japan. At nineteen, she had gone there to model, against the wishes of her family. I'd thought it was the start of her liberation, and mine too.

"That was a long time ago," said Esther. Her gaze returned to the woods and I wondered what she saw there. Since my time in California, the forests of northern Ontario were an unexceptional blur, even in the light of early summer.

Martha sat very still, head bowed over a book on her lap. On the cover, a bonneted young woman strolled through a hayfield, her face rosy-lipped and open, not unlike Martha's.

Already Martha had the sweetness of fundamentalist Christian womanhood. It was the sweetness of someone secluded from the world's chaos—not because she hadn't struggled, or wouldn't, but because whatever had happened, Jesus had removed the suffering from her heart, which was as tender again as her soft, white skin.

Finally Esther spoke. "Martha, the jars still need to be brought upstairs and washed."

I was disquieted by Esther's severity towards her daughter. Something in Esther had turned hard and small, I felt.

"What are you reading?" I asked Martha.

The book on Martha's lap was *Tess of the D'Urbervilles*. I too had read it as a teen but remembered little except the mood, which was grim, as the hapless characters betrayed each other and generally screwed up, while intermittently screwing each other. The book's bucolic cover amused me, a bit of false advertising that had helped me as a fundamentalist teen, packaging the most appalling stories—of husbands selling wives, children killing themselves, and worst of all, premarital sex—as gentle tales about simpler times.

"What do you think of it?" I said.

Martha hesitated. I remembered how I'd read at her age, torrents of strange words rushing through my mind, not always knowing what to make of them, until one day they began to sink in; around that time I lost interest in Jesus.

"It's lacerating," said Martha, her eyes growing glassy as she stared down at the book.

I was touched to see a young person moved by old art and asked, "Have you looked into universities?"

"Beth taught at university," said Esther, as if my question needed an explanation.

Martha contemplated the bonneted young woman on the cover and said it was probably a little early for that.

"Not really." I wondered if there was some idea in the family of Martha not going to university. My own mother had been less than enthused when a top American school offered me a scholarship, worried what it would do to my soul. She was not entirely wrong to worry.

"If you ever have questions, let me know," I told Martha. "I work next door to U of T, so I could show you around. It's worth looking into American universities too. Some have very generous scholarship programs."

"Martha, the jars," said Esther.

When the younger girls showed up, Esther doted on them, drawing them in for hugs and exclaiming at their accomplishments. Lydia and Violet had found mushrooms (early chanterelles!), and already at seven Violet was reading through the Pentateuch. When the boys returned from an expedition to the hardware store with Keith, I learned that Luke, now fifteen, was teaching mitosis to the children, while Titus, at thirteen, had designed an irrigation system for the garden. In fact, the children had decided to continue with their homeschool curriculum into the summer, because that's when the forest teemed with lessons.

In the garden, the late-afternoon sun filtered through trellises of pubescent beans and clouds of tangled dill. Here, university felt unreal as we gathered lettuce and radishes for supper. The children were good natured, Luke exhibiting none of the awkwardness typical of fifteen-year-olds, idolized by the younger children. As the food was carried to the table by Esther and the girls, Martha moved discreetly, while Lydia and Violet, still gangly and wild, held listing bowls of salad.

At the table, Esther brought up Keith's latest venture, which was to begin the next day. Called The Apostle Project, it was a retreat in the woods to build godly masculinity.

"So many young men are lost," said Keith. "They're hungry for guidance and real challenges."

Demand was strong, and already Keith was expanding the venture. "Finally, after fifteen years, the church is growing." He'd decided to go part time with janitoring. "It's a risk, but we're trusting the Lord."

When Keith learned that my husband was a documentary filmmaker, he was impressed. Among fundamentalists, non-fiction had a credibility that the best fiction could never match. A grocery circular was truer and, in some sense, more valuable than *Anna Karenina* could ever be. Or maybe Keith just enjoyed documentaries. I was surprised I didn't dislike him. He was a gracious man, which made it easier to ignore remarks such as "a family needs a husband's vision." I wondered how much he knew about Esther's past, whether he'd checked discreetly on their wedding night if she was a virgin.

"Excuse me, where is your husband?" asked Violet. The adults laughed, and I assured Violet that he would soon join me. A professional opportunity had presented itself, one which Jonathan could not pass up, so I was driving to our rental cottage for a few days' solitude. "What a great idea," said Keith. He had a talent for expressing approval.

Despite our differences and the absence of wine, I felt more relaxed with Esther's family than I had in a long time. The water I drank was reassuring in its simplicity, like part of a cleanse. It helped that I was beginning my first real vacation in years, away from spreadsheets and PowerPoints and endless graphs promising robust growth. If I had doubts about Esther's happiness, I began to reconnect with my own, as the children dispersed to play old-fashioned games, Martha leaping between jump-ropes and the boys roaming on stilts, while the sun sank behind the trees. I marvelled at how unneurotic they were, making reasonable requests their parents usually said yes to, and when a *no* was uttered, there were no pleas or demands for an explanation.

My own work involved frequent explanations and forcibly calm, optimistic problem solving, convincing clients about the value of short-term disruptions to boost long-term profits, then going home to convince myself of the same about my own life.

When the younger children retreated to bed and Keith learned that my cottage was still an hour's drive away, he invited me to stay.

"She can have my room," said Martha.

Esther had been staring at the darkening woods, no doubt tired after a long day, and took a few moments to second Keith's invitation.

I wondered if she would have spoken up had she not wanted me to stay. Perhaps Keith's invitation made her own assent inevitable. Still, any reluctance I felt at imposing on her was outweighed by the prospect of driving alone down a dark forest road. As Martha and I cleared the dessert plates, I told myself I would start out early the following morning.

I was the last to waken. Already the children and Keith were in the dining room studying, silent except for a whisper from Violet and the scrape of a heavy book pushed across the table. Not wanting to disturb them, I took my coffee outside, holding one of Esther's mugs, which was stippled along one side with delicate, spiky warts. My forefinger pressed against them, over and over, the way one might worry a sore tooth.

In fact it was Esther's mugs that had reconnected us. Earlier that year, one drizzly evening after wrapping up another project — the week's PowerPoint slide count was 117 — I stepped into a small café on a side street. I needed to stare out a window for fifteen minutes, alone, before returning home.

The cappuccino arrived in a small convulsive-looking mug. Even after it was empty, I held the warm clay, which seemed half consolation, half prank.

When the barista found the potter's name, the revelation felt providential. It was an affirmation of my and Esther's continuing bond after a gap of nearly two decades. In a way, it was not unlike the rhythms of Bible camp, when we had been infatuated with each other for a month in the summer before returning to our regular lives apart, until the following summer, when the crush renewed itself, with variations each year. Now, after two decades apart, the reunion felt likely to be even more intense.

Our early correspondence had been exuberant and photographic — mostly of the children from Esther, and of work trips to Zurich and Hyderabad from me. Esther invited me to visit her near South River, and finally there I was, and yes the children were delightful, but Esther's gushy Christian words felt unconvincing. They seemed to mask a sadder Esther who lacked the wit of her teen self, or even of the mugs, which expressed a restless, nervy spirit — her soul, I might have said at a different time. I couldn't help but feel that Esther was secretly oppressed, her only outlet those mute mugs. To anyone without much aesthetic sense (such as Keith, I suspected) they were simply useful objects.

I found her in the garden, kneeling behind one of the bean trellises and wearing a straw hat, two piles of weeds on a sheet of newsprint beside her.

I wanted to see if my extended visit bothered her. Her sweet Christian manner could not completely fool me, I believed, having once been a sweet Christian myself.

"Let me help you," I said.

"I'm almost done."

"Let me help you finish then."

In fact plenty of weeds remained along the trellis's opposite side.

Esther held up a silvery stalk. "This is edible. Lamb's quarters. Put it in a separate pile." Esther placed hers onto the newsprint. "It's high in iron. I pickle it, for Martha."

Esther worked quickly, and I struggled to keep up on the other side, hesitating before uprooting some of the weeds lest they be underdeveloped bean stalks, vigilant for lamb's quarters and checking with Esther that I had correctly identified it.

"Sheep from the goats," muttered Esther.

"What?" I wondered if she was finally acknowledging the fact that I no longer believed. In Christ's parable, the virtuous sheep are separated from the degenerate goats, who are sent to the eternal fire prepared for the devil and his angels.

But Esther didn't hear me, or pretended not to. The morning was dazzling, and I marvelled aloud at how peaceful the garden was. The bean and zucchini plants glowed, as bees clambered hungrily into the blossoms, and the sun drew out the prickling scent of the tomato vines. I could have agreed with Esther that life was filled with blessings then, when I noticed that she had moved to a more distant trellis.

As a girl, Esther had had a moody streak. Whatever the reason, now was not a good time for a visit. Probably as the mother of five children, she simply needed time alone and I was in the way.

When I finished my row, I stood up and headed to Esther's. "I should get going."

She remained on her knees, sunhat lowered, and kept tearing out weeds.

"You have a beautiful family, Esther." I thought of Martha, and Esther's abruptness towards her. "Martha is such a blessing." I meant it. God didn't have to exist for Martha to be a blessing.

The sunhat swung up, haloing Esther's face, still like a blooming Dutch girl's. She looked back at me with uncomprehending eyes. "Martha is pregnant."

The sunhat dipped back down as Esther dropped a weed onto the pile.

"It's a young man in South River. He drives an ATV. That's how they met, out in the woods."

The sunhat lifted up partway, revealing only Esther's lips. "Martha thinks he's her boyfriend, but what does she know? He's twenty-four and works at a gas station."

"My God," I said, and hoped it sounded like a prayer.

"He is not a Christian, obviously," said Esther. "She hasn't told him yet, and I haven't told anyone either, not even Keith. Of course, I will have to tell him soon. It will break his heart." Esther struck her bare knee with a fist. "I thought I could ensure that Keith's heart would never get broken, but I didn't count on what the children could do."

"You've done nothing wrong."

"I should have been more watchful. I should have remembered the way I was at her age."

"How could you have known? She's so" — I struggled to find the right word, rejecting *sweet* — "smart."

"I thought she was a sign that God had forgiven me. As a baby she hardly ever fussed. It was a blessing, a firstborn like that."

I kneeled beside Esther and placed a tentative hand on her back. It was like petrified magma.

"Martha has betrayed the family," said Esther.

"Why don't we sit on the deck? I can make tea."

"No, I shouldn't have said anything." She shook my hand off her back. "I'm sorry. You should go."

The children and Keith were still in the dining room when I came downstairs with my suitcase. I hugged each of them, Martha last, her shoulders slight beneath a loose T-shirt. "Feel free to message me," I whispered. Alone in the car, I drove slowly down the gravel road, reluctant to leave Martha with her furious mother, though once I reached the paved highway, I accelerated and felt a surge of vindication. Esther was unhappy. I had been right.

How terrifying the idea of sex had been at seventeen. A pleasure that could overwhelm your values, annihilate everything that made you recognizably yourself, and end with a baby, a stupefying transformation of your life — what could be more consequential, besides death? — as you became responsible for the survival of a new human who had no idea what a mistake its existence was, not to mention the daily humiliation you brought on your family, your parents especially, who had to live with the screaming reminder that they had not adequately schooled you in the ways of the Lord. Because an abortion was out of the question. You would have the baby, and unless you gave it up to an impersonal system controlled by the secular state, where babies were given to plausible-looking strangers who might misguide or abuse them — a cop-out if you thought about it, when God had decided that your actions merited a baby — then the baby was yours, forever.

The horror stories of fundamentalist girls. The camper who spent too much time in the woods with that guy and never returned the following year. The youth pastor who seduced his young charge, both exiled from the church, she to a farm north of the city. All those televangelists. The preacher's sweating agonized face on cable TV, as he apologized to God and to the millions of viewers he'd disappointed. A face not so different, perhaps, from the one he'd displayed at the height of pleasure.

Pleasure was the problem. Pleasure was a broad, slippery road with many alluring, winding pathways, all leading to torment. Anything too fun was dangerous. Who could know the consequence of watching that movie where a starlet cranes her neck ecstatically as her spectral lover kisses it? Or of listening to some boy band? Plus weren't half those singers gay, the devil's irony surely, all those gay boys paving the slick way to pregnancy for so many foolish virgins?

It had been Esther who loosened me up at camp, persuading me to sneak to the train tracks at midnight with the camp director's son and his friend, returning with a hickey on her neck. For the rest of camp she wore a scarf, like a lost Parisian who'd wandered too far north.

Esther's transgressions were merely funny because she had not gotten pregnant. But Martha was doomed. All that intelligence and promise wasted on a baby.

Martha haunted me as I walked barefoot along the dock of the rental cottage. Listed as a Zen boathouse, it was discreetly opulent — soapstone counters beneath pine rafters, a Danish sound system camouflaged by enormous lopsided baskets — but neither it, nor Muskoka's beauty, could distract me. I was in the hot tub, a glass of wine at my side, when Jonathan called that evening. I asked about the workshop.

"Sandra's a legend," he said of the teacher. It was a master class for young documentarians. Jonathan was forty, but one of the organizers liked him enough to overlook his age. Fortunately, he looked young.

I was happy for him, though growing tired of being supportive and hopeful. Jonathan had been on the verge of a break for six years, after a tiny break when his first feature was screened at a mid-size film festival. When we had decided he would pursue filmmaking, I figured that if I couldn't live my dream, at least one of us should. I hadn't counted on how exhausting hope could be.

"It's so relaxing here," I said. Jonathan had thought the Zen boathouse extravagant, but I was the breadwinner. I wanted to sit on a dock for a week, a first-rate dock, before returning to my job where I worked long hours for clients who expected solutions with long-term consequences that nobody really understood. That's what our clients paid for — for someone else to claim to know, someone who wouldn't bog them down with details, which grew more hazy the more you analyzed them.

During our argument about the boathouse, I'd told Jonathan that the splurgy rental reflected my faith that one day he would make more money. Jonathan had responded that he might need to keep working in Toronto during my vacation. Fortunately the master class opportunity came up, and feeling supportive again — or rueful? — I said he should take it. He said he'd join me as soon as he could.

I flexed my toes above the water, and Jonathan asked about the visit with Esther. "It's such a different life," I said. "It's like there's a girls' team and a boys' team. The boys build things and the girls make food and clean up and are really nice. Well, everyone's really nice. Nothing wrong with that, technically."

"It sounds awful."

"No, I think it works for them. They seem happy, mostly." I would not speak of Martha, who made my heart ache. "They're very independent. They grow their own vegetables and home-school the kids. Esther knows a lot about herbs."

"Are they doomsday preppers?"

"I don't think so. Just fundamentalists."

"Any of the kids planning to leave the faith?" joked Jonathan. His current project was on ex-fundamentalists, inspired partly by me, though I refused to be filmed. Jonathan called me his coy muse but didn't press, and anyway I was busy, often out of town.

But I also felt that Jonathan—raised in a blithely secular home—couldn't understand my fundamentalist past. For that matter, I didn't really understand it. As a child, the word *fundamentalist* had sounded to me as blandly neutral as *Canadian*. "I'm a fundamentalist," I told schoolmates who enquired about my religion, and they told me they were Anglican or Catholic. By the nineties we were using words like *evangelical* and *charismatic*, while continuing to believe that the earth was about ten thousand years old and biblical miracles were literal, including the prophesies of Revelation, when horses would make a terrifying comeback.

The word that had scared me as a child was *humanist*. Secular humanist. Liberal humanist. Words that implied an opening up to the world and its pleasures. Early in your exposure to humanism, you'd feel energized. Humanism felt good, a pleasant tingling during which all the values you'd worked so hard to maintain slyly dissolved, ending one day in isolation from God and all that was good, leaving you with only a flimsy cockiness, a veneer of self-satisfaction that masked your new reality of terrifying emptiness. Given how secular life was working out for me, sometimes, I couldn't dismiss the idea entirely.

"Did you turn off email notifications?" asked Jonathan.

"Yes."

"Promise me you won't read work emails?"

"I haven't. I won't."

"Have fun!"

"I will. I am."

"Good."

Being the laid-back spouse had become Jonathan's role. He was the artist now, though at the start of our relationship I had been the one who loved art, while he'd studied anthropology, viewing art as yet another form of culture, on a vast continuum that included burial rites and dental hygiene.

Alone on the dock, I gazed at the lights of four houses on the bay, contemplating my options for fun. A family with two children dined on their deck, and fragments of their conversation drifted across the water. *But you said you liked golden beets!* Even the most banal remarks made me wistful.

Everyone else was inside. Slight figures strode past picture windows or leaned against kitchen islands. As the mosquitos grew more aggressive, I lit another citronella candle and immersed myself almost fully in the hot tub, after refilling my glass of Viognier.

If we'd had a child, I would be inside too, putting them to bed. That spring, Jonathan and I had resolved to accept our childlessness. We had tried on and off for years, going from wanting two children to one, before three ruinous rounds of in vitro. Each time only one embryo was viable, and early jokes about being the kind of couple that puts one egg in one basket soon devolved into silence.

But the maternal reveries returned sometimes, of the ghostly child I had imagined for us, custard-skinned and sturdy, by turns spirited and solemn, with Jonathan's steady brown eyes. Usually it was a girl.

The infertility was mine and unexplained. Was it a fluke, or had I abused my uterus with stress? It was my mother who first posed the question, which I laughed at, asking if she had a nice rest cure to recommend. And yet the stresses of job-market disappointments surely didn't help, nor my schedule as a consultant, out of town Monday to Thursday, often working until eleven at night. I had tried the asanas and legumes celebrated for their fertility-boosting powers; I'd even packed a pineapple in my carry-on during my luteal phase, lest pineapples be scarce in Fort Mac in February. The third round of in vitro nearly precipitated a breakdown and hypnotherapy failed. My period was regular, often torrents of shredded tissue; one sad evening I fingered through the mess on my pad, wondering if the tiniest embryo might have gotten lost in there. When I thought of my uterus, it was not a pillowy receptacle but rubbery and inhospitable.

Yet in the hot tub, the warm water rippling around me, I felt almost pillowy. A tiny hope flickered, that if I relaxed rigorously for the week — sleeping in, jogging moderately, eating lots of fresh berries and greens — while remaining indifferent to outcomes, something good might happen. When you didn't care anymore was when good things happened, right?

I wouldn't have called it a prayer as I sipped my Viognier and thought of Esther's children, the joy they evidently brought her. Even Martha had once delighted Esther. Were I lucky enough to have a pregnant teen daughter, the problem had an obvious solution. "Any child," I said to the sky, where a few stars wavered. "Any healthy child would be a blessing."

It wasn't really a prayer — I didn't allow myself that indulgence anymore — as the steam rose in ethereal plumes, and a tiny part of my brain surmised that I was lowering my cortisol levels, thereby making my uterus more inviting to any hesitant future embryo. I hadn't drunk much, a couple glasses, when I experienced a vision akin to a shrooms flashback, though less psychedelic than gothic. In it, I stood at the edge of an oubliette, a shadowy dungeon where vermin skittered. Worried someone was trapped inside, I peered down into the opening. Pale light revealed interior walls not of stone but velvet, crimson and torn. From inside, something spoke in a low, gravelly whine. It said, *Nobody gets out alive.*

The oubliette was my uterus, I realized. The vision had the force of God's judgment, and I poured myself a more generous glass of wine. I thought of calling Jonathan, but what would I tell him? We'd had the infertility conversation too many times; now he said things like "We don't need a kid to have a good life," or simply, "I like our life!"

The family with preteens had disappeared inside. Two houses from my rental, a man stood on his dock. He was tall and shirtless and faced me. He could have been enjoying the view, but the evening was cool, and he must have been able to see me in the hot tub.

I thought of Jonathan's advice to have fun. It had become a refrain in our conversations. Earlier that spring, after I returned from a demanding project in Zurich, he expressed the worry that I was going to burn out. "You need more fun," he said.

"Zurich wasn't all stress." I'd had some very nice meals, including a fifty-dollar omelet made with a gruyère aged in a cave that played Mozart's *Requiem* in alternation with Tupac. (The bacteria were stimulated by the music's vibrations.) I enjoyed working with one of my Swiss colleagues — my feelings for him were crushy, I admitted to Jonathan, and this gave work a semblance of fun. But the fact was that as I reached middle age, I was not good at having fun anymore; excitement felt less exciting, the shrieking paroxysms of my twenties simply exhausting.

"Did you think of fooling around with the Swiss guy?" Jonathan had asked, as we reclined on the roof deck of our townhouse late one night.

"No!"

"I'm just saying that it wouldn't be the end of the world — I mean, it wouldn't be the end of *us* — if you had a one-night stand."

Jonathan seemed to think that a Swiss-Canadian extramarital coupling was just the thing to stave off burnout: that it would be invigorating and healthful and conclude with rational expressions of mutual respect. "I'm not saying you can have an affair. But a one-night stand, why not?"

Around us, glass towers blazed in the darkness, filled with empty offices.

I was hurt by Jonathan's lack of jealousy and asked, "Would you like that option for yourself?"

"No."

"Because documentarians are more fun than consultants?" Except for Remy, his co-producer, generally I found Jonathan's work acquaintances self-important, in a different way than consultants were. Consultants were equally game to reform national healthcare or to price a brand of beer or to help authoritarian governments monitor dissent — the project's content was incidental — whereas documentarians insisted on the importance of their work's content. Their pickiness evinced a self-regard that got on my nerves.

"Forget it," said Jonathan. If he wanted to fool around he would tell me, he said, because documentarians valued truth telling, however imperfect.

"Whereas consultants value perfect lies," I said, as Jonathan slipped a hand beneath my blouse.

I wondered if Jonathan wanted to reframe my infertility as an erotic opportunity, a kind of consolation prize. How I have fallen, I thought, to hear my own husband propose infidelity so casually. The fall didn't feel calamitous so much as irritating, like bumping your elbow and feeling an ache flutter along the bone.

Fortunately sex between us remained simple, reliably freeing my mind, absorbing me as art once had. Premium vanilla, I had called it to a colleague in a bar in St. Louis, after she confided to curating a vast erotic apparatus that required a spare room.

The shirtless man on the dock had disappeared into his dazzling house. I missed Jonathan. Even when his words annoyed me, his voice consoled me. I allowed my thumb to stroke my phone, and despite my resolve not to check email, absentmindedly opened the app.

Esther had sent a message. She asked forgiveness for ending my visit so abruptly, and hoped I understood the strain she was under. She was supplicating the Lord for wisdom about when to tell Keith, who was busy with The Apostle Project. *I cannot forgive Martha when I think of what her folly has done to the family,*

184

wrote Esther. How Keith's ministry would be hurt, after all his years of work, to say nothing of the girls. *Their innocence is over.*

Esther asked for my prayers. *The Lord sent you.* He knew she needed a sympathetic ear, from someone outside the family or church. She hoped to see me again, in happier times, and concluded with a verse about crying to God from the wilderness.

Martha's folly. *Folly* was not a word I used anymore, with its quaint intolerance, its moral certitude from an era before technology mitigated consequences.

I thought of Esther turning her face from Martha, in her daughter's time of crisis. How alone Martha must feel.

Martha had a Facebook account. Her timeline was brief—some photos of the family and a couple pre-Raphaelite paintings. She liked Emily Brontë and baby skunks.

I opened a message window and typed, *You did nothing wrong.* I believed the words, though they were not precisely true. Martha should have used protection. But did she even know what her options were? Surely she knew what a condom was, though it was possible she didn't, or only in the most abstract way, like how I knew that the large hadron collider exists somewhere in Europe.

I remembered how ignorant I had been about sex well into my teens, how I had believed it was possible for sperm to migrate through two sets of jeans, tenacious as bedbugs. Martha, it appeared, did not share my fears, and it was hard to believe that in the twenty-first century a Canadian seventeen-year-old could be ignorant of the consequences of sex. The family had a bulky desktop in the dining room, and Keith had professed gratitude for the existence of Wikipedia. Even so, Martha's online explorations would have been limited. Esther should have educated her.

I had slept in Martha's bed and watched the shadows of leaves tremble along her floor. I imagined how helpless she must feel, everything around her the same, but one astonishing change hidden inside her. Did she count how many days were left for her to appear as a regular seventeen-year-old? Was she able to keep reading *Tess of the D'Urbervilles,* or did she reread the same paragraph over and over? Martha could not possibly understand what her true options were. She was trapped in a world with only one. The injustice of her situation troubled me. Martha needed to be fully informed before she changed the rest of her life. And if Martha decided that she wanted an abortion, I would help her.

You have more options than you think, I typed. *I'd be happy to discuss them. Whatever you need, let me know.* I gave her my phone number. *You are a brilliant young woman with a promising future. We can sort this out. You are not alone, Martha.* ❤

The boathouse was a little too Zen. I tried reading a novel and jogged moderately, checking the phone signal in case Martha called. For the first time in years, I had free time to feel that something was missing in my life — some concern more human than how to disintermediate a supply chain or price a gourmet potato chip.

Wednesday evening I was relieved by Jonathan's arrival. When I invited him into the hot tub he said, "I don't have enough chest hair to sit in that thing," and eased himself into the dark water at the end of the dock. I listened to him paddle and huff while I sat in warm water with my Riesling.

Had Martha found my message pushy? When driving up to Esther's, I'd speculated that she might try to nudge me back to the faith. Not directly, but through her graciousness. In all my interactions with fundamentalists, an ulterior motive hovered behind their kindness, as they demonstrated how Jesus had changed them for the better. They wanted me to *see Jesus in them*, as the expression went, like when a man acts fascinated by everything you say, even the most banal statement, because he wants to get into your pants.

"So, here's something crazy," I said to Jonathan. "Where are you?"

"Over here," said a remote smudge in the lake.

I whispered loudly, unsure how far my voice carried over the water, describing Martha, her intelligence and general adorableness.

Jonathan grunted to indicate he was waiting to hear what I really wanted to say.

"And she's pregnant."

The remote smudge said "Shit."

"I want to help her get an abortion."

Jonathan paddled and huffed for a time. "Does she want that?"

"I don't know. I sent her a message offering, indirectly. She hasn't responded."

"That might be your answer."

"But the tech situation in that household is very basic. They have one old desktop on dial-up. I mean not really, but still. One desktop in a highly visible location for seven people. Maybe Martha is too scared to reply."

Jonathan slipped through dark water, while I shifted to a more comfortable position and said, "If she has a baby, her life is over."

Jonathan swam quietly. It was a maddeningly tranquil sound. "It won't be a baby forever," he said. "It'll grow up. She'll get her life back when she nears forty." I wondered if Jonathan was thinking of his own life, of his imminent break. "If she has an abortion, given her belief system, she'll have to live with the idea of herself as a murderer."

"You are assuming that beliefs cannot change," I said. "I'm proof they can." There was a solution, and it would be tragic if Martha did not take it. After that, I could help her apply to university. She would begin university when people were supposed to, in their late teens, when their minds are optimally receptive, when they have the guts that come with naïveté, and are more likely to get a break when they make mistakes. People at forty did not have the same opportunities.

I could help Martha see that life was so much more than what she had known. She must be terrified, living with her furious mother and waiting to find out what her father would do.

In bed, Jonathan and I fell into each other. On crisp unfamiliar sheets, with a bullfrog's stoic plaint in the background, sex was our reset button after a tense week. There had been another conversation about Jonathan's work situation at the bar of my favourite restaurant, where half a bottle of superb Beaujolais made me feel like anything I said would be understood in a sympathetic spirit. I'd asked Jonathan, "Have you ever thought about teaching prep school again?"

Jonathan had taught for four years, when I was on the academic job market. It was a time of false hope and great stress, for nothing, it turned out. He did not enjoy working with teenagers but the job covered our expenses.

"The documentary world feels very," I'd waved my wine glass, "vague." In my mind, the words were an invitation to candour, a chance for Jonathan to spill how he too found the documentary world frustrating, at least sometimes.

"Life is vague, Beth."

"But the arts," I said. "The arts are, I think, vaguer."

"Maybe. But documentaries aren't only art."

"They're artier than white papers and column charts. A column chart is *not* vague." I took a moment to enjoy this aperçu. "The thing is," I confided, "I gave myself four years on the academic job market. When nothing happened, I did something else."

"Nothing is not happening for me. Was the Zen doc nothing? The 20/20 grant?"

Jonathan would have to become very successful to justify more years without a full-time, paying job. The adjunct teaching gigs brought in little money, and the more I learned about the documentary world, the less likely success sounded.

"Just say it, you don't respect a man who made twenty-seven grand last year." Behind the bar, the bottles of alcohol glowed like colossal gems.

"I wouldn't put it that way." I smoothed out my napkin, an unusually soft linen. "You know what I think? I think you might end up fifty and frustrated."

"I got fifteen grand in grants last year."

"True." I tried to sound convinced, not wanting to ruin the evening, remembering how excited I had once been to make enough money for us both. When I got the consulting job, a year later we had money for a down payment on the townhouse. One Sunday afternoon, after walking through the narrow high-ceilinged rooms, up to the third-floor attic (which the owner used as a sculpture studio) I told Jonathan I wanted to live there. "I'll be your butler!" he said, and we made out beside a worktable heaped with chicken wire.

In grad school we had decided that our marriage would

have no script. The proposition excited me. Whereas Jonathan's father worked from home as an illustrator, my father managed a tax prep company and my mother stayed at home. When I was small, she excelled at what she called the "little extra touches" — spontaneously baking cookies for my Sunday school class and sewing costumes for plays, her Mad Hatter costume oddly preppy. "It's an honour to serve," she would say. I hated that line.

On the crumpled sheets, with the bullfrog still groaning, I thought of Martha and her prospects. My phone was on the night table, and I showed Jonathan the message I had sent her. He winced at the bright screen before placing it on his night table. There wasn't much more I could do, he agreed. "What kind of church does Esther's husband lead?"

"It's small, Bible based."

"Like the church you grew up in?"

"No, mine was bigger and louder."

"But it espoused the same beliefs."

"Pretty much." I didn't feel like talking about church, the old judgments and my mother's tears. A world at once overly emotional and dreary. Each Sunday morning during the worship service, while my father enunciated the words projected onto the wall in his atonal baritone, my mother cried. As the electric guitars twanged and the melody surged, her hands would flutter up to the ceiling, a tissue in one fist.

I never asked why she cried; nor did my father, to my knowledge. Sometimes after the service she'd marvel aloud, her soft, congested voice gaining power. "The Lord really worked on my heart today!" It was never clear what she had. Subclinical hypothyroidism, fibromyalgia, chronic fatigue syndrome: these were the words of her middle age and my teen years. By then I for what shall it profit a man?

was often out of the house, busy with a part-time job and the mounting extracurriculars that would get me into an American school.

As an adult, I came to think of my mother's condition as a slow-motion nervous breakdown. The cause, I believed, her life as a helpmeet. *It's an honour to serve.* How could that be enough?

"I can't believe how Esther has changed," I said to Jonathan.

"Aren't you proof that people can change?" responded Jonathan, giving my bicep a playful shake.

"What?"

"When you were talking about Martha, you said that beliefs can change, and you're proof."

"But Esther used to be so — " I didn't know how to convey the unnaturalness of her transformation. "The last time I saw her — I mean, really spent time with her — we were on shrooms. Something terrible must have happened in Japan."

Jonathan was silent and I could feel him think.

"What is it?"

"Why can't Esther prefer her fundamentalist life?" said Jonathan. "Why does it have to be because of trauma?" Sometimes Jonathan's empathy got on my nerves. Why couldn't he be a fucking person and judge her too? There was something superior about his empathy. As if he were above the fray of ordinary human gossip, keeping a kindly but above all safe analytic distance.

Jonathan rested against my back, and we listened to the bullfrog. It occurred to me that if we screwed again we'd have a slightly greater chance of conception. I took his hand and placed it on my breast, feeling his breath beside my ear. My hips gave a wiggle.

Jonathan exhaled and said, "I've been thinking about the doc."

191

My hips stopped wiggling.

"It's not working yet. Sandra said so. Even if she hadn't, I knew."

"What's wrong?" I tallied how long Jonathan had spent on the documentary already. Thirty months?

"It's the same kind of story, over and over. Some guy saying, I realized the Bible had all these contradictions. Or, the guilt was killing me. Or, my pastor or rabbi or imam was a hypocrite, talking about love and preaching hate."

"Those sound plausible."

"That's all they are. They're not surprising. Sandra thinks I should be transparent about my reasons for the project. She thinks I should interview you."

Jonathan had recorded friends. One was in the feature that got screened at the mid-sized festival where he got his first tiny break. But our relationship, I thought, was beyond ambition, away from the world's screens.

"You would have a say, of course, about what goes in."

"I don't know."

Jonathan didn't bring it up the next day. We swam and slept and read, taking breaks to finish the gallon of strawberries he'd brought.

At one point, as I swam, he sat on the dock and lifted his phone towards me.

"Are you recording me?" I asked.

"You look so happy."

"Turn it off."

"I hardly see you. I need footage of my happy wife. For the harsh winter ahead."

In the evening we sat on the sunporch and tried to read. Jonathan appeared more preoccupied by his weed pen, and I looked up from my novel and told him my answer was no. I would respond to questions off camera, and he could summarize them in the documentary if he wished.

Jonathan fiddled with his vape pen. Before each drag, he pressed a small button, and when the blue light glowed and he inhaled, I half expected the slim silver pipe to tinkle out a deranged arpeggio. He'd started smoking regularly that spring, after we decided to stop trying to conceive, and soon after turning forty. For me, the pen had become a symbol of Jonathan not giving a shit, which was simply a macho version of giving up.

I tried to focus on the novel I was reading. It was about three art-school friends in New York City, the most talented of whom, after a sensational gallery debut, descends into addiction, haunted by the traumas of his childhood. At twenty-six he moves to Amsterdam, where he executes brilliant forgeries in an attic (when he's not strung out or entertaining a patient, gorgeous architect). The scenes of the protagonist painting, as he meditates on the gritty genius of Rembrandt, are intercut with flashbacks of his traumas, beginning with his mother's murder, which he witnesses, followed by a string of heartless relatives and a predatory social worker.

The book's size was biblical, and I doubted I would finish it over vacation. I rarely read fiction anymore; much of what I picked up felt like a stylish daydream. Maybe people like Keith had a point, and fiction was a pallid little pantomime of reality. At least the Bible, however severe and clunky, had some plain insights on offer.

That evening at eleven, my phone rang. It was Martha. She apologized for the late hour and the delay. "I had to buy a calling card."

"No problem." I was elated to hear her voice and rushed to a guest room, closing the door behind me. "You found a way, Martha. Of course you did, clever girl." I flung myself onto a pristine bed.

"I might need to hang up suddenly," she said.

"Don't worry about me." I was giddy at her guts. Finally, we could talk frankly. "How are you feeling?"

She was okay, though sometimes sick. "I'm not sure if it's the pregnancy or because I'm scared." She was about seven weeks pregnant.

"What do you want to do with your life, Martha?" I asked. "Forget other people."

Martha said she wanted to be a teacher.

"You need to go to university for that."

She whispered yes.

"You can absolutely do that, Martha, but it's going to be impossible if you have a baby. University is just too demanding, not to mention the first few years of teaching."

I suggested we brainstorm together. It soon became clear that in her mind there was only one option: keep the baby. God had bestowed a baby on her, and she couldn't just give it away to a godless state.

The idea of a seventeen-year-old giving birth sickened me. Who could say how Martha would respond to an abortion, but at least then she could focus on her own needs.

"Growing up is about revising old ideas," I said, summarizing the options so far: keep the baby and don't be a teacher; give the baby up for adoption and become a teacher. I knew two couples who had adopted and each of the children was deeply loved, I assured Martha. One child had taken up the cello at three years old; another was animating her own short films at eight.

Finally, if we were bravely brainstorming all possibilities, I reminded Martha, there was the third option of terminating the pregnancy.

"I can't kill the baby."

It's not really a baby, I wanted to tell her. But I knew the videos and posters she had seen. The chatty fetuses with perfect fingernails who proclaimed, *I am fearfully and wonderfully made!*

Martha had brains and guts and just needed a nudge. To become Jane Eyre without the St. John, to push against the history of Christian girls being some man's helpmeet.

"You can still have your own life," I told her. "Why don't you visit us in Toronto? You could see the university and explore your options. Then you could make a truly informed decision." I told Martha we could pick her up on our way back to the city.

"I don't think my parents will let me."

"When would be a better time? Surely not in six months," I said. "The best thing for you and your mom right now is a break. I stayed with you, now it's your turn to visit me." I tried to sound jokey. "Promise me you'll think about it?"

It was an aesthetic decision, I told Jonathan. I couldn't feel the right feelings. Stories of sin and redemption, of being lost and then found: they didn't move me. Fundamentalist Christians expected zeal. Without feelings, what was faith?

In fact, my loss of faith wasn't even a decision. It felt like it happened to me, like temperament or sexual orientation. Like God's will. I suppose I decided to let it happen.

But those early years were useful, especially the Bible study, which taught me patience and how to pay attention. If I could no longer discern God's advice on the packaging of a frozen pizza (*Authentic Goodness!*), I could observe a still-life painting of medlar apples and find life and death entwined in the fruit's broken flesh. When a professor instructed students to sit in front of one painting for two hours and write down what we saw, I was exhilarated. There on the canvas was the ordinary, ephemeral world. Eternal life was never for me.

"Why haven't you told me this before?" said Jonathan. We were on the sun porch again — the day was hot — Jonathan with his vape pen and I with my novel.

"I have."

"Not in the same words."

"I guess I need a testimony."

"A testimonial?"

"No, a testimony. The story of how you found Christ, or lost Him, in my case."

I'd tried getting Esther to tell me hers, wanting to hear about Japan. All she would say was that it had been a confusing time, and that a beloved grandmother — who had not approved of the modelling — died while Esther was abroad. "Japan was a wake-up call," she said, skipping over her lowest point, which was the best part of the testimony, I'd always felt. It could be a struggle with depression or drugs, a near-death experience, or just a malaise. Those born into Christian families might talk about partying before realizing the dangerous empty road ahead. Then came the crisis and the cry to God, who gave a sign of His presence, as spectacular as a blockbuster or as quiet as a leaf. That's when you submitted to Him, and your life gained meaning and purpose.

Jonathan's silver pen lit up and he closed his eyes. "So your life's better now?"

I thought of Martha's fearful voice over the phone and of Esther's anger. "Of course."

"Then what's your infernal testimony?" said Jonathan.

"There isn't one," I said. "But Esther played a role. That's what gets me."

She and I had been on the train tracks at night, high on shrooms procured by the camp director's son. Esther dated him that summer and improvised herself into a hippie, wearing her hair loose and the same Indian-print sundress for days at a time. The best friend of the camp director's son was there too, reclining on the tracks as we sat on the rails, and telling us about a guy he knew who had been cured of his stutter by shrooms. "It rewires the mind, sparks a new paradigm." Around us, the trees pulsed violet.

"This must be how angels see the world." I forget who said it, but we all agreed.

"God created shrooms," said the camp director's son. He thanked Jesus, and we all murmured Amen.

"The Bible says nothing against psychotropic substances." I said this more to reassure myself, recalling Esther's pitch to me: "Look, Jesus turned water into wine when people were already drunk. Jesus helped everyone get *more* drunk."

Jonathan sat up. "Can I record this?"

"Do you need to?"

"It would help."

"You mean the doc will be finished sooner?" I said the words like a joke, but saw that Jonathan felt bad.

Then Jonathan was recording me on his phone, elbow braced against the armrest. "You were talking about Jesus getting people drunk."

There were other teen musings. Did the Bible acknowledge

evolution indirectly? Was the Apostle John on shrooms when he wrote Revelation? At some point Esther's voice grew expansive with awe. "I see Jesus," she said, and the camp director's son responded, "I see Jesus*es*."

Unlike them, I didn't see Jesus. I stood up and slid down into the stony trench beside the tracks, stopping at the blackberry bushes. Their delicate feelers pulsed restfully. Those blackberry bushes felt more alive to me than Jesus ever had.

I called to the camp director's son and asked when the train would arrive.

"Ye know not the hour nor the day," he said, and began laughing to himself.

It was our last summer together. I would see Esther once more, in Toronto, where she began Bible college; by the time she got married, I was in the States and low on cash. I also believed myself to be a different person, sure that my Christian friends could not understand me.

But that night I told Esther that I wished I could feel God's presence like she did.

"What if God decides that some people won't believe in Him?" said the friend of the camp director's son.

We tried to remember the word for that idea.

"But what would be the point of unbelievers? From God's point of view," I said.

"Jesus needed Judas," said the camp director's son.

"But even Judas was a believer, on some level," I said.

"I just mean that God needs the traitors," said the camp director's son. Around us, the trees grew upright, a mob of crosses.

"If faith is not doing anything for you," said Esther, "stop trying. There are some things we don't get to choose."

Maybe Esther wanted to relieve my worry, maybe she wanted to impress the camp director's son with her chill lack of dogmatism. Maybe it was the shrooms talking. Whatever it was, Esther planted in me a liberating idea: that in some things we have no choice, and faith is one of them.

The camp director's son spotted the train first. We stumbled down the steep rocks, holding hands when the train blasted past our faces. Esther and I screamed with delight, though our voices were overpowered by the machine, felt only in the vibration of my throat and along Esther's arm. Her hand crushed mine with a force that expressed both ardour and indifference — a vital selfishness that braced me — and I loved her then.

What I could not understand, two decades later, was why Esther had abandoned her freedom. The shrooms, the fooling around, the modelling in Japan: these were episodes in a story about finding her way back to God. It was the best kind of story, of being lost and then found. While in her eyes I could only ever be lost.

Jonathan's camera drew out thoughts I had never articulated, even to myself. Behind it, Jonathan's face had grown tender. It reminded me of our first years together. I made him put away the phone and straddled him, feeling more pillowy than ever. Not only did my body feel different, but my mind too, balmy with hope. If we were ever going to make a baby, now was the time. Surely such passion, I thought, would bear fruit.

Before leaving the Zen boathouse, I called Esther to say we'd stop by with gifts for the children. (After Martha had phoned me, I'd ordered books, which were delivered rapidly to the depths of the woods.) I had also answered Esther's email, urging her to let me know what I could do to help. Toronto was not so far from South River. *You are one of my oldest friends*, I'd written. *I'm praying for you all.*

Using Esther's language didn't feel dishonest, more like a translation of *you are in my thoughts*. To Esther, those words would sound thin. How could having someone in your thoughts compare with reaching out to the omnipotent creator of everything?

Jonathan doubted that Martha would be allowed to visit us. "This isn't your problem," he said, as I drove. He was annoyed by the two-hour detour to visit Esther's family. "Anyway, you can't force her to have an abortion and go to university."

"Nobody is forcing Martha to do anything. I just want to make sure she knows what her options are."

"She must know already."

"How can she, when she's so isolated? She probably thinks an abortion is like a horror movie. Not that she's ever seen a horror movie. Maybe she has. Who knows what Martha knows."

Jonathan placed his hand on my nape and began to press his fingers into the knotted muscle around the spine. "You sure there isn't a Martha spreadsheet somewhere? A plan to optimize Martha? One hundred percent reduction of pregnancy in year one, followed by thirty percent intellectual growth in year two?"

I pressed my neck into his fingers. "Esther needs a break from Martha. They both need a break."

When we arrived, I gave Esther a long hug. I didn't see myself in opposition to her, because of our shared past. I couldn't shake the impression that beneath her wifely surface, some part of her remained reckless.

"Keith is at The Apostle Project," she said, "so he hasn't noticed anything."

Titus took Jonathan to the swamp to show the irrigation project. Martha and Violet were in the kitchen cutting strawberries.

I found Martha hunched over a bowl of red pulp. "How's the garden?" I asked, placing a hand on her drooping shoulder. "Can you give me a tour?"

In the afternoon sun, Martha's skin blazed with a purity that made me wonder if it was the pregnancy or simply her youth. She seemed part of something primordially vital, expanding like the zucchini plant at our feet, with its huge tropical-looking leaves that canopied flaming tips.

Lovely doomed Martha, shoulders hunched with the strain of secret knowledge, or perhaps to shroud her swelling breasts. Soon she would be engulfed by the vegetation if I didn't get her out of that garden and show her how much bigger life could be.

"Have you thought about your options since we talked?" I asked.

Martha said she had.

"Has anything changed?"

There was still only one option, Martha said. Unless — here she broke down, as I put an arm around her, and she whispered that she couldn't bear her mom's hatred, nor the shame she was bringing on the family.

"Unless?"

"If God took the baby."

"Oh Martha." I squeezed her shoulder. "I hope you haven't tried to hurt yourself." I imagined her at the top of the staircase, praying to God that His will be done, before throwing herself down the stairs.

Martha shook her head. "I'd never do it myself, but God does, sometimes, take the baby. He did for Tess."

"Tess?"

"Of the D'Urbervilles."

I almost laughed at her naïveté, but her tormented face stopped me. "You have so many more options than Tess did!"

"Not really."

"But you do. I can think of at least three." Martha's bizarro Christian fantasy of a holy abortion was surely a hint of what she wanted. "Terminating the pregnancy, for instance."

"Please don't say that." Martha slipped from my grasp and turned a shoulder to me, arms across her abdomen. She looked ready to bolt, the only thing keeping her there politeness towards a guest.

"Okay, what about adoption?" I said. "Help me understand, Martha. What are your concerns?" It was a question I often asked clients. I was good at reassuring them, nicknamed the client whisperer.

Martha watched the zucchini leaves lift and sink in the breeze.

"I won't know who the adoptive parents are. I'm the one who brought this baby into the world. I'm responsible for it."

"Why is it impossible to know the parents?" I said.

"Maybe I'll meet them later, but the baby will already be theirs. I can't take it back."

"So you want to vet the parents."

Even now, I'm not sure whose idea it was first. Was it Martha's change of posture that gave me the idea, the way she turned towards me and unfurled her arms? Was it simply the train of my own words, as I went into problem-solving mode, combined with my renewed hope for a child?

Martha spoke first, in a half whisper. "Have you ever wanted children?"

I had to stop myself from laughing with delight at her nerve. "We did," I began slowly, "but haven't been able to have any."

"If you still want a baby —" Her shoulders trembled and I put an arm around her.

Jonathan and I had considered adoption briefly and dismissed it — a stranger's child was impersonal and risky, he felt — but if we knew the mother, then the calculation changed. I didn't yet know the result of the week's vacation, and still hoped I might be pregnant; but even if I were, Jonathan and I had wanted two children. Two was the ideal.

"Martha, you're a miracle."

Martha began to cry, and even I teared up as I held her, thinking how much fuller life could be. The moment felt providential, with Martha's future and mine clicking into a new, more satisfying, configuration. Martha could study at U of T and stop by on weekends to visit the baby. I would take time away from work and have other, more human, priorities.

Naturally I needed to speak with Jonathan. "But if you visit us now, you can see where the baby will grow up."

As her tears lessened, Martha spoke in thick syllables of her disbelief at God's goodness.

"He sent you." Earlier that week, her boyfriend had disappeared.

We stood in the garden a long time. Martha's eyes were puffy, so I went to the house to find Esther. "Martha wants you." Esther kept halving strawberries, pressing the knife's edge against her thumb even after the fruit dropped away. I took the knife from her and said, "Come," placing her hand in my own. It was a familiar intimacy from our camp days, when even as teenagers we'd held hands, as if acting on our instincts to nurture. Sometimes we did it in the presence of boys, flaunting our erotic indifference to them. It was a tantalizing display of chastity.

In the garden, I squeezed Esther's hand and said, "The Lord has made an amazing provision for Martha." I took Martha's small chilly hand, as if the three of us were about to pray, though Esther did not join her hand to her daughter's. I waited for Martha to second what I'd said, but when she spoke, the words came out garbled and desperate. The longer she continued, the more Esther's face hardened.

"I want to adopt Martha's baby," I said. "My husband and I have wanted a child for years."

Esther gazed at me neutrally. It wasn't clear that she registered what I'd said.

"It's an amazing provision, for all of us. That Jonathan and I want a baby, and that Martha has one. And that this is the summer when you and I finally reconnect. Surely this is the Lord's doing."

Martha's head was bowed and she murmured, "Thank you, Lord."

As the sun enveloped us, a bee scouted the zucchini flowers, its hum the only sound in the garden. At last Esther spoke. "God's loving-kindness," she said, squeezing my hand, though still refusing her daughter's.

It did not feel false when I began to pray. It felt like the return of an old instinct. How many times as a girl had I said *Thank you, Jesus*? Jesus had told us that *when two or three are gathered in My name, I am in their midst.* If anything, that prayer felt more cogent than mystical, a concise statement of an inspired solution, in a format more potent than the snappiest PowerPoint.

Esther had taken her daughter's hand in hers, because that was how believers prayed.

When Esther finished the prayer, we opened our eyes. Mother and daughter were teary, and Esther drew Martha to her, as we joked about excuses for getting emotional while praying in the garden. Keith was back, sitting on the deck with Jonathan.

I told Esther that I wanted to show Martha where the baby would grow up. "And maybe the university too." Martha would return when The Apostle Project was over. She would be refreshed, and so would Esther, ready to tell Keith the truth.

"As long as Dad says yes." Walking to the deck, Esther said, "Something bigger is at work here."

Keith was in good spirits. Already the Lord was blessing The Apostle Project: two days in, fourteen lives had been recommitted to Christ. He thought a visit to Toronto a well-deserved treat for his eldest child.

As Martha packed, I gave Jonathan a tour of the garden, pointing out the shoots of rainbow chard and the new beans, their white flowers intricately pleated. On this soil I had witnessed life take a new direction, as if Providence itself twinkled from the flowers' cool folds.

"I'm going to plant some vegetables when we get back," I said, uprooting a weed and feeling like a steward of Esther's realm. Last year I had bought a pot of climbing jasmine, which flailed briefly against the side of our deck, until Jonathan went away for a residency and it dried out.

"Just don't get too invested in Martha," said Jonathan.

"It's a campus visit." Now was not the time to bring up the baby. Jonathan was restless, wandering towards the garden's edge. "How was it with Keith?" I asked.

"Keith is a douche."

On the Don Valley Parkway, traffic gusted past us and I restrained myself from checking Martha's expression in the rearview mirror. I wanted her to love where we lived, because that's where the baby would grow up and where, I hoped, Martha would visit us. A family. I knew all kinds of families, and now a family I'd never imagined opened up for us, one with Martha as goddaughter, and who knew, maybe Esther would join, a second grandmother to the baby.

Martha loved our townhouse, the stained-glass transom of pale green lilies and the steep carved banister that zigzagged to the skylight on the third floor; and the kitchen, too, with its glossy white planes that hid even the refrigerator.

We ordered Korean and opened a Brouilly. Martha had her first taste of beef japchae, fiddling with the chopsticks, which she'd used only once before. "Isn't the texture satisfying?" I asked, feeling like I was weaning her on urban culture.

Jonathan joked to Martha that he was glad she was visiting, because it guaranteed that I wouldn't work over dinner.

"Two objections," I said. "First, I would never work over Korean food, which is too yummy. Second, my work pays for this house."

Jonathan alleged that he'd once witnessed me tinker with a spreadsheet while eating a kimchi pancake. I said that snacks didn't count.

Martha appeared bemused by our teasing, the unplacid back and forth, the raising of voices and brandishing of fingers as Jonathan and I each tried to prove ourselves right.

"Don't worry," I told Martha, "we're not serious."

"I am!" said Jonathan.

"Jonathan is correct that consultants work too much. One partner says we work five times as fast as most people."

"Check out the arrogance, Martha."

"What's a consultant?" asked Martha.

"Good question!" said Jonathan.

"Basically, we give advice," I said, "to companies and other organizations — governments, and universities too — about how to operate more effectively."

"Did you really understand that, Martha?" said Jonathan.

"A little." She drew the chopsticks to her mouth, as the glass noodles slipped down.

"See? Martha is still confused. It's not your fault, Martha. Beth's job is confusing!"

"Okay, how would you describe what I do?" I asked Jonathan.

"Let's see. It involves a lot of spreadsheets and PowerPoint presentations to create an illusion of order and, more importantly, a solution (or solutions, so the client can pick one and feel in control) while in fact contributing to the world's increasingly unstable economic landscape."

"I don't think that's any clearer," I said.

"Notice, Martha, that my wife is not disagreeing with me, because, as it happens, I am simply repeating what she has told me in unguarded moments." He refilled my glass.

After dinner Martha and I sat on the roof deck, gazing at the bright towers and listening to the distant rush of traffic along Church Street.

"This is how we relax," I said.

Jonathan's telescope was out, and Martha looked through it. Mars was visible, Saturn and Jupiter too. She was riveted.

"Jupiter just looks like an aspirin to me," I said, as her nape twisted around.

I allowed myself to think of the baby then. It was a girl,

wrapped in a waffled cotton blanket. I saw myself testing the temperature of the formula, the tip of the bottle's nipple releasing a warm droplet onto my inner wrist. Then I was carrying the baby, standing beside the sliding doors onto our small backyard where vegetables grew, murmuring soothing nonsense. Soon the baby was a preschooler, and I was delighting in her explorations — of a dandelion gone to seed, the community swimming pool, maybe a three-quarter violin. Then she was a sulky but conscientious teenager, in time confiding her worries to me; soon she was leaving for university, and already I was missing our life together.

That night, after Jonathan turned off his light, I said in a low voice, "Martha and I talked about her baby."

Jonathan made a listening sound.

"We want a baby," I said.

Jonathan adjusted the pillow beneath his head. "I thought you don't want to adopt."

"But this is different. We know Martha. She offered us the baby today."

Despite the memory foam mattress, I felt Jonathan's body grow tense. "If we're going to adopt, we shouldn't rush it. I need to finish the doc and I'll be teaching in the winter. When is she due?"

"January." I never felt like Jonathan was truly busy. When I imagined his work day, he was clicking unhurriedly at his desk, agonizing over nearly identical shots, or on the couch, reading for an upcoming class. When grading written work, he filled the margins with baroque scrawls. Meanwhile at my office, a kid named Charles completed a coherent 129-slide PowerPoint in four hours.

"Why the mission to save Martha?"

"There's no mission. I still want a baby. It's an opportunity for everyone."

"We can't lie to her. At least tell her we haven't reached a decision."

I rested a palm on my abdomen, as Jonathan said that he had a hard time seeing how the plan would work. Was I really thinking about what was best for Martha? If adoption was something I wanted, fine, but we shouldn't rush it. As Jonathan spoke, I felt subtle vibrations beneath my palm. Could I be harboring an embryo? That hope kept me from breaking down.

Had I pushed back, would Jonathan have reconsidered? Perhaps. But my own pliancy was undetectable even to me. Like a good Christian wife, I served at work, and at home too.

On the campus tour, Martha's gaze grabbed at everything — a gargoyle of a monkey, the dark wood ceilings, each doorway in a long hallway of nondescript rooms. Among the other teenagers, she looked like a kid, phoneless and wearing a loose striped T-shirt. The thought of her nine months pregnant, to say nothing of giving birth, was grotesque. The providential plan hatched in the garden now felt like a pleasant vacation reverie, reinforced by Jonathan's concerns and our return to the city, where cars rushed around Queen's Park, relentless as wolves, while teens of obvious privilege lounged on the campus grass, taking a break from a summer program. In such an environment, it was easy to be eliminated.

If I was being impartial, the best option for Martha was still an abortion. If that was impossible, then our adopting the kid was second best.

When the tour finished, and Martha lingered in the reading room, I excused myself. In an empty classroom, I called a pregnancy counselling centre, telling the receptionist it was an emergency. An isolated fundamentalist girl was in town for little more than one day. "I'm worried her parents will force her to have the baby," I told the receptionist, and finally she said to bring Martha in the next morning.

In the reading room, Martha sat on a bench beneath a lead-paned window, with a worn volume of poetry by Keats. The room was empty except for a lone old man napping on a distant couch. "You'll love university," I told her, remembering not just the books and ideas, but the campus too, the cool worn stonework and shaded lawns. In fact, the firm where I worked was on the edge of U of T's campus, and sometimes I almost fooled myself into feeling that I was still in academia.

As we walked past the azure domes of one college, it was easy to forgot the quiet desperation hidden inside, the rushed dinners of yogurt cups and bagels, the applications to jobs with four hundred other hopefuls vying for maybe five tenure-track positions that year. It was hard not to feel wistful about the freedoms of those years, exploring questions no white paper could answer.

At some point that afternoon I'd tell Martha about the appointment at the counselling centre. In the meantime, we'd do whatever she wanted.

Heading south, we approached the wide, reflective hull of the art gallery. "What is it?" asked Martha, and I strode inside.

I'd not been to the art gallery since moving back to Toronto. Jonathan had suggested a visit, more than once, but each time I was busy or tired. As Martha and I walked through the big cool rooms, we moved in avid slow motion, Martha leading us, stopping before a blazing Tom Thomson and Emily Carr's little white church stalwart in the woods.

In the European rooms, we looked at dusky allegorical landscapes and portraits of cagey aristocrats, one a young Florentine man with a jet beard and glittering, opaque eyes. Martha lingered before it, and I wondered how often she thought of her ex-boyfriend. Then *The Peasants' Wedding* by Pieter Brueghel the Younger. The son was not as talented as the father, but his work evinced similar features. The horde of humans dancing and drinking, each engaged with one or two others, sometimes embracing openly, oblivious to the rest. The red noses and the round bellies, the jutting pelvises of the dancers, one of whom gazed at his partner with open lust.

"This painting is by the son of the artist I wrote my dissertation on," I told Martha.

"Is that the bride?" Martha pointed to a distant, chubby woman.

In the foreground was a long-nosed man, a shocked expression on his face, though he had no moral advantage over the more orgiastic partygoers — his hand was ambiguously close to a woman's ass.

"What I like about Brueghel's art is the lack of judgment," I said.

Martha puzzled over my remark. "Don't the people look foolish?"

In the eyes of a lovely, devout seventeen-year-old, drunk middle-aged people were bound to look foolish. Still, I was surprised by her take.

"Isn't everyone foolish sometimes?"

Martha considered this proposition. She was always respectful, disconcertingly so; it seemed a kind of gallantry towards me, the weaker, worldly Christian (or unbeliever — what she thought I was, I didn't know). Clearly in her mind not everyone was foolish. Her father was not, nor her mother. Violet was, sometimes, but one day she would not be. Was it fundamentalism or youth that made Martha so serious?

"It's crowded," said Martha, of the painting, "but feels empty."

"You're right. There's nothing transcendent going on. It's all very earthly." One serious man, clad in black, stood among the dancers. His role was unclear.

"Do you ever miss teaching?" asked Martha.

I pretended to reflect and then said what I always did. "It was great while it lasted, but now it's satisfying to do useful work. I help all kinds of organizations be better at what they do. It's an honour to serve."

We passed a series of still lifes, including *Evisceration of a Roebuck with a Portrait of a Married Couple;* in it, the husband slices the animal's abdomen as his young wife looks away. I made sure we were in front of a pleasant painting (Chardin's *Jar of Apricots*) before turning to Martha and saying, "I know we talked about my adopting the baby, but I want you to have all the information you need to make the best decision for yourself. I've booked an appointment with a counsellor for tomorrow morning."

"A counsellor?"

"Someone to help you navigate this big decision. An expert. They know way more than I do, and they're impartial."

"I thought you're going to adopt the baby."

"I'd love to, but we should make sure it's what's best for *you*." Here Martha broke down. "You have so many options, Martha." I would not yet speak of Jonathan's concerns, wanting Martha to feel the full sweep of possibility — art, university, life in the city. I hugged her and said, "Think about it."

Jonathan was pissed that I continued to lead Martha on. Over Cubanos she brought up our adopting the baby, and I said, "If we can make it work, we'd love to!" while reminding her that she had options. In bed that night, Jonathan remarked that I talked to Martha as if she were a client, all while pushing her towards my own agenda.

"I might have preferences," I conceded, "but the choice is absolutely Martha's!" I felt that Jonathan was getting preachy; he reminded me of an old pastor who'd spoken against feigning a good heart.

The next morning Martha and I arrived for the counselling appointment. In the waiting room postered with images of pensive young women, I told Martha that none of this was her fault, her boyfriend should have used protection, but now the decision was hers and nobody else's. The appointment lasted barely ten minutes, Martha growing teary again when I asked about it. I returned to work that afternoon with the impression that outcomes were surer in the maelstrom of globalized capitalism than in the heart of a seventeen-year-old girl.

Fortunately, Jonathan was more pissed at Keith. Keith had bragged about The Apostle Project's successes, particularly one veteran "delivered" from PTSD. He'd also invited Jonathan to listen to some of the Project's online "life talks," which were basically sermons, liberal in their use of the word *awesome* and the expression *It's a God thing!* Other life talks were testimonies from participants, stories of being lost and then found after a week of prayer and fellowship in the woods.

Jonathan resented being evangelized to and regarded Keith with a contempt that puzzled me. He did not think that Keith was misguided or a joke, but a piece of shit. I had never thought of someone as a piece of shit, but there were people Jonathan met, albeit very few, about whom he held this view, and Keith was one of them. Later on, Keith would become a useless piece of shit.

At work, I was busy with a supermarket project in Oklahoma. Three mornings that week I breakfasted at Denny's, where my period arrived on a Thursday morning. In the restaurant bathroom, I stared at the rusty smudge, wondering if it could be a pregnancy complication, which felt like a semi-desirable outcome for a second. I hadn't bought a pregnancy test that month, wanting to play it cool, as if an embryo might be more drawn to my uterus if I were nonchalant.

That evening, Jonathan and I talked about Martha's baby. After three late nights on a vacuous project, the vacation still fresh in my mind, my unhappiness was in full flower. On the roof deck, surrounded by stacks of vacant offices, I teared up over my negroni and Jonathan said, "I didn't know you still want a baby so much."

"I misjudged," I sobbed, and Jonathan took my hand and said he needed a bit of time to reorient himself to this new reality.

From the top of our big, empty townhouse, we listened to the rush of traffic. I pointed out that a colleague of Jonathan had finished his documentary in record time because his wife was pregnant. The pregnancy was the push he needed to finish. Babies never arrived on schedule. Jonathan said he'd talk to Remy and see what they could swing.

Late Friday morning, Martha's number appeared on my screen. I excused myself from a meeting and rushed out to the atrium. It was Esther. Keith knew about Martha's pregnancy, and had decided that Jonathan and I could not adopt the baby. The light in the atrium was blinding, and as Esther spoke, I careened towards a window with a lowered shade.

The hopes for two children — Martha's and our own — were a distant delusion. Last night I'd believed that Jonathan and I had a shot at one baby, assuming Martha decided against an abortion, which seemed likely. Now we were back to zero. All I could say to Esther was, "The baby would be so loved."

"You don't share our values," said Esther. "I'm sorry, but it's true."

"I'm sorry too." From the window, I could see the sooty trefoil panes of the university's chapel, now a dining hall, where Martha and I had observed summer students eat enchiladas. "Martha could visit whenever she wanted."

"She told me," said Esther. "How you pressured her to go to an abortion clinic."

"It was a pregnancy counselling centre."

"Well, abortion was on the table. It was all over the table, from what Martha told me."

"I just wanted her to make the best choice for herself."

"It's not only Martha who decides. The whole family is going to be involved, one way or another. And ultimately the decision is the Lord's."

Coming from the friend who had initiated me into transgression, it was hard to take her words entirely seriously. I felt like if I dug deep enough I would find the Esther who had persuaded me that God's love was so big it includes even those who break the rules.

"I was worried about Martha," I said. "You seemed so angry with her."

"I was always going to forgive her. God has a lot of love for His children, even when they stumble. Anyway, this is really my fault."

"You're too hard on yourself." I thought of how chill Esther had once been, telling me to stop trying to believe. "Do you remember what you said on the train tracks, our last summer at camp?"

"Camp?" said Esther, voice incredulous. "No, but I can guess. I was full of lazy ideas. Probably something confused that I thought was clever."

Outside on the campus, a young woman wearing a romper entered the dining hall, and I begrudged her her relaxed life, so unlike Martha's. "The thing is, Beth, God created boundaries for a reason. You can't love both God and mammon."

"What do you mean?"

"Martha told me about your place, and the university too. It sounds impressive. But you know what Christ said: *For what shall it profit a man . . .*"

I honked out a laugh. "I haven't gained the whole world yet!" Had Martha seen me as a Satanic temptress when we sat on the roof deck, offering the world in exchange for her soul?

"I should have known the visit to Toronto wasn't a good idea," said Esther. "I should have listened when you said you don't have a church. But then you prayed for us. I thought you were reconnecting with God." It had been a farce, I thought to myself— Esther believing I was reconnecting with God when in fact I was trying to help Martha escape her small life. But I didn't laugh, because a new heaviness had settled in my heart. There would be no baby for Jonathan and me.

"Anyway, Martha and the baby are back safe," said Esther.

"I hope she's okay," I said. "I hope you're okay."

"We're fine. Don't contact her again. I have her passwords and am checking the phone report."

"Can I call you?"

"To be honest, I don't see why you'd need to."

"What will Martha do?" I pleaded.

"When the baby arrives, she'll know. I realize you're no longer a believer, Beth, but God is going to make something beautiful out of this, you'll see."

Esther hung up, and I walked numbly to the railing above a gathering space one floor below, with sculptural leather sofas and Afghan rugs, where a pair of colleagues bowed over a laptop and conversed in a staccato monotone. I saw myself topple over the railing onto the teak floor — the fall probably wouldn't kill me, leaving Jonathan and me more screwed. The idea was melodramatic and self-aggrandizing, absurd. I returned to the conference room and rejoined a spirited discussion about the imperatives of ultra-convenience in the new retail ecosystem.

Jonathan believed that Keith was behind the break with Esther. He faulted Keith for not calling me himself. "Probably he refuses to talk alone to a woman who is not his wife."

We were back on the roof with negronis — I couldn't eat supper — and I said, "I'm sure that as a pastor he speaks with women one on one." I was irritated by Jonathan's fixation on Keith and I was angry at Esther. She was responsible for vetoing the adoption, I felt sure. As for Martha, instead of gratitude, she had presented me as Satan tempting Christ, offering the whole world in exchange for her soul. *For what shall it profit a man,* Christ had said, *if he shall gain the whole world and lose his own soul?* The verse annoyed me, the smugness of its rhetorical question. What if your soul was small and scared — was it worth preserving then? Fundamentalism had taught me to fear the world, while academia had given me permission to be fascinated by it.

The world was chaotic, yes, but there were still some patterns and probabilities if you could access the data and analytics.

"What's sad is that it could have been win-win, for us, Martha, Esther, everybody," I told Jonathan.

"They're in a different headspace," he said.

"That's one way of putting it. A retrograde headspace. Every teen should be allowed to make a mistake and not be condemned for the rest of their life. It's deplorable to trap Martha like this. Poor girl. Have you thought what it will be like for her to be eighteen and dealing with baby shit, figurative and literal?"

On a nearby office roof, seagulls gathered and squawked. Jonathan said, "Lots of teens have done it."

"But not nowadays, in Canada. Nowadays it's disgusting. She is being sacrificed so the family can maintain their antiquated moral ideals."

Jonathan stroked my hand as I finished my negroni.

"Can I ask you about Keith?"

"Okay."

Did I remember how he and Esther had met?

Keith had been the assistant worship leader at camp. He crooned into a mic with a sweet tenor, as the women onstage harmonized softly. When he played volleyball, he spiked with a ferocity belied by his gentle voice.

Did he ever display any controlling behaviours?

"Why are you so interested in Keith?"

One of the testimonies on The Apostle Project's website was by the veteran who suffered from PTSD. He claimed that Keith had healed him. The man was receiving further counselling from Keith, but remained in a fragile state; Jonathan had spoken with him that day. "This man needs help, and Keith can't deliver."

"Can't you connect the guy with other services?"

"That's not my job. My job is to see how the situation plays out."

"But he's still with the church."

"He's ambivalent. If he leaves, I'll use him."

Ultimately the film was Jonathan's. If I worried about his prospects for success, I retained a belief in his brilliance. In graduate school, Jonathan had swept up prizes for innovative research, which included his first videography project. Soon after finishing his dissertation, he decided he couldn't stand academia, its fussy arguments and insularity. He began to work on the documentary about Jewish Buddhists that became his first small break. Meanwhile I, who had been methodical in my research and grateful for any small grant, was rejected by academia. From the start of our relationship, Jonathan was the brilliant one.

Even though I now made the money, I retained this idea of Jonathan and suspected he did too. I figured that it must be useful to think of yourself as brilliant, it must give you permission to do things others would not dare, like when Jonathan requested extra funding for a workshop in Cape Town and got it because he spoke directly to the department chair, who loved him.

Martha could be just as brilliant, I suspected, if she had the guts to act entitled. She remained heavy on my mind as work accelerated at a nauseating rate. One week it was a food-delivery platform, another a charter school; then two weeks on a potash mine, then three on an energy drink. Each site visit was a speedy, unsentimental assessment of a problem that felt as abstract as the questions from my job interview. *How many ping-pong balls can fit inside a 747?* Consulting was a kind of formalism, Sudoku with humans.

I was adaptable and good at communicating with clients. Thanks to my academic training, I anticipated objections and responded plausibly. My residual Christian-lady niceness played well in meetings, reassuring clients; it was one reason I was still at the firm, where we spoke of serving our clients and being honoured by their trust. I was a handmaid of globalized capitalism, brought in to *make things better*, as my mentor at the firm had told me during our first meeting. In those early days, I spoke readily about falling in love with operations management, marrying my passion for operations with food retail (and later, healthcare/mining/tech/etc.), in order to deliver value. With our tech clients, I wore novelty socks of Pac-Mans or winged toasters. With the mining engineers, I wore a boxy blazer and lowered my voice to a uniform alto. It didn't hurt that I was Canadian; in the eyes of some international clients, I was a peacekeeper of the free market.

When I thought of my baby prospects, I experienced sharp bouts of self-disgust. I began to wear black and charcoal, in kid mohair and baby alpaca. I ate baby arugula and baby squash, my sterile body consuming all forms of the infantile. I hadn't even had a miscarriage, and was naïve enough to wish for that devastating tease at maternity.

Sometimes, mid-meeting, I entertained reveries of a nervous breakdown. In one scenario it happened in a single outburst; in another, it was a steady trickle of sour remarks that led to my being sidelined and eventually terminated. Always it culminated in a stay at a sanatorium in the mountains where the air was sharp and cleansing. My breakdown would not be the whimpering decline of my mother's vague syndromes. I would have a better breakdown.

That fall, Jonathan was at a residency. I visited one weekend, and we hiked along an icy escarpment and ate in a glass-walled dining hall, surrounded by pristine peaks. It could have been a resort, the buffet loaded with brisket, polenta, tempeh Wellington, and tiny individual pistachio tarts.

One lunch we dined with a singer-songwriter, an experimental bassoonist, and a poet who had just won an award for her collection, *empath/telepath*. The artists reminded me of graduate students, clever sensitive people in their late twenties and early thirties. The experimental bassoonist might have been older. It was hard to tell.

When Jonathan introduced me, I said, "I studied art in graduate school."

"What kind?" asked the experimental bassoonist.

"Painting. Sixteenth-century Dutch and Flemish."

"Flemish?" said the singer-songwriter.

"It's a region of northern Belgium. A Dutch dialect, Flemish." I felt my tongue flap in my mouth.

"Your husband is super talented," said the experimental bassoonist.

"Yeah, Jonathan's a total guerilla empath," said the poet.

"Just don't get shot!" said the singer-songwriter, and everyone laughed.

"What?" I asked Jonathan.

"Nothing. Just a development with the doc, related to Keith's church, actually."

"You think Keith would shoot you?"

"No! It's a joke," said Jonathan, and I wondered what he'd told them about Keith.

The poet was saying something about genre. Poetry or prose, sci-fi or autofiction, as long as it was good, who cared?

"Everything's so fluid," said the singer-songwriter.

"Personally, my favourite fluid is the Rundle Old Fashioned," said the experimental bassoonist.

They were younger than us, but ages older than Martha, who at thirty would be raising a tween. I still thought of Martha too often. By now her pregnancy would be showing. The summer's anger and pity had given way to numbing loss — of the baby I'd never really had, but had believed in for one week, and of Martha, too, whom I'd imagined part of our new family, spending weekends with us while studying at U of T.

Over dessert the poet said, "I don't do hourly-paid work."

The experimental bassoonist groaned assent. When Jonathan gave a comradely smile, I said, "Why not?"

"I did once," replied the poet. "I worked a juicer but got fired." She gave a hapless laugh. "I was too slow, I guess."

In the afternoon, Jonathan took me on a tour of the compound. We tramped through a snowy forest of studios, one shaped like a conch, another like a fan, each original and charming.

"We're lucky," said Jonathan.

The day was cold, and I wore only sneakers. Nearby was a theatre, and we found shelter in a pair of seats, where Jonathan took one of my damp socked feet onto his lap. Onstage, two people were attaching an orange curtain to a long, horizontal rod. They chatted and laughed.

I asked Jonathan how the documentary was going.

"Great." Jonathan kneaded my arch. "I'm finding new connections between stories." Onstage, someone gave a vivacious hoot. "The veteran who was working with Keith? He left the church."

After an exorcism for his PTSD, the veteran had believed himself cured. He started to drive again, an activity which used to trigger memories of the jeep that hit a land mine and killed his friend. One night, driving home, the veteran had a flashback. His car swung off the road and one of his arms was crushed. Now he was more damaged. "Keith overpromised," said Jonathan with something like relish, as he kneaded my foot energetically.

"Do you hate Keith?"

Jonathan gave me a sidelong frown. "No. I'm not a fan of his work, but I don't hate him."

I retracted my foot and watched the two stage hands. They were still attaching the orange curtain to the rod. For the past ten minutes, they appeared not to have moved.

"Are you okay?" said Jonathan. "Is work extra crazy?"

"No, just regular crazy."

From the start, I had insisted that consulting was for me. I liked using my brain and being well remunerated. I liked the variety of projects and the travel, working with other clever, rootless types. Growing up fundamentalist, I had never belonged fully, in the world but not of it.

"By the way, can I do another interview while you're here?" said Jonathan.

"I thought you're editing now."

"I am. I've started. But the process is never linear."

"Right." My process was linear. Monday we implemented a methodology that spat out a solution by Thursday.

The stage hands were still chatty and immobile. No effort was visible.

My phone vibrated. It was an email from my mentor, responding to my latest memo on women in leadership. She would be chairing a panel on the subject, at a big international conference in January. When she'd asked if I'd help her review the latest research, I said, "I'd love to!"

Five years earlier, the partner who hired me had said he only worked with people he'd trust on a lion hunt. My professional confidence was at a low ebb after four years of rejection on the academic job market, and I was flattered. Would I trust the stage hands on a lion hunt, or the poet? She would empathize with the lion before being devoured by it. She would experience a transcendent interspecies connection, but I would survive.

Even then, part of me felt how adrenalized my consciousness had become. I had chosen to be an overachiever rather than a believer, preferring good works to faith, effort to grace, mindlessly committed to excellence.

At such moments, Esther's words came to mind. *For what shall it profit a man?* I felt the emptiness Christ prophesied, of the fool who says in his heart, *There is no god.*

Later, in the hotel room, Jonathan positioned a reading chair beside the window and set up his video camera. Outside, thick flakes obscured the spruce trees.

"Do any traces of your fundamentalist self remain today?" he asked.

"I hope not." I was no longer the flushed over-explainer citing Bible verses to no avail, insisting that the earth couldn't be billions of years old because under high pressure a barrel of crude oil could be manufactured in twenty minutes and anyway carbon dating was an inexact science. Now I talked about China's twenty-two city clusters, each designating a highly specific and fluctuating consumer demographic.

Jonathan asked if I ever missed fundamentalism, and what my fundamentalist self would think of the person I'd become. "I don't know," I said. Hypotheticals seemed pointless, though Martha's remark on Brueghel's painting came to mind. *Don't they look foolish?*

"Okay, let's turn it around," said Jonathan. "What about me? What am *I* a fundamentalist about? How am I inflexible?"

I laughed, confused. "Why are we talking about you?"

"I need to be transparent about our relationship. You're not just another interviewee. We're married."

"You can't show that in a subtitle?"

"This way is more honest. Tell me: what am I a fundamentalist about?"

I felt my mouth gape in a crooked half smile and grabbed at some low-hanging fruit. "Money."

Jonathan bobbed his head in a groovy nod. "Tell me more."

"The boathouse this summer. The renovations on the house. Even a cookie."

"A cookie."

"In grad school."

"Tell me about it."

"It's a trivial story," I insisted, while annoyed that Jonathan did not recall it.

Our final semester of graduate school, I taught less in order to finish my dissertation by spring. Jonathan and I were newly married and pooled our funds, with Jonathan contributing more. It was a straitened life; we lived in a studio and ate a lot of oatmeal.

After writing in the library one morning, we met for lunch at the business-school dining pavilion. The menu advertised items like white sturgeon saltimbocca and goat tacos, but I had a slice of pizza. When we finished eating, I was still hungry and short on money. I told Jonathan I wanted a cookie.

"We don't have money for that," he said.

"It's two dollars." I needed the sugar to keep working in the afternoon. Coffee I would filch from the departmental machine reserved for faculty.

Jonathan said that we should brown bag our lunches. I was wearing a drapey, open-backed blouse from a sample sale and felt wretched, unsated with greasy lips in my designer top, having been refused that most childish of requests, a cookie.

"Do you remember?" I asked.

"I don't." Jonathan was checking the camera, which gave a naïve-sounding little beep. "Why didn't you push back? I probably would have given you two bucks."

Even in grad school, I had acquiesced to my husband, in quietness and full submission. I believed he was smarter than I was, as if intelligence had a simple hierarchy among the highly educated. In a way, I still believed that Jonathan was smarter. Hence he pursued his vocation: this had always felt reasonable to me. I loved teaching and research, and could have taught as an adjunct, but both of us could not afford to do what we loved to do. Someone had to play the supportive role, someone had to serve. I was not so different from Esther, really. Helpmeet 2.0.

"Why are we talking about our marriage?" I thought of the baby we had given up on that spring. How Jonathan had shoved it into a box marked *impossible*.

"Okay, last question: what do you think of this project?"

"I don't really know much about it."

"The premise, then."

"It's great!"

Jonathan gave an arid little laugh. "Why is it great?"

"Making a documentary about people who once belonged to this misunderstood group, fundamentalists. The whole empathy shtick, really."

"The empathy shtick?"

"The open-mindedness. It's humble, but impressive. It's spectacularly humble, you might say."

Jonathan remained in documentarian mode, calmly curious, cocking his head to the side like a well-trained parrot.

"And the fucking nuance. Only people with lots of time on their hands can afford the luxury of nuance. As you have observed more than once, you get to be empathic and progressive because I'm a shameless materialist who does spreadsheets over dinner. Turn off the camera."

Jonathan fiddled behind it, though the red light remained on. I jumped from the chair and hurried to the bathroom, locking the door. I had to pee and sat on the toilet, my pee and tears drowning out Jonathan's voice. As I stared at our hair and fluff mingled on the black tile floor, I wondered if this was the start of my nervous breakdown. I was in the mountains.

From the other side of the door, Jonathan thanked me.

"What?" I shouted back.

"You were spontaneous and honest."

"The whole thing was upsetting. You can't use it."

"It was brilliant." That word again. Whatever was brilliant was good and holy. Both Jonathan and I had carried this idea within ourselves since graduate school.

"Would you hurt us to make this film?" I asked.

On the other side of the door, silence. Finally Jonathan replied, "Why would anything you've said hurt us?"

I didn't see how my outburst would help the film. But I also knew how desperate Jonathan was to make something brilliant, and this made me pity him, which made me resent him. I did not want to pity my husband. I would do no more recordings. What Jonathan did with the footage was up to him.

In the new year, I thought of Martha daily. I wondered what Violet had been told about her older sister, now big with child. God "blessing" Martha with a baby would make no sense. Keith's online holiday letter to his church alluded to no familial challenges, unlike previous Christmas letters, which had detailed God's blessings.

Martha must have many lonely nights in her room. Had she been forced to sit before a council of deacons who decided the terms of her penitence? Did she ever contemplate ending it all with her father's razors in the bathroom, or in the trout brook, where the water curled down to a dark silent place? Did she ever regret not having gotten rid of the baby when she had the chance?

I thought of emailing Esther, to warn her about Jonathan's film, but wasn't sure how to state the problem. (My husband's film contains information that might damage your husband's professional reputation?) Plus my schedule was punishing, a market-sizing analysis for a pharmaceutical firm to determine which anti-cancer drugs they should research. Whatever my ambivalence about Jonathan's film, my priority was supporting my husband. He was on creative lockdown, rush-editing in order to submit the film to festivals that year.

Late one Sunday afternoon, my mentor called me. Her father had died, and she could not attend the international conference to chair the panel on women in business leadership. Would I fill in for her? Normally a partner would do it, but I had reviewed the research and she wanted a woman; I had only to ask the questions she'd prepared. It would be like an academic panel. I'd also attend a bunch of panels and write a memo to the firm about the latest findings on gender parity in business. "You're perfect for it."

The conference was in the Swiss mountains, a concentration of power and intelligence I had never before witnessed. It snowed heavily that week, and attendees navigated icy sidewalks beneath the gazes of snipers on roofs. Inside, the panels were about disruption and inequality, animal spirits and uncertainty, and creating more robust systems through innovation-oriented partnerships between business and government. Nametags were objects of discreet fascination, indicating not only affiliation but also level of access, and occasioning a delicate choreography of eyeballs.

The event was at once exciting and dull. If anything, the dullness bespoke its prestige; nobody had to show off because they had "made it." It turned out that elites were in the best positions to *be themselves*. I was relieved to find most moderators uncharismatic, sometimes reading from notes and even once forgetting a panelist's name. At the panel I chaired, my own manner remained influenced by our managing director, an immaculately unobjectionable personality, calm and soft-spoken, a Canadian who liked to describe crises as opportunities. Only his hand gestures were expressive, softly chopping the air or caressing an invisible expanding balloon. I liked the expanding balloon gesture myself, which made me feel attuned to global fluctuations; it was a kind of brainy voguing.

Most of the action happened behind the scenes. The power players attended few panels, flying in for a day to network with industrialists and foreign ministers and maybe a celebrity. The world's most famous cellist played a Bach suite beneath a hundred-foot artificial sequoia. Constructed of domino-sized tiles shipped from Seattle, the tree spiralled grandly above my head. From where I stood, few observed it; it was one of many art installations designed to help attendees have the right kinds of feelings and thereby start to *make things better*. At the Hilton, executives pretended to be refugees, crawling under wires and through tunnels amid sounds of gunfire, filling out confusing forms, and learning to say land mine in Arabic. A man with a Russian-looking name emerged with straw on the knees of his nice navy suit.

As I stared up at the fake sequoia, transfixed by the cello's gorgeous purr, a man said, "Are you here for the skiing?" He had a Germanic accent and an unhurried manner. A camera hung around his neck.

We glanced at each other's name tags and exchanged nationalities. "I'm local talent." He smiled, which made him look even younger, maybe thirty.

"Are you a Young Global Shaper?" I asked. I'd read the title on someone's name tag.

We decided that I was an industrialist, in lumber, with designs on the sequoia.

"That's a lot of popsicle sticks," he said.

I joked that I was staying at the storied sanatorium up the mountain.

"Have you met the Russian princess yet? The Brazilian engineer?"

We agreed to visit the sanatorium before the end of the conference. From the icy sidewalks its lattice balconies were visible, where one hundred years ago the world's ailing elite had convalesced on lounge chairs, taking in fresh air and six meals daily.

At a panel on women's reproductive rights, an expert talked about a nation's high total fertility rate leading to poor educational outcomes for women. I briefly resented the effortless fecundity of poor women before thinking of Martha, again, and whether she'd given birth yet. Her agonized red face flashed in my mind.

I had once feared the world's empty pleasures and ghastly consequences. *For what shall it profit a man, if he shall gain the whole world and lose his own soul?* Now I wanted to understand how the world worked. It was why I stayed in consulting, why I'd been drawn to Breughel's painstaking realism. I wanted not to be scared of the world anymore. Wasn't that the definition of the elite — people who had the good fortune not to be scared of the world? People who, when faced by a problem, remained calm and broke it down into a bunch of numbers that could be rendered into a graph?

I never made it to the sanatorium with the Swiss photographer. Instead we met at the firm's party, which was modestly lavish, with hot-pink lighting and free brut. When it grew tiresome, we went to my room.

In bed the Swiss photographer repeated my name, each excruciating syllable. Jonathan remained at the back of my mind, enjoining me to *have fun!* Esther was on my mind too, my original role model for fun, even if she'd returned to the old small scared life, like a dog to its vomit. As I enjoyed myself laboriously, I did so with a mood of *See? The pit of hell is not opening up beneath the bed.*

And yet when the photographer climaxed and said whoa, to me it sounded like *woe. Woe unto you, hypocrites! For you devour widows' houses,* Christ had said.

I'd told the photographer I was on the pill, and that was enough for him. As we lay atop the rumpled duvet, I surmised that I could become pregnant. Unlikely, but not impossible. I tilted my hips in a way I hoped looked sexy rather than therapeutic. After listening to panels about fecund, underprivileged women, I was more desperate than ever. Eventualities — STIs, secrets about paternity, the demise of my marriage — felt remote, and my eyeballs prickled at the memories of accumulated disappointments. Was this the start of my breakdown, downhill from the fabled sanatorium? I closed my eyes and turned my face away, pretending to be sleepy.

When I did drift to sleep, a disjointed vision visited me, of how Breughel might have painted the conference. The busy panorama of important people, necks craned to read name tags. At a party, an industrialist danced the twist with a robot and, just outside the window, a foreign minister slipped on the ice. Along a mountainside, at an infernally prolonged panel, two speakers guffawed while three others slept; up on a roof, a sniper nibbled a macaron, while below an oligarch crawled through straw and two others played leap frog. Finally, off to the side, beneath a 747 releasing an avalanche of ping-pong balls, the Swiss photographer and I rutted. The whole of it foolish, as Martha would have said, a jolly, empty charade.

Editing continued into early February for Jonathan. He was stressed, and a friend invited him to work in a studio near Asheville. Jonathan cancelled classes before reading week, and that weekend I was on my own.

On Friday evening I sat in the small café where I had first encountered Esther's mug. I tried to write a note to Martha, to accompany the blanket I had bought for the baby in Switzerland. But I was unable to complete a coherent sentence that expressed simple goodwill. Each time the sentence curled into defense or apology. I was sorry but had meant well. I had not meant to hurt Martha and was sorry, and also concerned, not least because of Jonathan's documentary and what it might mean for a family already strained by a new baby, not that I blamed Martha.

Before leaving for Asheville, Jonathan had said the documentary was taking a new turn. "Is Keith in there?" I'd asked. "Oh yes, Keith is *in*," said Jonathan. Wanting to be supportive, I said nothing.

In the café, with one of Esther's mugs in my hands, I caressed its tender distortions and felt close to her then. It was hard to believe, as I held the cup shaped by her hands, that she never thought about me, that the cup wasn't a coded invitation to renewed intimacy with her and the family, even Keith.

Keith had a right to know. If Keith knew, then he could prepare what to tell his congregation. Yet on paper, my revelation about Jonathan's film was liable to provoke dire reveries. In person, I could see Keith's reaction and respond accordingly. I was the client whisperer, after all. *The Lord put it on my heart to speak with you*, I would say. In winter, their home was a four-hour drive north. Keith would give me ten minutes of his time. Of course, I wanted to see Martha's baby too. It would have been born by now, a few weeks old. How was Martha managing?

Early on Saturday morning I put the baby's blanket into a tote, plus booties and a bottle (bought years ago). It was a fantasy diaper bag, though I believed that I simply wanted to be equipped to assist Martha. For myself, I threw in a box of tampons, my period having arrived earlier that week.

North of Barrie, snow fell heavily. The tracks of cars ahead disappeared, and along the side of the highway the trees were vaporous. For nearly an hour I drove behind a spectral white pick-up, until it veered away to Huntsville and I was on my own, with the GPS woman who guided me to Esther's road. It was plowed, fortunately, and along the driveway I followed the tracks of Keith's truck, to the peaked gray house in the woods.

Titus answered the door. "Can I talk to your dad?" I said, and was invited inside. I couldn't tell if Titus remembered me. Unzipping my jacket, I listened for the raspy cry of a newborn, but heard only Lydia and Violet at the back of the house; then Titus's voice and Keith's.

The entryway was well organized, the coat rack labelled, an antique milk bucket filled with mittens and hats. Above the stylishly worn bench hung a wide plaque, its font an ecstatic cursive: *As for me and my house, we will serve the Lord. —Joshua 24:15.*

Keith materialized in slippers, holding a dishtowel. He seemed slighter than in the summer, despite a new beard.

"Could I speak with you for ten minutes?" I said.

Keith's office was by the entryway and darker than the rest of the house, with an old teacher's desk before a window. He gestured to an abbreviated sofa and sat at the desk, placing the dishtowel on a far corner. "The Lord put it on my heart to tell you," I began. As I spoke, Keith swivelled towards the falling snow. He looked tired, probably because of the baby, which I still hadn't heard.

"I think you have a right to know ahead of time." It occurred to me that in Keith's opinion, acting without the direction of my husband could undermine my case.

Keith continued to watch the snow, as I considered how to bring up Martha. I wished I had removed my coat or asked for a glass of water. "I never promised a cure," he said. "From the beginning, I called it a healing. A healing is a process, sometimes a long one. I told Rob that. I told that to Jonathan, too."

"You spoke with Jonathan?"

"He called me, for comment. He suggested we film, but I declined. He didn't have the right spirit."

"I could relay your concerns to him."

Keith appeared not to hear my offer. "There are so many variables. Belief, for one. You know, Beth, I've seen deliverances where the recipient experienced significant relief from suffering. But you need to submit to God first."

"Of course."

"After Rob's accident, I visited him in hospital. He told me off, he was upset. I called him later, left a message. Each time, no answer. The youth pastor called him, same thing. If we did anything more, it would be harassment."

We watched the snow homogenize the landscape, including my car, which was now mottled white. Finally Keith said, "How are you?"

A blankness heaved into my mind. "Great! Busy."

"Martha told me you're a management consultant."

I was glad Martha had come up. "Our team just completed a market analysis for a pharmaceutical company," I said.

"Sounds like important work."

"We're grateful to serve some influential clients. Each project is different, which I love, though I won't bore you with the details. Still, it's exciting to try to understand what's really going on in the world, such as it is." If I wanted to keep Keith's favour, I'd have to criticize the world a little. Not that doing so was unusual; these days everyone did.

"How's the family?" I said.

Keith smiled. "The short answer is, God's taking care of us." He stood up, and I asked to use the bathroom.

"Martha's upstairs."

He took my jacket and we climbed the stairs to her room. The door was ajar, and Keith said, "Let me give her a heads up." Through the doorway, Martha lay prone on her bed beneath a mauve quilt, which shifted when Keith bent over her.

The small room was crowded with a crib and a rocking chair. The desk had become a change table; a bag of diapers leaned against the bookcase, not far from *Tess*. When Martha settled into the rocking chair, I waved at her through the doorway.

I drew up a chair and admired the baby. It was perfect, even the bumps sprinkled along little lopsided cheeks. She was a girl named Robin.

When Keith left, Martha said, "The Lord told me you'd come."

A humidifier disgorged mist, but the air remained stuffy. With the sloping ceiling and the falling snow, and the sleepy mother and newborn, the atmosphere felt swaddled and unreal.

"Robin is teaching me so much." Martha leaned into the baby.

Was Martha implying that she didn't need university anymore? She seemed stoned.

Martha angled Robin towards me, and the tiny placid face winked. "Do you want to hold her?"

"If she doesn't mind."

"She won't, though I don't really know. You're our first visitor."

Robin was three weeks old. The soft weight of her was like

a drug, with the plump fists and pink eyelids. She felt at once delicate and indestructible.

"Some friends brought food," said Martha. "But we were sleeping." I wondered where Esther was. Beset by baby clutter, Martha looked lost. A teen mom. University was out of the question, for years.

My heart ached for Martha but was delighted by the baby, a cyclone in my chest. Outside, snow twisted in opaque gusts.

"Do you mind if I take a shower?" said Martha.

And there I was, alone with the dozy, trusting baby.

From Martha's room, it was a straight line to the front door. Martha would be in the washroom for ten minutes, at least. When she didn't see me and Robin in the bedroom, she'd assume we were downstairs with the family. A baby carrier hung on the closet doorknob. I had my fantasy diaper bag and could pick up formula somewhere. Robin would be okay. She would sleep for most of the drive. She was infinitely sturdy. I placed Robin in the carrier and found her little hat. Her face rested just below my clavicle. If at any time she cried, she would stay, I decided. Crying would be the sign that she should stay.

We walked down the stairs. My coat was on the hook and I zipped it up around her. Robin wasn't quite asleep, and she didn't cry, not even when I sat on the bench and bent down to put on my boots.

I believed the family would come around and eventually understand my solution. If I took Robin, they would be relieved of a burden. Keith would resign himself to his granddaughter living in Babylon, with all its amenities. The family would be welcome to visit.

I kissed Robin's tiny, hazy eyebrow, and she gave me a careful, sidelong look. Her face rested against my chest, even though I didn't smell like her mother. It occurred to me that I never would.

Robin was the most honest creature I'd met in years. She was the Truth and the Life. In her presence, my own artifice sprang into relief, and the words of a forgotten evangelist came to mind. I had feigned a good heart. I had feigned generosity and even lust; and now I was stealing a baby.

I began to cry. I hugged Robin, and still she didn't cry. Even now, I can't remember Robin crying that first afternoon.

Someone unzipped my coat, and the straps of the baby carrier were lifted from my shoulders. Someone led me upstairs, where I was laid on a bed and covered with a blanket. A hand rubbed my shoulders, a box of tissues was placed near my head. Words were spoken to me, then over me. Lord we come to you, for You know our hearts, You knitted us in our mother's womb. Sometimes a mug clunked onto the table beside me, dispensing sweet astringent steam. Sometimes a warm cloth rubbed my face and one time my feet. Somewhere in there, Esther's voice told me that God would send a sign, if I waited patiently on Him.

I wanted to stay until it was time to plant the beans. I wanted to watch them sprout from the earth and see Robin grow.

"Tears are your gift," said Martha. We joked that I cried more than Robin.

"I have been a viper to your breast," I said. Martha didn't deny it. Nobody asked why I'd been sitting on the entryway bench in my coat and boots, with Robin strapped to me.

Only once did Esther say, "God stopped you just in time." More often it was "God is doing His work," as she left a fresh mug of tea by the bed.

She wasn't around much, she had an order to finish. A big one, from a café all the way in Vancouver. It was an amazing provision from the Lord.

I told Jonathan it was a bad flu. He was still in Asheville. I didn't say anything about Martha or where I was. I didn't want him to worry, so he could finish the documentary.

Sometimes Robin cried at night. Then came the dreams about lost babies. One time the baby was found at last, skeletal. I thought it was dead, until I touched it and the head waggled into motion like a toy's. This was obscurely connected to the fact that I still hadn't gotten the STI-test results but had already slept with Jonathan. A doctor with my mother's congested voice told me that STIs also had nonsexual causes, including arrogance and deceit. I awoke to the blazing light of early afternoon.

For days I lay beneath a poster of a dachshund puppy inside a pink canvas high-top, and the words: *For it is God who works in you . . . to act for His good purpose. — Philippians 2:13.* It was Lydia's bed in the room she shared with Violet. "Lydia likes the couch," said Violet. "She gets a sleeping bag and the whole living room to herself." Nobody hinted that it was a burden to care for me with a newborn in the house.

One day I left the bed and walked down the stairs to the kitchen, where I rested on a chair. Keith was chopping onions for a venison chili. His wrist moved nimbly as he spoke.

He hadn't yet found full-time work. In winter it was tougher to find employment, but he didn't sound discouraged. If anything, he sounded exhilarated.

God was teaching him a lesson. "I became proud. Now God is setting me straight." His knife drummed against the cutting board. "Jonathan is doing the Lord's work, you know."

Sometimes Esther came upstairs from the basement for tea. It became our ritual at three o'clock. Keith was usually out of the kitchen then.

"God decided it was time to give you a breakthrough," she said, though I had received no heavenly sign. I didn't dispute her words. Her family had taken me in.

She was at work on a new series. It wasn't for the Vancouver café and she didn't know if it would sell.

In her basement studio, one wall was covered with shelves, the upper half crowded with the café order. Below them, the new series inched along—tiny, futile-looking cups and wide tottering bowls. A shallow chipped edge, an abrupt frill, an eruption of scales. The effect was daintily ruinous. Other objects appeared placental, mottled and darkly glittering.

My final morning there, we sat at the kitchen table, Esther holding Robin as Martha finished breakfast. Keith was outside shovelling. "You should let him drive you," said Esther. It was snowing again.

"I've already imposed on you too much." I drank more coffee, plus an alfalfa tonic, and invited Martha to stay with us in Toronto with Robin. Martha still planned to attend university one day. Robin beat the air with her feet.

When Martha went upstairs, Esther hugged Robin to herself and said, "Beth, the Lord gave Sarah a baby when she was ninety. He can do anything. God is going to give you a baby too."

Our therapist says it was irresponsible. Esther and Keith should have taken me to a hospital, or at least to a qualified professional. I needed more support than herbal tea and prayer.

Medication is an option, our therapist says. More important, however, are new behaviours. For a start, a hobby, something art-istic and personally meaningful. Every Sunday morning I spend an hour painting. This week it was the bean trellis in our garden.

Our therapist also recommends journaling. That way I can integrate past experiences and clarify my emotions. Journaling even boosts the immune system.

"Try writing about the breakdown," she said. "Put it on paper in a sitting or two."

"Like a testimony," I said.

"Absolutely!"

I don't think she understood what I meant, but she is upbeat and encouraging. Because if this were a testimony, I would be a changed person. Yet my life now is not so different. I draw and garden, yes, but I went back to work. My colleagues appear to find me much the same.

Granted, things will change when the baby arrives. Meeting Robin, and wanting her so badly, I saw how every baby is worthy of being adored, like Christ by the Magi. When Jonathan returned from Asheville, I told him, "I am going to adopt a baby." Then we went to see a therapist.

The first baby didn't work out, but I am believing the next one will.

Jonathan's documentary premiered at a big festival. We got a free ride in a limo. On the way to the screening, I told him, "I'm tempted to say we're blessed."

"Please don't."

A streaming service picked up the film and a few reviews came out. Jonathan's film was praised as a meditation on the losses that come with liberation and the stubborn appeal of certainty. Because the old ideas are never abolished entirely. Purity and impurity, man and woman, meaning and emptiness. The film's experimental digression on marriage was admired by one critic, who deemed Jonathan's editing brilliant.

During the premiere, Keith was on my mind. Onscreen the veteran called him a fraud. I had wanted Jonathan to record me one last time, after he returned from Asheville, but it was too late; by then the documentary was done.

Had Jonathan recorded me, I would have said that fundamentalists have a point about some things. Sometimes my life without God feels empty. My busy worldly work, my barrenness. But even this emptiness feels providential, the operations of a god I cannot believe in.

On the drive from Esther's, back to Toronto, snow fell the whole time. At Stirling Falls, I considered turning back, but then I would have had to tell Jonathan where I'd been. So I continued south, guiding the car along the disappearing road. When an accident was reported on Highway 11, I turned onto a two-lane highway, where oncoming cars flashed by in bursts of light. I drove carefully, but along a broad curve one of my wheels must have hit a patch of ice. My car slid out of the lane, through the terrifying whiteness, towards an advancing, exterminating light. Even now I cannot reconstruct how I got back into the right lane. For the rest of the drive to the city, my body vibrated with adrenaline, and I felt that I had been saved again.

Pieter Brueghel, the Younger
The Peasants' Wedding, mid-16th to mid-17th century
oil on wood
Overall: 36.2 × 44.2 cm (14 ¼ × 17 ⅜ in.)
Art Gallery of Ontario
Gift of Mr. and Mrs. W. Redelmeier, 1940
2557
Flemish, 1564–1638
© Art Gallery of Ontario

Acknowledgements

Bible verses are from the King James Version, the New International Version, or the New American Standard Bible. In some instances, a verse mixes versions, reflecting the oral culture in which verses are cited conversationally. Any dubious combinations are my mistake.

Elements in the story "Matsutake" were inspired by Anna Lowenhaupt Tsing's tenderly attentive *The Mushroom at the End of the World*, as well as by Carlo Rovelli's gracious and exhilarating *Seven Brief Lessons on Physics*.

This book would not exist without the help of many people. Sarah Albani, Amanda Ghazale Aziz, Kevin Birmingham, Rachel Ferry, Sarah Gilbert, Andrew Gray, Eric Idsvoog, Bret Anthony Johnston, Virginia Konchan, Tyler Krul, Miki Laval, Anna Marschalk-Burns, Sophia Ross Eckert, Sarah Selecky, Ayelet Tsabari, and Carly Vandergriendt: thank you for your insights and encouragements.

Thanks also to the English department at Dawson College, for supporting time away from teaching to write.

Kelsey Attard and Naomi Lewis at Freehand Books were essential in helping me turn the manuscript into a book, as was Deborah Willis for seeing its potential as one. Their guidance and enthusiasm have been hugely fortifying.

Above all, I am indebted to my writing group — Pamela Casey, Nisha Coleman, Nathaniel Penn, and Lesley Trites — for their sharp minds and generous hearts.